DECEIT IN PARADISE

PARADISE SERIES

BOOK 25

DEBORAH BROWN

This book is a work of fiction. Names, characters, places and incidents are either the product of the author's imagination or used fictitiously. Any resemblance to actual persons, living or dead, or to actual events or locales is entirely coincidental. The author has represented and warranted full ownership and/or legal right to publish all materials in this book.

This book may not be reproduced, transmitted, or stored in whole or in part by any means, including graphic, electronic, or mechanical without the express written permission of the author except in the case of brief quotations embodied in critical articles and reviews.

DECEIT IN PARADISE
All Rights Reserved
Copyright © 2022 Deborah Brown

ISBN-13: 978-1-7334807-9-6

Cover: Natasha Brown

PRINTED IN THE UNITED STATES OF AMERICA

DECEIT IN PARADISE

Chapter One

"I've had quite enough." I barely managed to stop myself from sending my phone into a skid across the kitchen island.

"Coffee?" Creole held up a mug, still in the process of concocting his morning brew.

I absently shook my head at my husband and pulled open the junk drawer, lifting out a pair of handcuffs and twirling them around my finger.

"Madison, babes, could whatever you're up to wait until I've had at least one cup of coffee?"

"I've got a busy day," I grumbled. It came out harsher than I wanted, so I blew him a kiss. I jumped off the stool and headed for the front door, stopping at the bench in the entry to grab my purse and briefcase, before stomping out to my Hummer, anger rising with each step. "When do I ever say no?" I muttered to myself, getting behind the wheel.

The passenger door opened, and Creole slid inside. "No way am I missing out on whatever's going on." His blue eyes twinkled as he leaned over the console and kissed my cheek. "It's prudent that I come along—keep you out of jail."

I humphed, then made the short drive to our

neighbors' house, Fabiana and Didier, who are also our best friends. As much as I wanted to burn rubber in the driveway, I managed to park without leaving skid marks on the brick pavers. I jumped out and rushed to the front door, not bothering to knock—a lockpick was faster. Besides, I wanted the element of surprise. I burst through the door, and Fab and Didier stepped into the entryway from the kitchen. It was clear both were caught off guard.

Creole closed the door and squeezed by me. "I need coffee." He headed straight to one of the kitchen cupboards, helped himself to a mug, and filled it from the ready coffee pot.

I hustled behind Creole and stood at one end of the island, Fab on the opposite end, Didier within arm's reach.

"What the hell are you doing?" Fab demanded, annoyance filling her face.

"Did you hear that, Frenchie?" I sidled up next to Didier. "You're the one with the no-bad-language edict. You need to get your wife under control." I caught his grin and the amusement in his blue eyes before it disappeared in a nanosecond.

"What do you expect when you burst into my house?" Fab practically shrieked.

"Yeah," Creole said from behind her, toasting me with his mug.

"I called again and again, and then you had the nerve to turn off your phone. You left me with no other option but to show up." I waved off whatever she was about to say. "Yes, I know you're busy. Slurping down that swill you call coffee with your husband isn't a good excuse for leaving me hanging. And when was the last time I blew you off?"

Creole laughed.

Fab leveled a stink eye at him. "What are you going to do about it?" Fab's smirk conveyed she thought the answer was *Nothing*.

We'll see about that.

I whipped out the handcuffs that I'd shoved into the back waistband of my skirt and slapped one on Didier's wrist (good thing he hadn't been paying attention) and the other on my own. "Ready to go?" I smiled sweetly at him.

"You take those damn things off," Fab screeched as she flew around the island.

Didier held up his cuffed hand and winked at me.

"Stop that," Fab practically spit. "It only encourages Madison's bad behavior. Can't you accept that I need a day off?"

"Fine. Take as much time as you need. If you can't step up and be my best friend, then I'm taking your husband as my partner. And the next time you call needing whatever, don't be surprised when I say I'm busy that month."

Fab shook her head with a snort and spun around, staring down Creole, who was grinning behind her back and didn't even attempt to cover it up, which only infuriated her more. "Aren't you going to get control of your wife?"

"I'm thinking Didier can take care of himself." Creole turned to his friend. "You so much as put a scuff mark on Madison, and I'll beat the *hell* out of you."

Didier grinned. "You'll have to cover for me at the office. But I'm ready to go." He shook our wrists.

Creole, Didier, and my brother, Brad, ran the day-to-day operations of The Boardwalk, a joint family-and-friends real estate venture that consisted of attractions, shops, restaurants, a collection of rides, a hundred-slip marina, and continued to expand.

"I'll fill you in on the game plan once we're in the car," I said, steering Didier to the front door and managing to stop short of banging it closed.

"You're going to have to take this off to get me in your SUV." Didier shook the cuff as I reached for the car door. "Heads up: I'm going to run." He laughed, clearly enjoying himself.

"Your wife…" I unleashed a disgruntled sigh.

"Hold that thought… five, four, three…" The front door flew open. "Faster than I thought," Didier said, laughing.

"Stop right there," Fab yelled as she stomped across the driveway, Creole behind her.

"Happy now?" She jerked open the driver's door, her purse flying into the backseat, and slid behind the wheel. "You can let my husband go," she yelled across the car.

"As a matter of fact, I am happy." I took the key out of my pocket and unlocked the cuffs, then stood on my tiptoes and kissed Didier's cheek. "Thanks for being such a good sport."

"Anytime." He laughed.

I left Didier, who'd already gone around to the driver's side, and walked over to Creole, giving him a big kiss. "Have a good day at the office, honey, and behave yourself."

Creole laughed and tugged me back for a second kiss. "I'm sure when you said 'behave,' you meant yourself."

"If there's an exchange of gunfire, I'll get hot on the phone and report in." I hustled back to the car, knowing Fab had had enough kissy time with Didier, since he'd joined Creole and she was gunning the engine. I got in and closed the door, and Fab skidded out of her driveway. I rolled down the window and waved to our grinning husbands. "Since you didn't answer my question, I'll do it for you: I always say yes when you need backup." I ignored her shaking head. "Coffee's on me—a triple espresso latte will put you in a perky mood."

"What's so important that I had to give up a day of doing paperwork by the pool?" Fab roared out of the private gated neighborhood nicknamed 'the compound.' She owned two of the houses and rented one to Casio, a retired Miami detective, and his family. Creole and I owned the other two, and we were renting one to Emerson, a family law attorney who was dating my brother.

"My phone rang early, and that's never good."

Fab groaned, signaling *hurry it up*.

"It was Mac, and you know how she often forgets who's the boss." I relayed the short conversation: "*'You need to skedaddle over here and prontola.'*. Then she hung up. Before you ask, I didn't call back because when she's done that in the past, it meant that something smelly hit the fan. I figured it was faster to get on the road. Although this morning, I was slowed down by you-know-who." I jabbed my finger at her.

Macklin Lane was the manager of The Cottages, a ten-unit beach property I owned. She kept the full-timers and guests herded up and made sure that they stayed out of enough trouble that the cops didn't get called. Most of the time anyway.

Once Fab hit the main highway, she drove like a pack of wolves were chasing her. I'd mostly gotten over hanging onto the door handle, but this was one of those days. Call me a wuss, who cares. She did manage to slow and enter the coffee drive-thru on all four tires. She ordered for both of us, handed me my cup, and whizzed back out. I'd heard her ask for extra whipped cream for me, and I was already smacking my lips.

"You're going to thank me later for dragging

you out of the house—because of it, you're not going to miss out on one moment of the fun and excitement, which you know is never-ending at The Cottages." I flipped the lid off my cup and licked the inside.

"Basically, you don't know anything and don't have a particularly good reason for not getting more information. So... I'm ruling out a dead body, since Mac would've led with that tidbit as soon as you answered," Fab reasoned.

I made an X in front of my face with my fingers. "No dead-body talk. We've had more dumped on the property than anyone else on the block."

Fab squealed around the corner to The Cottages and was about to turn into the u-shaped driveway when she hit the brakes. A boat blocked the entrance, leaving little room to squeak past. And not just any boat—a damn big one.

"Where the heck did that come from? Better yet, how did it end up in the driveway?" I inwardly groaned, hoping this wasn't some bargain one of my tenants, namely Professor Crum, had found and managed to somehow get back here. Crum wasn't one to pass up anything he deemed a good deal, no matter how big a piece of — it was.

Fab backed up into the driveway of Mac's house across the street and parked next to her truck. Mac had gotten a good deal on the property, and it didn't bother her to live within arm's reach of work. All the better to spy on people, she'd told me more than once. We sat there and stared out the windshield.

"Pontoon boat. Guessing about thirty feet... maybe more," Fab informed me.

We had our hands on the door handles when two police cruisers came around the corner.

"I'm going with 'maybe' on a dead body." Fab had the nerve to smile. "No lights or sirens... That's a good sign? Or..." She tapped her cheek, enjoying herself way too much.

"Mac could've at least given me a heads up if there was going to be a hint of police action," I grouched. "How about we sit here and see how things play out? Or scoot through the trees and hide out in the office?"

"The heck with that." Fab opened her door, one leg out. "You know I'm not one to mix it up with the cops, but if we don't go over and get in the middle of whatever's going down, we're going to have to rely on a retelling, and we both know firsthand is better. Just try not to be too annoying and get yourself arrested."

"Me?" I squealed. She laughed as she shut the door. I hopped out and caught up. "If I have to call hubs for bail, I'm telling him this was your great idea."

Chapter Two

Kevin Cory, resident sheriff's deputy, was the first to pull into the driveway and get out of his car. The other deputy parked in the street and joined Kevin in checking out the boat. Kev hadn't looked our way, so I didn't bother to call out a greeting. It was a toss-up as to how it would be received, since our relationship ran lukewarm. That was because more often than not, I found myself in the middle of whatever illegal activity was going down.

The two officers stood at the far end of the boat, Kevin doing most of the talking as he pointed around. The two laughed. Laughter was a good sign... hopefully.

"You take the lead." I attempted to step behind Fab, who blocked me.

"There must be a simple explanation." She eyed the boat with appreciation. "Appears to be a custom-built party boat, twin aluminum pontoons, easy thirty feet." She stood on her tiptoes. "Nice interior finishes, bar down the center, seats eight or ten."

I shook my head in wonder, as Fab had already established the ability to identify a car at a glance, and now boats too. "How do you know this stuff?"

Fab's answer was a smirk.

A door slammed behind us, and Mac came barreling out of the office, a hot-pink tent-shaped dress swirling around her body. Normal by her standards, but the shoes... She slapped up in pair of slip-on sandals that were a replica of a man's veiny feet.

"Where's the rest of the guy?" I eyed the shoes as she came to an abrupt stop in front of me. "Did you by chance leave him in your living room?"

Fab stared, turned to me and conveyed, *Why are you asking?*

"Aren't they the cutest?" Mac held up her foot, shaking it around and smiling. Then her demeanor changed. "I expected you to hustle." I was surprised she didn't tap her watch for added effect, but she didn't have one on.

"Don't look at me. There stands the reason for my tardiness." I stabbed my finger in Fab's direction. She took a swipe at it, and I stepped back.

"This isn't the cops' first trip here." Mac nodded at Kevin as he closed the distance between us. "It's a two-part story," she whispered.

I nodded at Kevin and pasted on a pleasant smile. I'd been practicing in the mirror and hoped it paid off.

"Not sure if you know there's a city ordinance against keeping a boat in the driveway of a residential neighborhood. You wouldn't want to get fined." His smirk got bigger with each word.

So much for pleasant.

The other officer had finished his walk around the boat and, with a wave to Kevin, headed back to his car.

"Saunders didn't believe it when I told him someone had dumped a pontoon boat, so he had to see for himself." Another smirk from Kevin.

When word got out about the boat, every lookie-loo on the block would be down here.

"As for the county issues, that won't be a problem once you have it towed. I'm surprised it hasn't already happened, since you're law enforcement, and since you live here, you know that it was dumped or offloaded, or…" I trailed off, hoping Kevin would step in with some kind of explanation, but he only smirked at me. He was enjoying this way too much. "Would you happen to know the details of how the boat came to be in the driveway and care to share?"

"A call came in during the early hours—loud music, carrying on, and at an address I recognized, which was shocking," Kevin said, still amused with himself.

"You're in a good mood today. Coffee? New girlfriend?" I asked.

"Where was I?" Kevin asked. Another smirk—he was going for a record today. "I pulled up and found the pontoon blocking the driveway, drunk partiers crawling all over it, a few hanging off the sides. Since I take it that you're not claiming ownership, you won't be upset to know it has major back-end damage."

"How many of your neighbors were you able to squish into the drunk wagon? Are they still in the slammer or did they sober up and get sprung?" I asked.

Fab poked me in the back.

Nothing was ruining Kevin's good day. "Being the good guy that I am, I gave them a warning to quiet it down and told them I'd better not to have come back. The best part: I asked that they save me a drink for when I get off work. I'm here to collect once I change out of my uniform."

"I'm going to need a drink," I mumbled. "Could we rewind the story? I solemnly swear that the boat doesn't belong to me. In your investigation, did you determine who the registered owner is? How it got in my driveway?" Kevin's shrug irked me, and I knew he was doing it on purpose. "Seriously, when is the tow truck arriving?"

"When you call one." Kevin leveled a stare at Mac and raised his eyebrows.

Mac rubbed the tip of her shoe (the man's toes) into the ground. "Late... uh... around midnight, a truck pulled up—really nice one, by the way, all tricked out. Where was I? Oh yes, it was towing the boat. Not sure why, but the driver stopped, and once again, not sure what all went on, but the dude got back in the truck and left, minus the boat."

"And?" Fab glared at her. *What about the rest of the story?*

"Nice of the driver to dump the boat in your driveway. Mighty convenient." Kevin almost couldn't contain his laugh.

If I knew there had to be more to the story, then so did he. It surprised me he was letting it go. "Did you by chance run the tags? Registration?" *Whatever.* "Contact the owner and ask what the flip?"

"Turns out, the pickup—a Ford F-650, by the way—was hauling the boat to a customer and the boat and truck got stolen," Kevin relayed. "But the *dude*, the one committing grand theft auto, apparently wasn't interested in the boat and was kind enough to dump it in your driveway. The owner of the towing company contacted Mr. Roof, the owner of the boat, and his reaction was more muted than I would've expected. I'm assuming both men will be out to inspect the boat, although Roof wouldn't commit to exactly when that would be. If it were me, I'd call my insurance company, especially after being informed of the damage."

"You're telling us that Mr. Roof made no mention of when or if he'd be getting his butt out here? Isn't that unusual?" I asked.

"Since the boat's on private property, yours,

remember when I said it was your problem? That hasn't changed."

Fab laughed behind me. I didn't bother to retaliate, knowing that the only way was to run around after her.

"This has been fun." I glared at the boat. *Now what?*

"Here's a freebie for you." Kevin edged his way back to his car. "You might want to think about tacking up a 'Keep Off' sign to stop the partying. Besides cutting down on calls to the police, you could be liable if anyone were to get hurt." He waved, climbed back in his patrol car, and managed to maneuver around the boat and into his parking space. The boat blocked a couple of other spaces, which thankfully didn't have cars in them at the moment.

Fab turned on Mac. "What really happened? Even Kevin has to know that he didn't get the whole story. Maybe he decided that because no one died, he'd let it play out. If he finds out you were holding out, good luck."

Mac's cheeks bloomed pink. "We don't need to be airing laundry out here in the driveway; you never know who's lurking around. Come into the office. Have a cold drink." Without waiting for an answer, she took off.

I watched her disappear into the office, leaving the door open, and took one last look around. "It's shocking, considering we attract guests that love drama, that no one is sitting out on their porch soaking it all up. Could it be that they're all guilty of something?"

Fab linked her arm in mine. "If the whole boat thing played out as Kevin suggested, I'm thinking you just got lucky."

"Except it didn't sound to me like he was convinced he'd gotten the whole story." I tried not to snap.

"Doing my part to be helpful, I've ruled out anyone living here as having stolen it." Fab propelled me toward the office. "Not a one of them has the chops."

Thank goodness.

Once inside, I took my usual seat in front of the desk. Fab staked out the couch under the window. Mac handed out cold water from the refrigerator in the corner, then plopped down in her chair, changing her mind midway to putting her feet on the desk.

"Out with it," Fab directed.

"Most of what Kevin said actually happened," Mac hedged, downing half her water bottle. "I wasn't about to tell him the rest, as I don't want him knowing that I have security cameras. A couple of the guests were drinking on their porches and watched it all go down, and after the truck took off, they knocked on a few doors, and party time." She shifted in her chair. "I did hear the truck pull up out front and checked the security camera. Saw that the boat wasn't sitting right—it appeared to have lurched to the side.

Two guys, not just the one reported, got out of the truck and unhooked the boat on the street, leaving it partially blocking the driveway. I didn't get a good image of them or I'd have turned that over."

"How the heck did it get into the driveway?" Fab demanded.

"Made a couple of calls. Figured it was better than blocking the street." Mac nodded, agreeing with herself.

"Who'd you get?" I asked.

Mac zipped her lips. "If I tell and word gets back, there goes that connection."

Maybe I didn't want to know. "Did you happen to get the contact information for the boat owner and his insurance company out of your friend Kevin?"

"About that…" Mac drawled.

I leaned my head back and stared at the ceiling.

"We want to hear everything," Fab said, glee in her tone. "Don't we?"

I assumed the question was for me and didn't answer.

"I wouldn't want it to get out that I did such a thing…" Mac weaseled.

"We're good with secrets," Fab assured her. "Aren't we?"

Another question I ignored.

"I lurked around, eavesdropped on the cops talking, and got the name of the company hired to tow the boat. Made a call and got Roof's number. Interesting couple of calls, listening to both men's side as they pointed fingers, each thinking it was the other's responsibility to figure it out. The tow guy went on about how the truck was worth more than the boat. As it stands, we're waiting for the insurance companies to show up."

"Any clue how long that's going to take?" Fab asked.

"I'm going to call our own insurance company this morning and make sure we're covered, and I'll get an idea then. Let's hope it goes through the weekend."

"I'm afraid to ask, but why so long?" I blew out a long sigh.

"Party time." Mac threw hands in the air and gyrated in her chair. "Look, pooper," she directed at me, since I was known to squash a good time, "until it gets hauled out of here, I'm going to milk every bit of hot fun I can."

"Since I'm willing to bet you were one of the partyers, when you checked every nook on that boat, did you happen to stumble across any dead bodies?" Fab asked.

Mac laughed, shaking her head.

I squinted at Fab. *Did she want a yes answer?* "I'm thinking it's legal to drink in the driveway, but double-check with your friend to make sure."

"Checked that one out a long time ago, and as long as there are no noise complaints and no one stumbles into the street, we're good."

"I'm going to make this your problem," I told Mac, and she nodded, having expected me to do just that. "Tell the owner of the boat to get his butt moving or I'll have his expensive toy hauled to storage and he can pay the fees."

"We don't need to do that right away," Mac insisted. "Let's take a 'wait and see how it plays out' approach. Before you get all grumpy, think about the fun to be had, and how much easier my job is when it's sitting in the driveway."

The woman was exasperating when it came to her ideas for entertainment. "Code violations," I reminded her.

"Think compromise. Knowing this very subject would come up…" There was a ta-da in Mac's tone. "We've got friends in the code department, and surely there's a workaround if we don't milk it."

"Do you need to be reminded that a cop lives here?" Fab demanded.

"I'll assure Kevin that I'm working on the issue."

"When you make another call to the owner of the pontoon, make it clear that he gets the boat moved now. And I want to know right away, not the next day."

Mac nodded, which meant maybe.

"Time to check out this pontoon for ourselves." Fab stood, phone out and ready to take pictures.

The three of us went outside and made our way over to the boat. As we walked around, Mac pointed out the back-end damage. It was hard to miss, as it looked bashed in.

Done with her picture-taking, Fab hauled herself up the skinny ladder and over the side. "Great bar," she yelled.

From the excitement on Mac's face, she hoped no one claimed the pontoon, wanting to keep it like a lost puppy, only nine hundred thousand times bigger. It wouldn't surprise me if she was working on a place to park it and still have it accessible should the parties in question drag their feet. "Any other problems I should know about?"

"The party went on until almost dawn, so it will probably be afternoon before anyone is sober enough to stick their head out the door."

"I wondered where everyone was." I took a second look up and down the driveway. Then checked out the apartment building next door, which I also owned. It was quiet too.

Fab finished her inspection and hopped down. "In addition to the obvious damage, there's quite a bit more to the underside. The new owner isn't going to be happy."

Mac shuffled her feet, getting the man's toenails all dirty, a sign something else was up.

"You're holding back on something. Just tell me already, or I'll sic Fab on you." Idle threat, as she fan-girled Fab.

"Just a reminder about our meeting tomorrow. If there's some kind of agenda, you need to add my name, as I have a few ideas we need to talk over," Mac said.

"Since when are we so formal? You can tell me now."

"Today's not good; there's already enough going on." Mac's phone rang. She pulled it out of her pocket and looked at the screen, then nodded at me and answered. "Mr. Roof, I've been waiting for your call."

It was clear that Mr. Roof was doing all the talking, and Mac listened intently. This wasn't a quick 'I'm in the neighborhood' call.

"Okay, well, we'll keep in touch." She pocketed her phone. "Roof's in discussions as to who's liable and will let me know by tomorrow what's happening next. Kind of disappointed if this turns out to be the last night we can use the boat. I'm thinking barbecue and open bar." She grinned, clearly liking her impromptu idea.

"No wonder the guests love you. Never a dull moment," I said.

"If you have any problem with Mr. Roof, give me a call," Fab offered.

"You still annoyed that I dragged you along?" I asked as we walked back to the car.

Fab made a non-committal noise. I poked her, and she laughed.

Chapter Three

Fab maneuvered out to the highway, jammed on the gas, and headed towards home. "You haven't heard the last of that boat," she predicted. "It's a big investment for the new owner to be showing such casual indifference. If it were my purchase, I'd be all over it, hounding the insurance company to get it out of there, and they'd do it just to get me off the phone."

"I've got a plan for that boat."

"That's a shock."

"The next time you want me to pull a plan out of somewhere, I'm going to serve up sarcasm. When you hop all grouchy, I'll remind you of this moment, although there are others I can pick from." I gave her my practiced smile, which I knew she caught out of the corner of her eye.

"And your plan?" Fab asked.

"Rather than looking at it as an inconvenience, have someone come out and relocate it to, say, the barbeque area… although it might not fit."

"Oh brother. You need another reminder about code enforcement? You can't turn it into party central without them being all over it." Fab honked at someone, who returned the favor. "The only way the boat's going to be accessible to your drunken guests is that ladder. Hate to point out the obvious, but bad idea."

"You come up with a better one and tacos are on me. I found a shabby, run-down place, no curb appeal—you know, the kind you hate—but great food."

"Always a shab hole. Why is it you never have a five-star restaurant to try out?"

"It's not like one of my choices has ever made you barf." I briefly thought about making the sound effect and passed. "Back to the subject at hand. Plan B is to have step-daddy come out and tow it. The owner can deal with Spoon, and if he doesn't want his behind rearranged, he'll hop on it."

Mother waited a long time after my father died to tie the knot again. Jimmy Spoon couldn't be more different, but he'd swept her off her feet, wooing her with a cigar and a shot of Jack Daniels, and soon they were doing the happily ever after.

"You know Spoon thinks that title is yucky."

I'd bet that Fab was rolling her eyes, but she had her head turned. "Sometimes I say inappropriate things to amuse myself—like now." I grinned at her and flipped the visor down, noting that she was glaring at the road. "What's caught your attention?"

"Roll down your window," Fab barked, then

turned sharply to the curb and slowed. She hit the door locks, and they all flew up. "Tell that kid to hurry up and get in if he wants to lose the two on his tail."

I stuck my head out the window, making eye contact with the running boy, a backpack slung over his shoulder and an oversized thug not far behind. "Hop in! You can trust us to get you where you need to go," I yelled. "Are you sure about this?" I said over my shoulder. No answer.

The kid sized me up, then glanced over his shoulder and, like me, knew he wasn't going to outrun the man. He flung open the back door and hopped in. The man pounded on the back of the Hummer with his fist as we pulled away.

"This probably wasn't a good idea," the kid said, almost out of breath. "They're already mad, and this will really piss them off."

The kid turned, as did I, and we both saw a pickup truck squeal to a stop and pick up the man who'd been chasing him, then pull back into traffic and speed up in hot pursuit.

Fab adjusted her rearview mirror. "Where do you want to go?"

The kid dragged his eyes away from the back window and turned around. "Drop me off at the beach. I'll lie low and wait until dark to move on."

Fab rubbed her fingers together.

I grabbed cash out of my purse — going by his disheveled state, he could use a meal — and handed it over the back seat. "Grab something to eat."

The kid nodded and locked eyes with Fab.

"Do exactly what I tell you, and they won't get their hands on you," Fab told him, *for now* left unsaid. "I'm going to drop you off up here at the liquor store. Run around the back and head straight for the dumpster. There's an opening behind it that will take you to the street right behind this one. Hide out there, and when I'm certain they're not tailing me, I'll double back to pick you up and take you wherever you want to go."

I didn't know anyone that knew shortcuts like Fab, and now actual holes in walls.

"Get ready to jump out." She sped up and squealed to a stop on the side of the store.

The kid didn't hesitate, but leaped out and ran.

Fab backed up, forcing the truck to stop or rear-end the SUV, and ended up with a tire on the curb. The man who'd been chasing the kid jumped out of the truck and took off after him. Fab pulled into traffic and continued south.

"Can't believe you figured out that kid was in trouble." My eyes were glued to the side mirror.

"I watched the man toying with the kid for a couple of blocks. He was prolonging the chase, wanting to scare the devil out of him, and from the look on the kid's face, which only intensified as he got closer, he succeeded." Fab sighed. "It didn't look right to me, instinct or something, and I just reacted."

"I had a few questions, such as his name and age. I'm hoping the latter doesn't get us arrested. I didn't think about giving him a business card."

"Whether he's related to those two men or not, helping him run will only give him a short reprieve. He's not going to be able to hide forever, and when they find him…" Fab shook her head. "The good thing is the driver was more interested in getting the kid back and didn't follow me. I know these streets, and I'll be able to circle back without them knowing we're still in the area. If they're still hanging around, we'll know how badly they want the kid. Let's hope he did what I told him and got away."

"What if it's his dad or brother? Then what?" I asked. "And even if they're not, depending on his age, helping him in any way might get us in legal hot water."

"Since when have we shied away from a little trouble?"

Never.

"I'm only offering to give him a ride to wherever he feels safe." Fab u-turned and cruised past the liquor store. The truck was parked off to the side of a neighboring business, a lone man behind the wheel. She turned into a strip mall directly across the street and found a space under a tree. We both scooted down and peered over the dash, and for a long time, nothing happened. Eventually, the man on foot reappeared from the other end of the block and got in the passenger side of the truck. They sat there for fifteen minutes, then finally got back on the road going north.

"Please don't follow them," I implored. "This SUV is conspicuous. I mean, how many Hummers do you see on the road? They're sure to pick us up in the rearview mirror, and I'm actually surprised they didn't see us sitting over here."

"No worries on that one, though I'd like to have gotten the license number of that truck. Now I'm going to make good on my promise and look for our runner." Fab pulled back onto the highway, turned south, and drove several blocks before turning off. It didn't take her long to reach a nondescript residential road one street behind the liquor store.

"You're a human roadmap," I said in admiration.

"All that late-night driving around I used to do has paid off more times than I can count." She cruised the block slowly several times, checking out potential hiding places.

After the fifth time, I said, "You cruise this block one more time, and someone's going to call the cops, worried that you're casing it. My guess is the kid only took the ride because we were a better option than the two men. Now that he's escaped, he's back to whatever his original plan was."

"We both suspect the kid is underage and on the run; it's not going to be a happy ending."

"Agree with you there." I felt bad about the pure frustration on Fab's face. "If you had caught up to him, then what? I know you well enough to know that you're not going to dump him somewhere with a few more bucks."

"We're always helping someone, two-legged or four. Okay, mostly you, so it's my turn to be a do-gooder."

I laughed.

Fab hit her hand on the steering wheel. "Time to go home." But not before she took one last cruise around the block and a couple of side streets.

Once back at the compound, a frustrated Fab went home. Knowing her, she'd come up with another plan to find her new friend. I shared the whole day with Creole while he fixed dinner and suggested that we go to bed early.

Chapter Four

The next morning, Creole and I were up early, and being a good wife, I made coffee and offered to put a waffle in the toaster, but he turned up his nose. More for me.

After I assured him that I wouldn't get into trouble—nothing planned, anyway—he kissed me and left for the office ahead of me. There'd been a last-minute change to our group meeting, it now included Boardwalk issues, had been pushed to lunchtime, and included food.

Finishing my coffee, I opened my laptop and looked for anything needing my immediate attention.

"I'm home," a male voice called from the sliding pocket doors, startling me.

I looked across the living room to the deck that ran along the back of the house, overlooking the beach. "Good way to get shot. As an ex-detective, you should know that." I glared into the smirking eyes of my neighbor, Casio Famosa, the man's bulk filling the doorway. Maybe this was a sign that I needed a dog, who'd have announced his arrival long before he got to the door. My cats, Jazz and Snow, didn't even acknowledge his existence. Nothing disturbed one of their naps.

"I come bringing neighborly felicitations." Casio closed the distance between us. "I'll have a cup of coffee." He nodded to the mug in my hand.

I waved for him to take a seat at the island, then got up, filled a mug, and set it down in front of him. "You never stop by in the morning, or ever, actually, so something must be up."

"Just thought I'd come by with a reminder that you owe me," he said with a faint smile. "You remember those IOU things you flaunt? Let's hope this isn't where I find out they're useless."

Amongst family and friends, we traded IOUs for unspecified future favors, and when one party was ready to cash in, no crabbing and making up some feeble a— excuse.

"Hardly." I squinted at him, which made him smile. "You need a favor, just ask; skipping around the bush wastes both our time."

"Seems as though I have an unexpected family issue or two," Casio hedged.

I suspected he took the deep breath in an attempt to stall for time so he could come up with a way to be more vague.

"You're probably not aware that my nephew Marcus, Brick's oldest, is staying with us for what I thought was going to be a few days but is clearly going to be longer."

Brick, Casio's rodent brother, was a gigantic pain whose involvement in anything was bad news. But he did get all the hair—not sure what happened to Casio's. In his defense, he did rock the bald look.

I pasted on a *that's nice* smile.

"Marcus brought a dog. There were conflicting stories about how he ended up at our house, but I'd had a long day and didn't ask for clarification. The dog was sitting in my entry, and it was too late to evict her anyway. The next day while I was at work, canine love bloomed—first with my kids and then my Australian Shephard, Larry—it was love at first bark with Melba the Border Collie."

"That's sweet."

He laughed at my sarcastic response. "When it became clear that there was no love between Marcus and Melba, I brokered a deal, and now Melba's the newest member of the family." He sounded disgusted.

I'd guess money was involved and he paid too much. "How long has it been since I last saw you? A week maybe? And in that time, you've acquired a kid and a dog."

"Sums it up." Casio stared down into his mug, then made eye contact and tapped the rim.

"Here, let me." I stood and grabbed his mug, pouring him the last of the coffee.

"When Fab rented me the house, your *friend* made a point of saying 'No pets,' then amended it to 'No more pets' when we got Larry. You need to break the news to her, possibly pouring it on that my kids love Melba, and while you're at it, mention Marcus, though he's not permanent. Although his departure date's unclear."

"Melba, huh? I'm guessing that your kids named this one too?"

"Once the vet confirmed Melba was a girl, they weren't going for 'Dog,' as they didn't care for the name to begin with. My kids told me Melba was a natural choice. No argument there; I save them for important issues." A single dad whose wife had died from cancer, Casio had promised her that he'd step up, and his four kids had the tough-as-nails detective wrapped around their fingers.

"Done. I'll tell Fab. As for who owes who, you now owe me *more*, not the other way around." This was going to be fun, but he didn't need to know that, or that all he had to do was ask, without going the favor route, and I'd have done it. "When I mention that Marcus has taken up residence and she asks why, what do I say? And how old is he?"

"Issues, to answer your first question. The latter, seventeen going on fifty."

It shocked me that Marcus's mother would let Casio within ten feet of her son. The two loathed one another, and that was putting it mildly. "Can't wait to meet him." If he was anything like his father, I'd muster up a cheery hello and hightail it home.

"I'm off to the office." Casio shoved his empty mug at me. "Finishing up a divorce case and have a report to type up for the not-so-happy couple, one party of which doesn't want to pay alimony."

"How have you adjusted now that you're not chasing down hardcore criminals?"

"My current cases are a bore. But I've got to be around for my kids." Casio stood. "So we're agreed?" I nodded. "Just know, anytime you need anything, I'm your man."

He was halfway to the front door when it blew open and Fab crossed the threshold.

Casio leaned towards her, and whatever he said, she smirked. He raised his brows at me over her shoulder, telegraphing, *Don't forget*.

Fab shut the door behind him. "Grab your stuff. We've got a busy day." She tapped her foot in an exaggerated motion, amused with herself. "When we're in the car, you can tell me what Casio wanted."

"Give me a minute." I ran across the room and locked the patio doors. Already dressed for the day, I slid into sandals and grabbed my bag. Fab had the front door open, waiting for me. "Where's the fire?" I asked as I passed her.

Fab didn't bother with an answer and didn't waste time in getting behind the wheel of my Hummer. Who drove didn't bother me anymore. If it came down to a game of bumper cars, I'd prefer she be in the driver's seat. I slid into the passenger seat, and she backed out onto the street and cruised slowly through the compound. The security gate opened, and a white Porsche came roaring towards us and turned into Casio's driveway.

"Who the heck was that?" Fab demanded.

"I only got a quick glance, but he appears to be Brick Famosa's twin but a lot younger, so I'm guessing he's the oldest spawn, Marcus."

Fab stopped in front of Casio's driveway and powered down the window. "Slow down," she yelled when he got out of the car.

The bulky dark-haired male didn't acknowledge Fab, ignoring her completely and not breaking stride as he went into the house, slamming the door.

"That charmer is part of the news I have to share. But first, let's hit the coffee drive-thru. I have it on good authority that lunch is going to be served at the meeting, and an extra shot of caffeine will keep my stomach from grumbling until then."

Fab went through the security gate, waited for it to close, then continued out to the highway. "Your rambling makes me forget what I want to know. Almost."

"Marcus is staying with Uncle Casio for... he was vague when it came to how long. 'Issues' was the reason for the visit. He offered up no further explanation as to what the heck was going on. You'd think Marcus would be in school like other teenagers."

"Brick calls on occasion. Usually he's wanting a sympathetic ear for his complaints and to see if I'm willing to come back and work for him. Before you ask, I tell him it would be a choice between him and my husband. Anyway, next time he calls, I'll find out what's going on."

Fab cruised through the drive-thru and got us coffees.

"There's more." I took a long drink. "Marcus showed up with a dog, and the kids fell in love with Melba just as fast as they did Larry. She's now a permanent resident, and that may violate the pet rule that I didn't know you had. I won't be the one breaking the kids' hearts—and Larry's heart—by telling them Melba has to go; you can meanie up and be the one to do it. I wouldn't suggest telling Casio to dump the dog roadside."

"I'm ignoring you because you're ridiculous."

Chapter Five

I thought we were headed to the office after grabbing coffee, and it surprised me when she turned off the highway. It took me a minute to recognize the neighborhood where she'd been looking for the boy yesterday. "I'm surprised you didn't come back here last night and ferret out the kid's hiding place."

"After I told Didier what happened, the two of us cruised the area, but no sign of him. I'm pretty sure Didier was relieved. Yes, he wanted to help, but he didn't want either of us to get into trouble doing it."

"What do you suppose happened to the kid?"

"Probably still on the run," Fab said with a sigh. "I'm hoping he went home and that neither of those men were waiting for him."

After two slow passes through the neighborhood, Fab headed over to the office... sticking to the speed limit—she must not be feeling well. Or it could be that she only had one eye on the road in front of her. She suddenly hit the brakes, the car behind us laying on their horn, and made a fast turn that garnered more honking.

"Trying to get us killed?" I snapped.

"I found him," Fab said excitedly as she whipped around the block and pointed off to one side. "He's panhandling at the convenience store."

"That's a bad location. Anyone going in there with spare change is buying beer and lottery tickets." I easily spotted him at the side of the building. "Now what are you going to do?"

"Offer him a ride. He must have somewhere to go."

"Probably not or he wouldn't be here. Whoever he was running from, they must be worse than living on the street." If Fab could find him, the two men wouldn't be far behind.

She turned into the parking lot and parked on the side of the building a foot from where the kid stood, holding a plastic sand pail.

"Do you want backup?" I was surprised that he hadn't attracted the attention of the police.

"I've got this." She got out and approached him.

He looked up and, after a quick jolt of surprise, nodded. They talked long enough that I was beginning to think I should have gone along, just so she wouldn't have to repeat everything. They must have come to some kind of compromise, as they both walked back to the car. I wondered, as I had several times already, what next? Maybe he'd coughed up an address, but I highly doubted it.

Fab came over to the passenger side and motioned for me to roll down the window. "Would you vouch that I'm not some weirdo?"

"Whatever she promised, she'll come through; she always keeps her word," I said, noting that he didn't appear to be too worried about dealing with two women he didn't know. "I'm going to be the voice of restraint here and ask what's going on and will we get in trouble for helping you?"

Fab didn't give him a chance to answer. "I can give you cash and leave you here, but that's not a good idea because whoever you're running from is likely to find you."

"You're probably right." He shuddered.

Fab opened the back door, apparently confident she'd convinced the kid she wasn't some kook-nut. "Hop in, and I'll take you to get something to eat. After that, I'll drop you wherever you want, even if I don't like it." She walked around and slid behind the wheel.

To my surprise, he got in. I imagined his rumbling stomach was calling the shots. I turned in my seat. "Madison. And that's Fab, if she hasn't already introduced herself."

"'Hey you' works for me. Been called that plenty of times." He settled back in his seat and stared out the window.

"If someone else asks your name, you might want to make one up," I said. He cracked a brief smile. "How about going home? I'm sure they're worried about you, and whatever the problems are, maybe they can be worked out."

"Home—no such place." He sniffed. "I was in foster care, and I'm not going back there. I just need some food, then I can take care of myself. Just need to get a job."

"How old are you?" I asked.

"Eighteen."

Yeah, sure. "You'll have to have an ID that verifies your age or no one is going to hire you." His eyes shifted to the window and he didn't answer.

Fab rolled through the drive-thru. "Roll down the window and order whatever you want."

He ordered enough for a couple of meals and was handed a large bag and soda. "If you could drop me at the beach, that would great." He dug into the bag.

"I've got a better place in mind; you can eat in peace and won't have to look over your shoulder," Fab said to his responding grunt. He'd turned his attention to his food and was barely listening.

"Hmm…" I reached out and flicked Fab's arm. She ignored me. I suppose it wasn't the best time to ask what she planned to do with the kid in the back seat, but a telepathic message or two would be nice.

Fab maneuvered through the streets and took a shortcut or two to get to the office in record time. She turned into the large warehouse that

Creole and I owned and pressed a button on the visor, opening the security gate. It wasn't much to look at from the street, but we liked it that way. We'd bought three side-by-side properties, and the other two were now leased to a boat dealer. My first warehouse purchase was a little farther down the street, and all its floors were rented.

Fab owned two buildings of her own at the other end of the street, where we'd had our office until recently. But at Didier's suggestion, we took over the top floor of this warehouse, which put us two floors above The Boardwalk offices and our husbands. The second floor was leased to the ex-chief of police out of Miami, who'd opened his own security company upon retiring and hired Casio after he left the force.

"What's this place?" Hey You asked, turning around in his seat as the gate closed.

"My guess is that my friend here wants to help you out in some fashion. Just know that anytime you want to leave, say the word," I told him. He nodded, but wasn't quite sold. "Whoever was chasing you yesterday won't find you here, and if they do, we've got alligators in that murky strip over there that're always looking for a meal." I pointed to the far end of the property.

Fab parked, got out, and opened his door. "There's a table over there where you can finish your food. Afterwards, we can talk. I'm not generally the do-gooder of this duo, but I'm willing to help you out and find someplace safe for you to go."

I gave him a reassuring smile.

He'd only taken a couple of steps when Arlo bounded up. Dropping the Frisbee from his mouth, the Golden Retriever gave the newcomer a thorough sniff.

"Arlo, meet Hey You." I was about to give him the "he doesn't bite" speech, but the kid was already patting Arlo's head and feeding him a French fry.

Lark Pontana, office manager extraordinaire, came chasing after her dog, her long brown hair swinging side to side. She made her own introduction and bumped knuckles with the boy, then threw the frisbee for Arlo, who went romping after it.

Fab led Hey You over to the table, and the two sat down. I ignored her glare, which said it was a private conversation, and sat down next to them. She'd do the same.

Hey You sucked down the last of his soda.

"You want something else to drink?" Lark asked and ran down the choices.

"If you're sure… okay." He nodded at her.

"What about you two?" Lark asked, and we both nodded. "I'll be right back." She headed back to the office.

"Not quite sure how to start this conversation…" Fab started.

I bet. She was probably in wing-it mode.

She slapped her hand on the table. The kid and I both stared at her in surprise. "Let's cut to the chase here. Tell us how we can help. Don't dance me around, thinking I won't see right through any nonsense. That will aggravate me."

"What my friend is trying to say is that we're very resourceful when it comes to solving problems," I said reassuringly.

Hey You stared back and forth between us. "Those men I was running from are bad news. No telling what they'll do if they catch up to me." A shudder ran through his slight frame. "And if they find out that you helped me in any way, they'll take their anger out on you. Their solution to problems is to beat people up, and they never cross them again… or they disappear."

"Why don't you start by telling me your real name?" Fab said.

"Kyle Dow."

Fab introduced herself and shook his hand, then abruptly shoved up the sleeve of his long-sleeved t-shirt to see that his arm was covered in bruises. She smoothed it back down.

He jerked his arm back, his face conveying that he didn't think this was going to end well. He took a shaky breath. "I was a street snitch and runner for Burrows and Cabot, the two guys that were chasing me yesterday, and thankfully got tired of it. I wanted a normal life, even though I don't know what one looks like. Finally, I couldn't go along anymore, so I bided my time and made a run, even though I knew getting out was a long shot. I'm tired of being the reason people get into trouble and their butts kicked, or worse."

"I'm surprised that you didn't get your own butt kicked digging up dirt on people," Fab said.

"It happened a couple of times, and the last time was the worst. That's when I decided it was time to go before I ended up dead. Made my plans to leave but didn't get far. It didn't take long before Burrows and Cabot showed up and started taunting and threatening me. Then you two appeared out of nowhere. I didn't think about all the ways jumping in your ride could go wrong, just hoped it wasn't a setup when I hopped in."

Lark came back and placed a soda in front of him and waters in front of us. "You need me for anything..." She pointed to the grassy strip and went off for another round of Frisbee with Arlo.

"You said something about foster care. Did you have anywhere to go after you aged out?" Fab asked, and Kyle shook his head. "So you need a place?" She pinned me with a stare I couldn't decipher.

"What would you like us to do?" I asked.

"A ride out of state would be good. It shouldn't take me long to get a job."

"And just drop you off?" My eyebrows went up. "You never said whether you have a valid

ID, which is what you're going to need to get a job."

"I've never had any paperwork. Always thought maybe, one day, it was something I could work on." Kyle looked wistful.

"Now there's something we can easily help you with." Fab turned to me, with a head nod, letting me know she wanted a few minutes alone with Kyle.

Fine with me. It wasn't that I thought Kyle was lying, but I did think he was leaving out big details that could come back to bite both of us. "I'm going upstairs. When you're ready, come and get me." I stood and waved for Lark to wait up, as she and Arlo were headed back inside. "Not sure how long that's going to take." I motioned to the table. Knowing that she could be trusted, I gave her the quick version of how Fab met Kyle.

"Your new friend better watch his back. Snitching on folks for a couple of thugs will get you dead."

"Pretty much what he said." I sighed.

"And if he was good at it, they're going to want him back on the job." Lark stared back at him. "If not, doesn't mean they want him running around, possibly blabbing and bringing trouble down on them."

"I know we weren't followed here, but if anyone shifty shows up, call the cops. Let them deal with it."

"Do you mind if I just shoot them?" Lark grinned.

Chapter Six

I walked up the stairs to the third floor, opened the door to our office, and entered the wide-open space. Fab had put her massive desk on the far side of the room, making sure that if someone came through the door, or anything else happened, she had an unobstructed view. My office was an oblong space around the corner. The sliding doors to the deck and view of the murky strip of water had been the clincher for me. My eight-foot-long desk, made out of shiplap, had been a gift from Fab. I shared it with Xander Huntington, our smart as a whip Information Specialist. He'd been told he could park a desk of his own anywhere that wasn't taken, but he'd yet to make a change. When word got out that he was good and fast at digging up information, he'd easily grown his own client list beyond Fab and me. I also knew that he'd sold an app he designed for six figures and was close to selling another one.

It surprised me to hear voices; I recognized Xander's but not the female one. My ears perked up, and I stopped out of sight when I heard him say, "I'll transfer the money today. Next time you have an appointment, I'd like to be included."

"Oh Xander, you're the sweetest," the female gushed.

It was impossible to figure out what was going on based on the little I'd overheard. I pasted on a smile and walked into my office. Xander looked up and waved, and a young blonde turned and checked me out from head to toe. It was hard to tell if I passed muster, as she didn't show any emotion. I put my briefcase down, pulled out my chair, and sat down.

Xander made the introductions. "This is Krista."

"I should go." She stood, her form-fitting dress outlining her baby bump.

I couldn't help but stare, and Xander answered the question I wanted to ask.

"I'm going to be a father." He smiled faintly, and the lines in his forehead deepened a bit.

"Congratulations to you both." How did I not know that he not only had a girlfriend but a baby on the way?

Xander stood and put his arm around Krista. "I'll be back."

"Nice meeting you," I said.

Krista nodded but didn't say anything, and Xander walked her out.

It wasn't long before he was back. He sat down at the other end of the desk, his attention immediately focused on his laptop.

I had a list of questions running through my

mind but opted to tell him about the morning instead. "I'd like you to run a check on Kyle Dow, supposedly eighteen years old. You're probably going to need more information, but I don't have it. The kid's tight-lipped and was reluctant to tell us his real name; it surprised me when he did."

"It's easy enough to check, if he's been reported missing."

"That would be swell. Uhm…" I screwed up my nose. "Totally none of my business, but you know that's never stopped me." He grinned, which was encouraging. "I overheard part of your conversation, about you transferring money. I hope there's not a problem."

He arched a brow at me, probably a polite way of saying "mind your own business." If it was, I ignored him.

"If you've got a problem, I'm here for you. I'd be insulted if I thought you didn't already know that, so instead, I'm thinking it just slipped your mind and you need a reminder. You're like a brother to me, and since you haven't had a sister, you wouldn't know this, but we can be pushy."

"A lot's been happening, and all at once. It's kind of overwhelming."

"You've got a girlfriend?" How did I not know since we were friends and worked together? "I meant it when I said congratulations."

"About six months ago, Krista and I started

dating. We were together for a couple of months and then decided we were better off as friends. She called last week and wanted to meet for dinner. That's when she told me that she was pregnant and I was the father. And that she's in need of financial assistance."

"How far along is she?" I asked. "Not to be rude, but are you sure you're the father?"

"Four months. I want a paternity test; in fact, she offered to take one but told me it would have to wait until the baby's born. In the meantime, I'm taking her at her word. There's no question about me helping her out."

"That shows what a standup guy you are." I was pretty sure that the test could be done at any time, but I'd check before mentioning it. There might be health issues.

"It's still shocking that I'm going to be a father, since I just barely got my act together. But I'll just have to learn. Did you know there are pre-dad classes?"

"You're going to be as great a dad as you are everything else." I smiled my reassurance. "More prying: the appointment I overheard you talking about… I'm assuming it's for the baby?"

"I'd told Krista that I wanted to go to her next prenatal appointment, and she agreed but then forgot to tell me. It was yesterday. Frankly, I was surprised that she didn't tell me about it. Maybe she wants to see if she can depend on me first." He picked up his phone and scrolled across the screen, then held it out. "The ultrasound."

"Why do I have to eavesdrop to find out what's going on?" Fab strode into the office and leaned against the desk.

"That's how I found out... sort of." I smirked at her. "Then I got to meet Krista."

"The blonde I saw you with in the parking lot?" Fab asked. Xander nodded.

"Keep your questions to a minimum. Lunch is about to be served downstairs, and I'm hungry. Whatever Lark ordered, I'll make sure she sends some up to you," I told Xander.

"No worries there. Lark's always got everyone in the building covered, and anytime food's involved, she comes around and takes orders." Xander grinned.

"I happen to know that your girlfriend can get a paternity test while she's pregnant," Fab said. "You should tell her that if she wants your continued financial support, she needs to get the test. You also need to tell her that your other sister wants to meet her."

Xander's eyebrows rose, and he appeared a bit shell-shocked at Fab wanting to meet Krista.

I stood, grabbed my phone, and nodded to Xander. "If you need anything, you better ask."

"Before we go, I want to introduce Xander to Kyle. I told Kyle that you could get his birth certificate so he can start getting his life together. In the meantime..." Fab pointed to me. "You need to figure out a safe place for him to stay until we get something more permanent figured out."

I rolled my eyes at her. Catching Xander's smirk, I knew he'd seen me.

"If you could talk to Kyle..." Fab said to Xander, leaving it up in the air what exactly she wanted.

Xander followed us out of my office, and the three of us stopped short of the couch, where Kyle was sacked out, fast asleep. The television was on, so he'd found the remote.

"Intros will have to wait." Fab shrugged.

I waved to Xander as we went out the door. "I'm telling you now: Kyle isn't eighteen, and you're walking a felonious fine line. The person you need to talk to to keep your behind out of the clink would be Emerson."

Emerson Grace was a family law attorney and currently dating Brad. The family loved her, as she was one of the few non-crazy women my brother had gone out with.

"When you saw Xander with Krista, did you happen to take pictures?" I asked. Fab gave me a curt nod. It was one of the few times that she'd bypassed the elevator for the stairs, and she didn't say anything all the way down. "Are you planning on taking Kyle home with you?" I asked.

"He asked if he could camp out by the fence, and I gave him an emphatic no." Fab screwed up her nose. "He told me he feels safe behind the security fencing. That's when I told him that if it didn't creep him out, he could stay at the office and sleep on the couch. And also that he needs to come up with a plan before he just walks off. He liked that idea."

"Did you happen to remember that the building is filled with ex-cops?"

"They'll just have to mind their own business, won't they?"

I laughed at her as we walked under the roll-up doors. "Let me know how telling them that works out for you."

Chapter Seven

Creole, Didier, Brad, and Casio were sitting around the conference table. I walked up behind Creole, wrapped my arms around him, and leaned down to kiss his cheek. Then I shot a thumbs up to Casio and mouthed, *Told her*. He winked.

Mac came barreling through the door, a big pink box in hand, which meant she stopped at the Bakery Café and brought something we'd all love. "Cookies." She held it up before setting it on the counter in the strip kitchen, pulling down a plate and arranging them.

Lark, who'd set the table, now placed a large platter of sandwiches in the middle, followed by a couple of salad choices. Everyone already had a drink, as they knew to get one before they sat down.

I claimed a chair next to Creole but kissed Brad's cheek before sitting. "You staying out of trouble?"

He snorted. "That question would be better directed to you."

"You know how it is."

Brad's look told me no, he didn't.

I looked around the table. "Where's the Chief? He's going to be ticked if he finds out he missed food."

"He's playing golf over in Naples," Casio volunteered.

"No worries, I've got him covered." Lark waved her hand.

"I heard a rumor that you take good care of everyone in this building," I said, followed by a chorus of ayes from the guys.

Lark blushed.

While the guys wolfed down their food, we got an update on the various projects—Boardwalk and elsewhere—that were currently underway. It didn't take long for the food to disappear. The table was cleaned off and the cookies appeared—a variety of favorites and certain to please everyone. I grabbed one quick before they disappeared, too.

"What's happening with your pontoon boat?" Creole asked me with a wink.

"When did you get a boat?" Brad demanded.

"You're the only one who can own one?"

Brad spent years on the open water, making his living as a fisherman and doing quite well. He'd sold half the business to a friend several years ago and didn't miss the water as much as I'd thought he would. Now he had two children and was a hands-on dad, involved in every aspect of their lives.

"Let me tell him." Fab waved.

"Be sure you start your story with the fact that no one was found dead." I laughed at her groan.

Fab sauced up the retelling. I'd already told Creole what happened and could see that Fab had told Didier.

"We need to stop by The Cottages on the way home so I can check on the large intruder," I told Fab.

"Something's going on there." Brad shook his head. "The owner not making an effort to recover the boat is a big red flag. I'd have already been out there inspecting it for myself."

"There's kind of an update." Mac inched her fingers in the air. "In the early morning hours, two guys pulled up in a truck, and not the stolen one. They got out and crept around the property before boarding the boat. It was about an hour before they hauled several canvas bags out. Threw them into the truck bed and roared off."

"Did you call the police?" Didier demanded.

"They never do," Brad answered.

If the cops had been called back to The Cottages this morning, I'd have heard about it, so no, but that was none of anyone's business except Creole's, and he wasn't the one asking. "I'm sure there's a good explanation." I made a face at Brad.

"I didn't know about our visitors until my morning walk, and I wouldn't have at all if they hadn't left a ladder behind. Guessing that they didn't know the boat had one... or they were making sure they wouldn't need to make a second trip." Mac was enjoying every minute of relaying events. "Once I was done checking the property for drunks and dead people, I went back home and reviewed my security feed. Too bad I didn't have some kind of x-ray lens for a looksee inside the bags."

"Just the two men?" Creole asked, and Mac nodded. "You recognize them?"

"Nopers, I sure didn't." Mac pulled out her phone. "Only got a partial plate and managed to forward a couple of screenshots to my phone, and I'm sending them now."

"Any word on the owner or the insurance company coming by to fetch the spendy boat?" I asked.

Mac shook her head. "I told the owner any time after the weekend would be best. I didn't tell him that I had a party planned and wanted to use the bar."

"We have an impressive tiki bar by the pool, in case you forgot," I reminded her.

"The guests love the pool area, but the new attraction is getting rave reviews, so might as well milk it while it's hanging in the driveway." Mac stared. "No squatting on my plans."

"When do I ever do that? Only when it's illegal," I answered for her, and this one might be, but it was vague at this point.

"Yeah, squatter." Creole poked me.

I gave him a squinty side-eye. "I've got a great

idea for your party plans—one that will elevate your already high standing—Creole and Didier are available to bartend."

Fab laughed.

"Please don't wear shirts." Mac rubbed her hands together. "The women will faint." She sighed, clearly thinking that would be the best thing that could happen.

Both men glared at me.

"It was so thoughtful when they volunteered, and I knew you'd love the idea." I poured on the sweetness.

Creole and Didier both shook their heads at Mac. She winked and grinned, letting them off the hook.

"Send me the contact information, and I'll get that boat moved." Casio cracked his knuckles.

"We're not in a hurry, are we?" Mac turned to stare at me. "Dragging our sandals for a few days isn't going to matter."

"Yeah," Creole growled in my ear.

"I have more news, personal though. Did you want me to spill in front of everyone while we're all sitting around all cozy like?" Mac arched her brows at me.

"Madison would love to hear what's on your mind," Fab said with a crafty smile. "You've got our attention."

The guys all nodded with grins on their faces.

I glared at Fab.

"I'm branching out and opening a vacation

rental business." Mac preened.

How did I not know that she was even thinking about the idea? That was the second time in one day, and I didn't like it. "I feel like I should warn you." I bit back a growl. "My Glock is strapped to my thigh, and if your next announcement is that you quit, you might want to rethink that idea."

"Not going anywhere." To everyone's amusement, Mac shot up the room with her fingers, complete with sound effects. Lark clapped. "I already have two clients. Make it three if you let me rent out that house at the end of the block for you."

"Don't you need a real estate license?" Brad asked.

"I can do rentals without a license, but I think it would be a good idea to have one. That's why I signed up for night classes." Excitement radiated from Mac.

"If you have any questions, I'll be happy to help," Brad offered.

Mac nodded and then stared at me. I knew more was coming. "There's one other little thing. I want to use The Cottages office for my business and thought we could work out a deal."

"We'll figure it out," I said.

"Well then, I guess the meeting's over," Fab said.

"Not just yet, as I'm certain that everyone would like to hear the latest on the runaway you're harboring upstairs." Didier leveled a stare at Fab. "It doesn't surprise me that you were able to find him."

Fab gave a quick rundown on how the morning had played out and how she'd found Kyle and decided to bring him back to the office until something could be figured out that didn't include calling the police.

"Since you don't know a lot about Kyle, you should talk to Emerson," Brad said. "I'm hesitant to suggest her, but she'd kill me if I didn't."

"Great minds, bro." I tapped my temple. "Who better than an attorney that specializes in family law?"

Brad groaned.

"*Now* the meeting's over." Fab stood and was almost to the elevator by the time I caught up.

"I noticed you didn't mention that you invited Kyle to be our office guest," I said as we rode up in the elevator together.

"I'm calling Emerson as soon as I get back to my desk."

The two of us walked into the office and found Xander and Kyle sitting in chairs in front of the couch, laughing it up.

"We've got a temporary solution to Kyle's problem," Xander said as we approached and took seats on the couch. "Was just telling him how I met the two of you and how you both helped me."

Xander had bounded into our lives by

attempting to snatch Fab's purse. He wasn't very good at it. Turned out he was down on his luck and happened to be wicked smart, and we hired him to work in the office.

"Figured it's time for me to pay it back." Xander flashed Kyle a reassuring smile. "He can come stay at the house for a few days. I checked with Billy, and he's fine with it. No one's going to come sniffing around with Billy in residence unless they're stupid."

Billy Keith was a long-time friend, and anytime we had a problem, he stepped up, no questions asked. Tall and lean, he appeared to be your everyday Joe… until you ticked him off. If you were lucky, you'd walk away with your head still attached. It sounded like a good temporary solution, but something told me there was more to the Kyle story.

Fab motioned to him, and the two went to her desk.

I went back to my office, Xander behind me. I gathered up my files and shoved them in my briefcase, then decided to wait at my desk while Fab talked to Kyle.

"I think what you're doing is great, but know that at any time, it's okay to say you've had enough," I told Xander. He nodded. "You should also give Kyle a heads up that Billy's a great guy but has another side if crossed and it won't be smart to screw the man."

Xander laughed. "Billy will make that very

clear to Kyle, like he did me. Along with you and Fab, Billy helped me get my life back on track, and maybe he can do the same with Kyle. He's the one that'll get the kid to talk, give him the assurance he needs that something bad won't happen when he does."

"You ready to go?" Fab showed up in the doorway and nodded in my direction. "Give Kyle a burner so he has a way of staying in touch," she said to Xander.

On the way out, I nodded to Kyle, who was sitting on the couch, remote in hand.

Riding down in the elevator, I threw out, "How about something cold to drink?"

Chapter Eight

Imagine my shock when Fab pulled into the parking lot of a dumpy shack of a restaurant that offered outside seating and a glimpse of water. "Have you been here before?" I asked.

Her look said, *Have you lost your mind?* "It's just the kind of 'leave your attitude at the door or get out' type of place you seem to like."

We grabbed a table on the deck next to the railing.

"I'll have a margarita," I told the server.

Fab held up two fingers. "Make hers a double. I'll have an iced tea."

"Iced tea? Who are you? You're up to something, and your need to get me sauced in the middle of the day can only lead to trouble, which you know."

Fab shook her head like I was overreacting. "Can you keep an open mind until we get our drinks?"

I squinted at her while reminding myself not to let my guard down.

The server returned with our drinks.

"I'll have a piece of key lime pie," Fab told him.

"Two forks please." I smiled and sipped my drink, making a face.

"Take a good long drink, and the rest will go down a lot easier."

After another sip, I wondered if I could get a to-go cup. "Is this about Kyle? You helping him is super swell."

"Those men that were chasing him? I did find out that someone else is calling the shots, but I know there's more to the story and intend to find out what it is. I proposed that Kyle become a client—pro bono, of course. Told him he needed to know what options he had that would keep everyone out of trouble. I called Emerson while he was sitting at my desk and gave her a brief rundown, and we're getting together."

"Don't be disappointed if there's not a simple solution." Neither of us were good at taking no for an answer or accepting that a problem couldn't be worked out.

The server set the pie in the middle of the table.

I licked my lips. "Why don't you just spill whatever it is you've got cooked up that you want to rope me in on—so much so that you feel the need to get me liquored up?"

"You know how you've mentioned on more than a half-dozen occasions that we should go into business together?"

Maybe this wasn't going to be so bad, but I needed a clear head and slid the drink away.

"Drink up." Fab pointed to my glass.

I shook my head and reached for a fork. *Yum!* "Reassure me that whatever you're about to propose is legal, and then get to the good part."

"There's a dress designer on the Overseas who offers several other related services. I met Lucia when I needed a dress altered; she did an amazing job, and I've been back several times. It's clear that her business has begun to falter, and I thought an infusion of cash and an advertising campaign would be just what she needed. She's too talented to close up shop and take her skills elsewhere."

"You never cease to amaze me. Sounds like a great idea, but not a business that needs two investors."

"I'm thinking we partner up and buy the strip mall where the shop is located. It takes up an entire block and is flanked on both sides by other strip centers. I've been trying to contact the owner to make an offer, but he hasn't returned my calls." Annoyance kindled in her blue eyes.

"How long have you had this partnership idea? How would it work? Not sure why you need me, since you're more than capable of strong-arming the guy, and it can't be about money, since you're a billionaire's daughter. Where is Papa Caspian these days, anyway? Cruising one of his private islands?"

"Any more questions?" Fab rolled her eyes. "Caspian has been encouraging me to branch out. He hasn't said it directly, but I know he worries about my private investigator jobs."

For good reason. I didn't know what kind of noise slipped out, but she glared.

"I made the mistake once of mentioning your idea of partnering, and since then, he's asked several times if we've made progress. He likes you and the idea of us working together, and he has been pushing me towards real estate."

"What am I bringing to this partnership besides cash? I'm paying my share or not interested. We'd also need to hash out who does what, so there are no misunderstandings."

"You have more experience with rentals than me; not sure my warehouses count since I rent to associates. The strip mall has four businesses—Lucia's Couture, a real estate office that's never open, and two other spaces that are vacant. It's unclear when they were last rented, as there's no signage and Lucia didn't know."

"This venture doesn't seem quite highbrow enough for you," I said.

"Probably not, but I like Lucia—she's talented, hardworking, and deserves a break. That's why I thought we'd lease the other storefronts to businesses that would complement each other and hopefully bring in more traffic."

We both turned our attention to what was left of the pie and devoured it.

Fab settled the check and, as always, left the server a huge tip. "Time to go for a ride. The property is just a couple of miles north." We walked out to the SUV and got back on the main highway, where she was forced to slow for traffic. "Probably a good time to tell you that there might be a slight problem or two with the property."

I groaned loudly. *Here it comes.*

Fab made a face and continued, "Just yesterday, when I was in the dressing room, I overheard a man strong-arming Lucia for what was basically protection money. He threatened that if she wanted to continue to operate her business without any problems, then she'd better pay up and stop with the excuses."

"That's the first I've heard of an extortion racket here in the Cove. Don't be surprised if this fellow turns up dead. I'm not suggesting that Lucia would do it, but if he's hitting up other folks, it could shorten his life. Do you have the man's name? I know a couple of people that would be more than happy to run him out of town."

"Lucia was scared and refused to talk about it. I think it's someone she knows." Fab pointed off to the side. "The white building over there."

She turned into the gravel parking lot, and we both checked out the string of stores as she attempted to circle the building. Unfortunately, the back was fenced, the large entry gate closed. She pulled back around to the front and parked.

The street number had been painted in the

middle of the long, dirty building. Of the four glass entrance doors, two were covered with brown paper, and the real estate company and dressmaker were the only ones with signs. There was only one car parked at the other end—a white SUV.

"Is there parking around the back?" I knew she'd have checked it out, even if it meant jumping the fence. She ignored my question. "Are you going to give me a tour? I'm certain not having a key isn't going to stop you, since you've probably already been poking around and know your way in."

"I've been wanting to check out each space more thoroughly but need a lookout. I do know there are a couple of storage rooms in the back."

"Lookout is something I'm good at." I smiled at her and climbed out of the car.

The two of us stared at the building. I watched as Fab went over to the gate and found it locked.

"This sort of fits in with my idea of becoming real estate moguls. Draw up the contract, and I'll have my lawyer look it over." I almost laughed at her look of annoyance. "My two cents: unless we can buy the property, think about moving the existing business to another location—something with enough room to accommodate your expansion idea."

Fab took out her phone and snapped a couple of pics.

"The whole block is in need of serious curb appeal. Among other things, and at a minimum, the dead plants need to be replaced," I said as I turned and checked out the traffic as it cruised by. "There needs to be an eye-catching sign to get people to notice."

Fab motioned for me to follow her to the dress shop. As she opened the door, a bell rang overhead.

A paunchy middle-aged man had a slight woman with long dark hair pushed into the corner, anchored with his hand around her neck, his face in hers—yelling.

Fab and I drew our weapons.

"Step back," Fab yelled.

The man turned, one hand holding the woman in place, and his eyes went wide at the sight of the gun in Fab's hand. I moved to one side so he could see mine.

"Get the hell out of here. This is none of your business," he barked.

"That's where you're wrong." Fab moved forward in a blink and kicked him in the groin.

He doubled over and dropped to his knees.

Fab reached around the man and dragged Lucia out of his reach. "You alright?" Lucia nodded. Fab pointed her gun in the man's direction. "Do you want me to shoot him?"

Lucia shook her head vigorously. "No," she murmured.

"Your lucky day." Fab kicked the man in the

hip. "Because I'd prefer to shoot you. Now get out of here."

I was already holding the door open, and once he staggered out, I locked it.

"You shouldn't have done that." Lucia trembled. "Feld will be back and madder than ever." She swiped at a couple of tears. "I'm moving. I've been looking, and nothing's affordable, so I'm going to go back to working out of my house until I can find something." She sighed and stumbled back into a chair.

I sat on the arm of a chair across from her while Fab checked out the showroom.

"What's Feld's story?" I asked, surprised that wasn't Fab's first question… unless she already knew.

Lucia mumbled something unintelligible, which irritated me.

"Look." My growling tone caught her attention, and she stared at me wide-eyed. "My friend here is talking about investing in your business, and you owe her the truth about whatever's going on here so she's not blindsided. And how about a thank you for saving you from more bruises?" I stared at her neck, which had started to discolor. Fab should've snapped the man's fingers one at a time.

After some hesitation, Lucia said, "Feld works for the owner—collects rent, that sort of thing. Recently, he started squeezing me for more money, saying it would protect my business from vandalism. He didn't want to hear that I'm bringing in just enough to pay the rent."

"Do you think your business is a good investment?" I asked the woman.

"Granted, it could be doing a lot better. I think that could be remedied with a social media presence and aggressive advertising." Lucia nodded with assurance.

"You also need to figure out a way to put a stop to Feld's threats, because even if you move, that won't necessarily stop his extortion attempts. Fab and I have friends that can help you with that and discourage him from showing up again."

"I've put everything into this business. I don't know how I'd start over." Lucia started to cry.

Done with her snooping, Fab walked over and awkwardly patted her shoulder. "Do you have another number for the owner besides the one you gave me?" She took a seat on the arm of the other chair. "Any other contact info? What about for this Feld cretin?"

"I've only ever dealt with Feld. The one time I called the owner's number, I had to leave a message, and it was Feld who showed up to find out what I wanted. I was given a post box to send the rent to, but Feld always collects on the first day of the month." Lucia blew her nose, then took out her phone and scrolled across the screen, shaking her head. "The first time Feld showed up, he parked in the back, which no one ever does. Since I didn't know what was going on, I snapped a picture of his car." She held her phone out to Fab. "Is this helpful?"

Fab nodded, took it, and forwarded the picture to herself, her phone pinging a confirmation.

"When Feld is here, which isn't often, he spends most of his time at the real estate office." Lucia pointed. "Thought maybe he was a broker or an agent, but I've never seen anyone come or go. There's a name on the window but no phone number. I checked and couldn't find a listing."

I held out my hand to Fab and mouthed, "Your phone." She handed it over. I scrolled through it and forwarded the picture to Xander, then texted, *Find out who owns this car. Sooner would be better*, and signed my name so he'd know it was me.

Fab told Lucia that working from home for a couple of days would be a good idea. "That will give me time to figure out how to get rid of Feld, short of murder."

Lucia jumped up and packed a couple of bags. When she was ready, we waited while she locked up her business, then helped her out to the car.

Chapter Nine

Once Lucia pulled out onto the highway, I turned to Fab. "Why are we hanging out?" The words had barely come out when she beelined down the walkway.

She stopped in front of the real estate office, whipped out her lockpick, and opened the door. Time for me to show off my backup skills. Though I didn't doubt she could single-handedly keep a few men at bay.

Drab was a good way to describe the large one-room office. The only furnishings were an old desk and a recliner, and both had seen better days. Fab whipped out a pair of gloves, which meant that part of her plan was to toss the office. Disappointment bloomed in her eyes as she scanned the space; it was clear there wasn't much going on. She stepped behind the desk and threw open the drawers. "Nothing. Not even a pen," she said in disgust.

I hung out by the door, which I'd locked, Glock at my side.

Fab crossed to the strip kitchen, turning her nose up at the coffee maker, a model that was no longer sold. She opened the cupboards and found a can of no-brand coffee. Of the two doors on the far wall, one opened into an empty closet and the other a bathroom. Fab's nose pinched as she jumped back and kicked that door closed.

The only other door was in the center of the back wall, an "Exit" sign overhead. Fab opened it and stuck her head out. From my vantage point, there was only a view of the dumpster. She stepped outside and disappeared from sight.

I left my post at the front door and moved to stand on the threshold of the rear exit, where I watched Fab pace the small parking area with room for only a couple of cars, and walk up to another locked gate at the opposite end.

"Where does that go?" I pointed to the fence.

"There's a short alley that dumps out into the neighborhood behind here." Fab inserted her lockpick in the door of the empty space next to the real estate office and stuck her head inside. "I knew Lucia's store had a back exit and assumed it would be the same for the rest. Better to enter this way to snoop around; that way, no one will see me."

"Hold up," I yelled and, with one last look inside the real estate office, closed the door.

This space, the same size and layout as the previous, was filthy. Who knew how long it had been empty, and the last tenant hadn't bothered to clean up after themselves, leaving boxes and trash behind. The man who owned the building hadn't checked... or had decided it wasn't his problem and the next tenant could take care of it.

Fab made the same walk-through as in the first office, this time kicking a couple of boxes left behind.

I was happy when she finished and locked up. "What are you hoping to find?"

"Just want to know what I'm making an offer on." Fab opened the door to the last space and, a second later, drew her gun and stepped inside.

"Don't freaking shoot," a man's voice yelled. "I'm not even armed."

I moved into the doorway.

The man—who'd been lying on the floor, jacket under his head—attempted to sit up, then rolled on his side and pushed himself into a sitting position. "Fabbie. Sweetie. How've you been?"

"What are you doing here, Bert?" Fab snapped, holstering her Walther.

The dark-haired man, decked out in wrinkled tropical shorts and shirt, unleashed a smarmy smile.

Another one from her old life. I rolled my eyes.

"Oh man, it's good to see you, babes." Bert gave her a toothy grin. "I could use a favor. Old times' sake and all. Keep in mind all the times you asked and I delivered, and with no complaints. Mostly anyway."

"You haven't answered my question," Fab reminded him.

"I'm in a bit of trouble and needed a place to lie low." Bert swiveled around and leaned against the wall. "Happen to know the owner of this place and knew it was empty. What better place to hide for a few days with no one the wiser?"

"What about your house in Miami? When did you start doing business down here?" Fab demanded.

"My house isn't the hideout it once was; you never know who might be lurking around." Bert squirmed. "Once I get my current situation straightened out, it'll be time to find new digs."

"Cut the bull and tell me what you're doing here, living in squalor. You have more tricks to make an illegal dollar than anyone I know, and I also know you're close with a buck, so reach into your stash and find a new place. Knowing that your first inclination is to lie, don't go down that road; I'll sniff it out, and if I do, I'm out of here." Fab leveled a stare at him.

"I'm the best at what I do." Bert checked me out, undecided if he could trust me.

"She's a friend and not interested, so back to whatever you were meandering on about. Time to get to the point." Fab turned to me. "Bert's a money launderer."

"Hey!" The man snorted. "Okay, okay." Fab's burning glare was enough to get him talking again. "Got on the radar of the Feds, and they shut down a couple of accounts pending investigation, which left me owing a client big money."

"That's hardly going to matter when the Feds cart you off to jail."

Bert snorted. "You know I run a legit investment operation. I can cover this slight glitch, but I need time. But my client doesn't want to hear 'more time.' I either cover the loss now or I'm a dead man, and not a quick bullet." He grimaced. "I tried to cut ties previously, when I heard his banker turned up in pieces, but death is the only way out."

"If you're going to cry poor boy, you should save it for someone who doesn't know you. You've got other sources of cash—pay the man off and be done with it," Fab snapped.

"I hit hard times, and my cash flow isn't what it once was. I inadvertently made things worse and ripped off a drug shipment. It wasn't worth as much as I was led to believe, and now I've got two boss men after me. I got wind coming back from Key West that there's a bounty on my head, and knowing there's eyes everywhere, I remembered this place and got off the road. Just until I can get my finances together." Bert had a river of sweat rolling down the sides of his face.

I stepped into his sight and stared him down. "How in the heck do you expect your old friend Fabbie to help? Whatever cockamamie idea you're about to spout, I'm guessing it also puts her life in jeopardy. Forget it."

Calm down, I've got this, Fab telegraphed.

Sure you do.

"What do you know about Feld, and what happens when he finds out you're holed up here?" Fab asked.

So she can remember names when she wants to.

"Feld's an acquaintance who owes me. But once he figures out how to make a buck off me and keep his head attached, he'll sell me out."

"Fabbie, a minute of your time." I motioned for her to get her butt in gear and, while she was at it, wipe the annoyed look off her face.

Fab moved over in front of me and whispered, "Bert's helped me out in the past. Before you explode with 'tough,' help me figure out a solution other than minding my own business."

I stepped around her and stared down at the man. "What is it you want?"

"Get me out of Florida. No one needs to know. It's been forever since Fabbie and I had a connection, and no one will link us together."

I turned my attention to Fab. "Good luck explaining a road trip to Didier. I'm telling you now, I'm not going because my husband will sit on me if he has to."

Fab pulled out her phone. "How much more time do you think you have before someone shows up here looking for you?"

Bert shrugged, but fear filled his eyes. "Hard to say, but I do know that I can't stay long."

"You said something about coming up from

Key West; how did you do that? This isn't an area for getting around in without a car. Hitchhiking?" I asked, noting that I hadn't seen a car parked in the front or back other than Lucia's.

"I stopped for gas and noticed that I had a tail. Left my car parked in front of the convenience store, fled out the back, and disappeared into the neighborhood. Made my way over here via side streets, where I could find them. Good thing I have a map app on my phone or who knows where I would've ended up."

Fab stepped outside, leaving the door open. She turned her back and made a call, keeping her voice low.

I glared at Bert. "Anything happens to Fab because of you—that includes one hair on her head rearranged—and you'll have a third person wanting you dead."

Bert held up his hands in a conciliatory gesture. "I got you."

I turned away.

Fab stepped back inside. "Got you a ride to Miami. Where you go after that is up to you. You've excelled at sneaky in the past, and I suggest you trot out those old skills. Once it gets dark, a man will pick you up here. He knows not to park out front and will come through the back like I did. Be ready to go." She pocketed her phone, eyeing his backpack and some junk food wrappers. "Try to pull a fast one with this man, and he'll rearrange your brains and enjoy every minute." She unleashed one of her creepy-girl smiles.

"Dude have a name?" Bert picked up a soda can and downed it, then pitched it across the room.

"No, and neither do you," Fab snapped. "Give him the address of where you want to go; you've got time to come up with one. No need to get friendly."

"Give me your phone." Bert held out his hand.

Fab handed it over before I could scream *no*.

Bert made a call and handed it back. "You've got my number, and if you ever need anything, I'm your man."

"I've got no advice for how you fix screwing big-time criminals, but I have a different life now and won't be involved. I have every confidence you can figure out a way around the Feds and be back in business," Fab told him, leaving *if you live long enough* unsaid.

"You know…" Bert gave her a lovesick smile. "Anything… I'm your man."

To my credit, I didn't get sick on his dirty bare feet or in the boat shoes parked nearby. I preceded Fab out the door and stood waiting, hand on the knob, missing her parting words to Bert.

Fab turned in the opposite direction than I thought we'd be going, which led to another gate tucked at the opposite end of the building. "Now where are you going?" I hissed. Not wanting to be left behind, I ran and caught up to her. Not sure why I'd hesitated, since she just cut down a path that ran down the side of the property and out to the street.

Once in the car, I said, "Thanks for thinking of me on this deal, but not interested." I let the sarcasm pour out.

"Just hold your skirt; this deal may turn around. Give it a couple of days."

"Are you going to tell me who you called?" I drummed my fingers on the door panel.

"It's better not to know."

"What are you going to tell Didier?"

"The truth. But after sexy time. He's going to be happy that I didn't personally involve myself."

Her moony smile had me inwardly groaning. Except that she *was* personally involved, which I was certain that Didier would point out if he were told the whole truth. As for the bad guys, they wouldn't take it lightly when they found out she'd helped Bert go wherever. I hoped far away—in fact, voted for another country. "We going home?" It looked that way, but one could never be sure. I'd had my fill of excitement for the day.

"Just a slight detour. We need gas," she said, turning into a station that we never used and choosing a pump on the far end. She got out and stood behind the driver's door snapping a couple of pictures before getting back in.

"Hmm..." I tapped my cheek. "I'm assuming that we're at this dump of a station because it's where Bertie left his car. Which one of the wrecks is his?"

"The brown thing over there."

It was hard to tell the make and age of the rusted, beat-up sedan. Surprised me it ran. "I would've thought money laundering paid better."

"Bert likes to maintain a low profile and has an affinity for cars that appear to be on their last tire."

I stopped myself from rolling my eyes for fear of them getting stuck. "You might want to mention that an old piece of... also draws eyes."

Fab had gotten her fill of watching people pulling in to get gas. She cruised out to the highway and made a call. "It's the brown eyesore parked in front of the ice machine. Next to the air hose, there's a newer sedan, two guys slumped down in the front seat." After a pause, "Uh-huh." She hung up.

"You gripe to no end when I don't put my calls on speaker, and once again, here I am with no clue what's going on."

"Ignorance is bliss in all things Bert."

"I'm impressed you spotted the two men in the car." I tried to check them out in my side mirror, but it was too late.

Fab turned off the highway and onto a road that dead ended. Before that, she veered off into the trees—if you didn't know the road was there, you'd miss it—and continued into the compound.

Larry was doing his business on the lawn, another dog I assumed to be Melba following suit. A burly young man with lots of black hair paced the road in front of Casio's driveway, a phone to his ear—the same one we'd seen disappear into the house earlier.

"What's going on?" Fab demanded.

"The call Marcus is on appears to have his full attention, and whatever the conversation is, he's not happy. Also, since he doesn't have a bag in his hand, he's not cleaning up after the dogs."

Fab cruised up and stopped beside him, rolling down my window and leaning across the console. He totally ignored her and continued walking, and she coasted after him. "Marcus," she bellowed. He stopped and turned, *how dare you* on his face, and just stared. "Be sure you clean up after the dogs."

"Yeah, right," he said with full-blown arrogance. "If you don't mind." He pointed to his phone and walked away.

I laughed and got a shove to the shoulder. "He's a younger version of his old man. No denying that DNA."

"He's lucky I didn't get out of the car and kick his butt," Fab grouched. "Isn't it common sense to clean up after your animals?"

"You'd think so, but not for some people. I'd

word it a little nicer when you stomp over and give the 'welcome to the neighborhood' speech and, while you're at it, 'here are the rules.'"

"You know what he looks like to me? Trouble. What's he doing here anyway, and how long is he staying?" Fab cruised into my driveway and parked.

"As I already reported, Casio was vague on the details."

"Since I know you're about to offer to make the 'welcome to the whatever' speech, I accept. That little toad looks at me again like I'm a bug he wants to squash and it won't be pretty."

I laughed, much to her disgust.

"Happy you find this amusing."

"I volunteer to be the welcome committee." I had her attention, suspicious that I'd given in so quickly. "As a backup plan, get daddy dearest on the phone and have Brick give his kid a heads-up that you're not someone to fool with."

"I may do just that, and then get the whole story about why his kid is camped out at Casio's."

Fab had worked for Brick Famosa for a number of years, and though he professed that she was one of his favorite people, he never thought twice when it came to putting her in danger. I couldn't think of a job we'd done for him where an exchange of gunfire wasn't involved. She'd finally told him sayonara, can't work for you anymore.

Fab parked in my driveway, and we both got out, grabbing briefcases and purses. She stood at the end of the driveway, one eye on Marcus. "We'll talk tomorrow. Tonight, I'm going to entice my husband to come home early."

"I'm calling mine and suggesting a low-key evening and that he bring food."

A shrill whistle filled the air. It got the dogs' attention; they stopped chasing one another and turned their attention to Marcus. He waved them over, and they came running. Marcus made eye contact with Fab and waved.

"Don't shoot him," I warned.

Chapter Ten

Creole brought home pizza, and the two of us curled up on the couch. On a full stomach and after he'd had a couple of beers, I told him about my day. Fab's business idea had slid off the rails as far as I was concerned.

He turned my face to his. "And you said?"

"When I first heard about the idea, I was in, sort of—not totally wild about the idea of a strip mall. But after meeting Feld and Bertie, any kind of a deal screamed trouble. If Fab is set on growing Lucia's business, I've come up with an alternate plan, and you know I'm good at those." I winked at him, noting he wanted me to move it along and not leave out any pertinent facts. "If Fab gets all 'tudey with me—not wanting to take my advice or come up with a better plan of her own—I'll have you confront her. She responds well to threats of bodily harm to her husband, so go with that."

Creole laughed with a shake of his head. "Know this: you'd owe me big."

"If I need you to gallop to the rescue, I'm willing to up the ante." I held out my hand, and we shook.

"When you find out who she called to solve Berto's problem, I'd like to know."

"Just a friendly tip: if you pick up on my tendency to butcher people's names, it's going to become a habit." I shook my finger at him, noting his smirk. "Let's hope it's the last we hear of Bertie." Enough of that man. "Sort of met Marcus today — twice." I told Creole about both sightings and my offer to spell out the compound rules, once Fab told me what they were.

"I'm telling you now, Marcus will look like he's listening, but he'll tune you out," Creole said with a shake of his head. "Casio brought him to the office, introduced him around. Came off as a full-of-himself, arrogant know-it-all — but then, it runs in the family. Apparently, the kid got in with the wrong bunch at school, and his old man thought a change of scenery would do him good."

"I'm still surprised the mother went for it."

"Brick laid down an ultimatum. I waited for the details on what it was exactly, but Casio didn't elaborate. He's proud of himself, thinking that he and Marcus are on the way to being best friends. I told him to keep his eyes open, when what I wanted to tell him was to watch his back. There's just something about the kid."

"Same sentiment as Fab's."

* * *

Creole and I were having a lazy morning, drinking our coffee outside on the deck, the cats at our feet, enjoying the waves that gently lapped the shore. It was our favorite place to sit any time of day.

Both of our phones rang at the same time, and we laughed.

Jake's, the bar I owned, popped up on my phone screen. This early wouldn't be good news. I ignored the call so Creole and I weren't talking over each other. His was a work issue that he took care of in short order. He hung up and pointed to my phone, which rang again. This time, I answered and put it on speaker.

"Oh, there you are," Kelpie, one of my bartenders, said in a chirpy tone as soon as I answered. "I knew you wouldn't be avoiding me."

"Tell me the cops haven't surrounded the place." I knew the chances that they had were slim, since we weren't open yet, but later in the day, it was always a possibility.

"Good news," she cooed.

Creole chuckled.

I visualized her gyrating around, as per her usual. "Which is what?"

"There was a bit of a fight last night. More good news: no one got hurt. Okay, a couple of black eyes and bloody lips. But better news, the bar's getting a good cleaning, and we'll be open on time." There was a ta-da in her tone.

I swear she lived to make these phone calls. "How many of our patrons went to jail?"

Creole held up his thumb and forefinger in a zero.

"I'm full of good news today—no one. You know why?" Not waiting for answer: "It's because I had the bright idea to have a few regulars spread the word that if anyone was caught calling 911, I'd shoot them and ban them for life." She sing-songed the last part.

Creole looked down, shaking his head. I patted him on the back and got a stink eye. I stopped short of laughing.

"Should I ask the cause of the fight?" And if she somehow instigated it was left unasked.

"Oh you know, two guys get into a whose is bigger spat, and the next thing, fists fly. A couple of our other patrons thought what the heck and hopped into the fray. That's my interpretation anyway. As far as fights go, it was a four." The disappointment in Kelpie's voice was clear.

"Any more good news for me?"

"Cook marched up here and informed me—in case you come in the front door, which you rarely do—that he wants an audience."

"Do I get a clue?"

After a long pause, Kelpie lowered her voice to a whisper. "Friend of the family issue. But you didn't hear that from me."

"Tell Cook I'll be there in about an hour."

"Okie-D!" she stopped just short of yelling

and hung up.

"Do you think Kelpie's running a pay-to-fight scam?" Creole asked, annoyed.

"Wouldn't surprise me, since you and I have been told on several occasions that it's good for business. You can't be too irked, since no one went to the hospital or got arrested."

Creole didn't appreciate my attempt at humor. "You have another scheme for getting Fab out of the house?"

"Not today. I'm giving her a rest. I'll use my Glock for backup." I shot my finger into the air.

"These antics of yours aren't funny," he grouched.

I launched myself into his lap. "You take that back." I hooked my arms around his neck.

"Make me."

***

After Creole and I went inside, showered, and changed, he got another call and flew out of the house ahead of me. I grabbed my briefcase and headed out the door. The engine of my Hummer was already running, Fab behind the wheel.

"What are you doing?" I asked, sliding into the passenger seat.

"You think I'd miss the aftermath of a bar fight?" There was incredulity in her tone.

"How did you find out?" I asked as she cruised slowly down the block, one eye checking out the neighborhood, Casio's house in particular.

"I have my sources." Fab drove out of the compound and out to the main highway.

Chapter Eleven

"I'm happy that you decided to grace me with your presence," I said as Fab cruised towards Jake's. "So you don't flip, Cook wants a minute of my time... about a family issue, it was whispered confidentially."

"Must be some real trouble or one of his hundred relatives would take care of it."

I agreed. If you needed a job done and it was legal, Cook had a family member in the business and you always got quality service.

Traffic was light, and it didn't take long before Fab pulled into the parking lot of the short block I owned, where Jake's sat at the back of the property. As we cruised past the lighthouse, I issued an ultimatum: "You either make it start paying for the space it takes up or I'm going behind your back." Where did it come from? Good question. A flatbed is all I knew. Why take cash for a job when you can get a lighthouse?

Fab ignored me.

She'd find out I wasn't blowing hot air. "Go slow," I said as she coasted by Junker's, an old gas station given a good scrubbing and turned into an antique garden store that was rarely open. "There doesn't appear to be any new deliveries." If you wanted first choice on anything, you practically had to be standing there when the truck was unloaded or you were out of luck. Inventory turned over fast. Junker mainly sold to other dealers, who hawked the items in their retail stores.

A huge piece of cardboard tacked up on the front door of Jake's caught my attention. "I'm betting that reads, 'Cleaning up from humongous bar fight, but opening on time.'"

Fab laughed as she cruised around the back and parked. "Not taking that bet."

We got out and trooped through the kitchen door. Cook's door was open, and he was on the phone. I waved and pointed to the bar, and we continued down the hallway. I stopped at the office door, which was cracked open, and after a knock, stuck my head in, while Fab continued and grabbed a seat at the bar. Doodad, aka Charles Wingate III, was kicked back in his chair, feet on the desk, a clipboard in his hand. I credited him for getting a desk, chair, and couch in the miniscule space.

"I see you're working hard." I waved.

"Don't you worry. Once I'm done placing a couple of orders, I'll be back to doing nothing." He grinned. "I'm claiming most of the credit for cleaning up the mess, even though I did get some help. You could bring me a beer."

"I'll be sure to do that." I wasn't able to back

out of the office before he stopped me.

"Heads up: There's some termite in the bar that wants to talk to you. Told him we weren't open yet and to get the hell out, and he laughed. That's when Kelpie pointed her handgun. Bummed me out to have to give her a headshake to put it away."

"Any clue what Termite wants?"

"I asked that and got the finger. And I waved mine right back at him." Doodad smirked. "If you want to be my favorite boss of all time, dawdle a bit so I can eavesdrop."

"You can't take away a title I've already earned." I saluted and left him as he opened his laptop and furiously clicked away.

Termite? I assumed it was the twenty-something seated at the end of the bar—just barely legal, I'd guess—a po'd expression on his face. Fab and Kelpie were at the other end, engaged in conversation and completely ignoring the variety of noises the guy blew out of his mouth. I slid behind the bar with Kelpie, feeling staid in my t-shirt and raspberry cotton skirt when standing next to a woman clad in a full-length bathing suit top, shorts, and tutu, wings clipped to the straps of her suit. Her pink hair was in a messy bun, drinking straws poking out in several directions.

I filled a glass with 7up and took a long drag before loading it up with cherries. Then I turned to the man furiously tapping his finger on the bar top. "Mr. Termite, I understand that you're waiting to speak to me." Out of the corner of my eye, I caught Doodad sliding into the bar and taking a seat at one of the tables.

"Very funny. Ha-ha. It's going to give me great pleasure to kick all your asses to the street," Termite sneered.

"Why don't we skip the pleasantries and you get to the point of why you're here? I'm the owner, and I'm telling you now that you're not kicking anyone anywhere unless you want two broken legs."

"I'm pleased to announce that you are no longer the owner." After a dramatic pause, he said, "I am."

"Congratulations. Now get out." I pointed to the door. Whatever con he was running, it wouldn't work.

Termite produced a manila envelope and shoved it across the bar. "You might want to read this. Then we can make this a smooth transition. Or not. If you choose the latter, I can promise you it will get nasty."

I grabbed the envelope and removed the single-page document, then scooted down the bar and stood next to Fab. She read faster than me and hissed in a breath. It was a deed signed and notarized by the previous owner, Jake Cedric, to a Jason Shields—aka Termite, I assumed. "I have one of these, also signed by Jake, if this is indeed his signature. And I have bank verification that the amount agreed upon for the sale was deposited into his account." Why would Jake sign over the bar—of which he only owned half at the time, but I had no intention of sharing that tidbit—to someone else, and then sell that same half to me? At the time, he was on the run from loan sharks, and because of me, he was able to beat it out of town alive.

"You might want to check the date on yours, as I'm certain mine supersedes it," Termite gloated.

"What took you so long to get your scam together and claim supposed ownership?"

"Nothing supposed about it. I am the owner, and you're holding the proof. So take your friends and get out, and as you so kindly pointed out, the door's that way." Termite flicked his finger. "I'll be posting a sign that Jake's will reopen in a few days, after it's been fumigated."

"You're not the brightest bulb. I'm not going anywhere based on this." I held up the paper, wadded it into a ball, and tossed it in the trash under the counter. "The only chance you have of getting your grimy fingers on *my* bar is to file a lawsuit and let a judge decide."

"Asking questions here and there, I knew you'd make that dick move, and so you know, I have the original document in a safe."

"That's swell. Now get out. I wouldn't hate to shoot you; in fact, I'd enjoy it." I flashed him one of Fab's creepy-girl smiles. "I think it's typically a count of three, but I'm thinking two for you to get out." I drew my Glock, keeping it at my side.

"That's a felony. I'm calling the cops."

"Go ahead and make the call, but you're doing it outside, and while you're waiting, use the time to brush up on the law. You'll be the one escorted off the property after they've told you the same thing I just did. A court will decide whether you have a claim or not."

"Who are you to Jake?" Fab demanded.

Termite ignored her, shaking his head with a grin, and then spew every dirty word he could think of.

Fab pulled her Walther and pointed it at him. "You were asked nicely; now I'm telling you: Get. Out."

"I'll be back." He slid off the stool.

"You show up again, and I'll have you arrested," I yelled after him. "Another thing, you'll *never* get your hands on this bar."

"Bitch." Termite disappeared out the door.

I knew we hadn't seen the last of him.

"Who was that?" Fab demanded.

"Heck if I know," I said. "I won't be asking Jake, since I heard that he met with an untimely accident. I never verified whether it was true or just a story to get the loan sharks off his back. I don't know why he'd screw me, since I was under the impression that he had a good relationship not only with my aunt but me."

"Car accident," Fab said. "Xander put an alert

on his name, and an article came up. You should have him follow up to verify that a death certificate was filed and it wasn't some scam story Jake paid a friend to write."

I pulled out my phone and texted Termite's name, along with the message: *Who the heck is this guy?* Then asked for a death certificate for Jake, even though it wouldn't matter if he was dead or alive; the legal fight would be with Termite.

"There's more than a few places around here that a body can be tossed. One I've heard of is a bit of a drive, but chances are good that it will never resurface." Kelpie nodded, liking her idea.

"If Termite comes back, he's not allowed inside. We have more than a few regulars that would be happy to show him the door," I said to Kelpie and Doodad. "Spread the word. I caught Fab pointing her phone at the man, so she can forward a picture."

Fab picked up her phone and scrolled across the screen, followed by several phones dinging one after another with incoming message alerts. She looked up and asked, "What are you going to do?"

"I'm not waiting to see if Termite's able to pull some legal maneuver and get control of my bar. I'll be calling a lawyer and my CPA about protecting my assets." Fab and I had a criminal lawyer on speed dial, and he could recommend someone. I bent over, retrieved the balled-up legal document, and shoved it in the pocket of my skirt. "Bar fight and now this; swell start to the day. Do you think you could hold off on any more problems until next week?"

"Don't forget Cook," Kelpie whispered, loud enough for all to hear.

I nodded and slipped down the hall to the kitchen. Cook's door was wide open, and he was still behind his desk. As soon as he saw me, he motioned me inside, Fab taking a seat next to me.

"I eavesdropped from the deck and heard what that twat wanted, and my money's on you," Cook grouched.

I smiled my thanks at him. "I hear you have an issue you need my help on."

"There's a friend of the family, Charlie Miller, who served in the Army. While he was deployed, a friend offered to store his '63 Porsche."

Fab hissed out a breath. The woman knew her cars.

"A car he restored himself," Cook added with a smile. "Charlie's back and wants the car, but the so-called friend has danced him around, ducking him, not taking his calls. He showed up on the friend's doorstep several times to demand his car back. The friend's story has changed several times; one's that the car was stolen. But the last time Charlie tried, the friend called the cops and claimed not to know what he was talking about. The cops checked the property and found nothing. Charlie then talked to a couple of the neighbors. One remembered seeing it parked on the lawn, a 'For Sale' sign on it. The man was interested in it himself, but the price was too steep."

"One of two things happened, maybe three," I mused. "The friend forged Charlie's signature on the title and the buyer had no clue, or the buyer overlooked the lack of legit paperwork in favor of negotiating a lower price. It sickens me to say that a number of people don't care about the legalities. My third option, which I doubt, is he wrecked it, had it junked, and doesn't have the big ones to fess up."

"What do you want Madison to do?" Fab stared down Cook.

"This is a job for both of you. I had no doubt you'd be sitting right where you are," Cook directed at Fab. "I want you to find the damn car and get it back to Charlie. He's off serving his country and his car's stolen by a supposed friend—no way does this guy gets away with theft. Don't think so."

"Set up a convenient time for Charlie to come in for a meeting; there's information we're going to need from him." I eyed Fab. "No weaseling out." She made a face.

Cook laughed as he watched the byplay between us. "Charlie's out of town for a family reunion; he'll be back in a couple of days, but I've got everything you need." He opened a desk drawer, withdrew a sheet of paper, and handed it to me.

I glanced at it and handed it to Fab. "Where this gets complicated is if Weasel forged the signature and the buyer thought they were getting a straight-up deal," I said. "That would mean going to court, and how a judge will rule is never a certainty. If there's no way of getting the car back, I'd like to know that there's leeway to come up with an alternate plan." I didn't like our chances of finding such a hot auto.

"I'm giving you the okay on Charlie's behalf, and only because I trust you both." Cook picked up his phone and scrolled across the screen. "Almost forgot." I heard my phone ping a couple of times and then Fab's. "Texted pictures of the Porsche and the so-called friend. Also included two of Charlie, one in his uniform if that would be helpful."

"It might motivate people to talk to us," Fab said.

"I'll get back to you." I stood, as did Fab.

"No doubt." Cook smiled at us both. "I know that you'll do your best… and also know that there might not be a solution, as much as I don't want that outcome for Charlie. It is what it is."

Back in the car, I said, "So sad it's too early for alcohol, for me anyway. Zip through the coffee joint and get me something with extra whipped cream."

"I'm ordering you a double, maybe a squirt of caramel," Fab said. I couldn't help licking my lips. "Got a call while you were talking to

Doodad, and there's an issue with Kyle. I have to deal with it, and you're coming with me."

"I'll put a smile on—no matter that it might be fake—if you can promise that afterwards, we can go home and sit by your pool."

"You're on. I'll make this as quick as possible."

Chapter Twelve

It surprised me when Fab pulled into JS Auto Body and parked. I'd assumed we were heading to the office to talk to Xander. On the drive over, I'd been on my phone the whole time, talking to my CPA—Ernest Whitman III, aka Whit—telling him what had happened at Jake's and that I wanted all of the bar's assets protected. He assured me that if the paperwork was legit and I was served by Termite, he had a good lawyer on speed dial that could handle it.

The bar had been on the skids when I bought out Jake, and Code Enforcement had been days away from shutting the business down for filth issues. I'd poured time and money into making it the popular dive bar it was now and wasn't about to give up without a fight.

"Let me guess, car trouble?" I asked, wondering what the heck as I shoved my phone in my pocket.

"Sometimes it's fun not to tell you everything and just fling it at you, see what kind of reaction I get." Fab laughed.

I climbed out with a shake of my head.

Jimmy Spoon had the door open and was standing on the threshold, beckoning us inside. I kissed his cheek on the way in, surprised to see that he had a full office. I waved to Billy and Xander and acknowledged Kyle, all of them sitting in chairs lined up against the far wall.

"Mother's not going to be happy with you when she finds out she missed the party." I raised my eyebrows at Spoon, taking a seat next to his desk.

Westin family quirk—no one wanted to be the last to know about anything, and if there was juicy news, then everyone wanted to be the first to tell everyone else.

With hellos all around, Fab claimed the couch, as per her usual.

"I just sent you a couple of emails," Xander told me.

"I'm going to the office as soon as we leave here," I said. "Where's the food?" Another Westin tradition.

Spoon snorted. "I've got drinks."

Fab and I waved them off.

"This little sit-down is due to events that happened at the warehouse. It's been decided that Xander will give us the details." Spoon pointed in his direction.

"There was a problem at the office late yesterday—" Xander started.

"Does Creole know?" I cut in. Would've been nice to have heard about this last night.

"He got the update just before you got here," Spoon assured me.

"Kyle and I were getting ready to leave when the gate buzzer sounded," Xander continued. "Knowing everyone in the building had split, I checked the video feed before answering. Kyle looked out the window, recognized the pickup from the men that were after him, and yelled for me not to let them in."

"Forward the images from the feed," Fab said.

Xander nodded. "Figured they'd go away if they didn't get a response and sighed with relief when they backed out. Except they then turned around and backed up to the gate. One man jumped into the truck bed and started to climb over, and I hit the alarm."

"It was loud." Kyle snickered. "Bet you could hear it out on the highway."

"No need to worry about noise complaints from the neighboring businesses; if anyone was around, they weren't getting involved," Xander assured us. "Not a soul came out to the street. The guy jumped back in the truck bed, and the driver took off."

"Why do they want you back so bad?" I asked. My guess was that what Kyle knew about their criminal activities made them nervous.

"There's no quitting unless you're dead," Kyle said. "I asked around if anyone had been allowed to leave and got a warning to drop the subject and never bring it up again."

"I'm surprised they were able to track you. It's not like we left a trail," Fab said.

"Thinking along the same lines as you, with Kyle's permission, I went through his stuff and found a tracking device in his backpack," Billy grumbled. "No worries, I took care of it."

"Emerson should be in on this." *Weren't you supposed to set up a meeting?* I turned to Fab, who gave a slight shake of her head. What did that mean? I pulled my phone out of my pocket.

"You might want to hold off on the call until you hear this next part," Spoon said.

"The three of us went out for burgers last night," Billy said. "Kyle went to the bathroom and, on the way back, was waylaid by a guy twice his size. The man slammed him up against the wall, hand on his neck. Lucky, I'd kept an eye out. Jerked the guy off Kyle and got in a solid punch before he pulled a gun. Got to say it surprised me when he backed up and disappeared. I'm also happy that I didn't get shot, knowing I couldn't return fire."

"He got away?" Fab asked, definitely disappointed.

"Took a minute to make sure Kyle was okay and then checked the parking lot—no sign of the man anywhere." Billy nodded at Kyle. "Why don't you tell everyone who he was?"

"An undercover cop. I've done business with him before, if you can call it that. He knew I was working the streets running errands for the other guys and wanted to squeeze me for the same information. In exchange, he gave me enough money for a burger and promised not to haul me off to jail for being a runaway. It didn't take long for the pressure to get to me, and that's when I decided to get out of town."

"Which you were going to do without a plan and not much money," Billy grouched at him.

Kyle's cheeks turned red.

"It's disgusting that a cop would put the squeeze on a teenager." I didn't know any that would use that tactic. "How are old you?" I asked, since I was certain he had yet to tell us the truth.

All eyes were now on Kyle.

"Fourteen," he squeaked.

Fab sat up straighter. "How did you meet this cop?"

"Detective Brand cornered me one day, said he knew all about me and that unless I agreed to cooperate and provide information, I was headed to jail. I told him running from a foster home wasn't a crime. That's when he told me that the family had filed charges against me for theft. It's a lie; I didn't steal anything from them," Kyle stated adamantly.

"Since you have more than a couple of people looking for you, you need to lie low," Fab advised.

"Kyle thinks all he needs is a ride to the Georgia border, where he can disappear and get himself a job. Told him it was highly unlikely without ID." Billy shook his head, his expression conveying that he thought it was a bad idea.

"Harboring a runaway is a crime," Spoon said, in case we didn't know.

"Time for some legal advice." I picked up my phone and called Emerson. "If Brad's around, you might not want to tell him it's me on the phone," I said when she answered. She laughed. "You know how he gets when I call asking for a favor."

"I'm here at the office." Emerson had lowered her voice.

"I'm at Spoon's business, and there's a legal problem we could use your expertise on. Would you mind coming over and giving us some advice?" I asked.

"I'll be there in five." She hung up.

"Emerson's on her way, and she can tell you what your options are," I told Kyle. "Ones that will keep us all out of jail."

"I told Kyle that Emerson's always upfront with everything she does." Fab gave him a reassuring smile.

It didn't surprise me when Emerson showed up with Brad at her side.

"I tried to shake him, but he wasn't having it." She smiled up at him.

"Once I heard the urgent request came from you, and knowing that, like you, Emerson has a hard time saying no, I came along to say it for her." Brad hooked his arm around her.

Billy had gotten up and grabbed a couple more chairs from a nearby closet, and they sat down.

I introduced the two to Kyle. "I asked you here for legal advice," I told Emerson, ignoring Brad's glare. "I'll let Fab take it from here."

Fab made a face but launched into the retell, surprising me by starting from when she picked Kyle up on the road and not leaving out any details.

Emerson listened and nodded several times. When Fab finished, Emerson asked Kyle a series of questions about his family, which he answered with little hesitation. According to him, there was no one. "Legally speaking, the court would ideally like to see you placed with a suitable family member. If there isn't anyone, then you'd be looking at foster care again. It has to be done this way to prevent anyone from going to jail for helping you out."

Kyle shot forward in his chair, shaking his head vigorously. "I'm not going back, and if you make me, I'll just run away again."

"If you do that, the next time you get picked up, it would lead to a different set of legal problems for you," Emerson said.

Kyle crossed his arms and glared.

Billy patted Kyle on the back. "Any reason I can't be his guardian?"

"Are you telling me that you're related?"

Emerson asked. "If so, that would certainly make it easier."

"Kyle's mother and I were cousins—second or third, I believe." Billy's stare defied anyone to say otherwise. "At one time, we were close, and then lost touch."

I looked down and grinned at the floor.

Emerson's laugh conveyed that she didn't believe a word. "If you're willing to fill out the paperwork to be a foster parent, I have connections that can expedite the process."

Billy turned to Kyle. "I get that you don't know me very well, but are you willing to give it a try? Before you answer, know that you're not going to be a dick kid and put something over on me. Grown men don't get away with that." His smile would put the fear in most people. Kyle nodded without hesitation.

Billy's offer surprised me, but he'd be good for the kid. He had been for Xander.

"I'm thinking that Kyle should share his situation with the Chief and Baldie," I said. "The people he was involved with need to be in jail, and if that's not possible, then run out of town."

"I dare you to call Baldie that to his face," Fab challenged.

"How much?" I didn't think she'd put up cash, and her silence told me I was right. "The Chief and Baldie, who prefers to be called Casio, are both ex-law enforcement, but you can trust them not to screw you. When they give their word, they keep it. No phony, waffley excuses." That got a smile out of Kyle.

"There isn't anyone in this room, or that we'll introduce you to, that will screw you over. If anyone tries, you let me know." Fab air-boxed.

That got more than a few grins.

I gave her the *behave* stare, which she ignored. Thankfully, she hadn't shot up the room, even with her fingers.

"You keep a low profile while I get the paperwork expedited," Emerson told Kyle. "I'm assuming that if I have any questions, I can get ahold of you through Billy?"

Kyle nodded, appearing overwhelmed by the conversation. "I should probably warn you that the guys I was working for aren't nice and don't like it when they're crossed. In fact, they respond with something painful. There was talk of people disappearing or ending up dead, but I never saw anything and knew not to ask."

"That needs to be shared with Casio," Spoon said. We were all in agreement.

"Any questions?" Emerson asked Kyle, who shook his head. She handed him and Billy her business card, and the meeting broke up.

"Mind if I take a lunch break?" Billy asked Spoon, who responded with a snort. Billy turned to Kyle. "Probably should've discussed my idea with you before throwing it out there, but it was last-minute, and just blurted it out. How about we go to lunch and talk about expectations on both our parts?"

"That's a great idea." Emerson beamed at them. "Let me know if anything changes."

I gave Spoon a kiss and was about to dash for the door when Brad cornered me. "Before you start crabbing at me about getting Emerson involved, just answer: who else?"

He hugged me hard. "I'm not averse to Emerson helping Kyle get his life figured out. But all of you need to watch your backs. I intend to give Emerson the same advice."

"You really like her, don't you?"

"Stop it. You know I do."

Chapter Thirteen

Fab made the short drive to the office, cruised into the lot, and parked. Her phone rang a couple of times along the way, which she ignored, sending it to voicemail. Probably a client. I had several calls to make but needed more information before I started. Knowing Creole and Didier were in a meeting, I went upstairs, leaving Fab sitting at one of the tables outside as her phone rang again.

I'd just settled at my desk when Xander walked in. He was also on the phone, agreeing to send money. He hung up and sat across from me, and I said, "You need to put your baby mama on a budget."

Xander wrinkled his nose. "I tried to get Krista's next appointment date out of her, and she was evasive. You'd think she'd be happy that I want to support her through her pregnancy."

"If the two of you haven't had this conversation already, you should sit down together and talk about expectations."

"I assured her that I would be there for her and our child. And also that I'd do my best to be a damn good father."

I smiled at him, noting that he didn't look as shell-shocked as when he first shared the news. "You two need to come to an agreement, one that you're *both* happy with."

"I'll ask her out to dinner again. Maybe this time she'll say yes, and we can have that talk."

I hoped that the two would be able to work it out. "Were you able to find out anything about James Shields?" Termite was more fitting. I opened my laptop.

"Jake Cedric is listed as the father on his birth certificate."

"That was a well-kept secret on Jake's part. He never mentioned a word about a son, and neither has anyone else that knew him."

"Ran a credit check, and Shields has a low score due to delinquent accounts. His criminal background check came back clean."

"Would you see if you can locate a death certificate for Jake? Notification of his demise came through the rumor mill, and it wouldn't surprise me if he put out word of his death and is still sucking air somewhere warm."

"Wouldn't it be something if he's still walking around somewhere?" Xander said with a note of disbelief.

"If it turns out he's still alive and pulled some shady deal with the bar, I'll be tempted to shoot him." I sighed. "I haven't spoken to a lawyer yet, but if Jake transferred the bar to his son and then sold it to me, I'm not sure how that plays out in court." Why would he do that when I'd been more than fair with the man? "If Termite does win, he won't get much. One thing he can't change is that I own the property the bar sits on. He'd have to negotiate a lease to stay, and I'd kick the business to the curb. He could bring in a flatbed and haul the building off to another location, but that would be costly."

Xander laughed.

Fab came in and sat down on the far side of the desk. "That was Gunz." She set her phone down.

Gunz was currently Fab's biggest client. One good thing: he never knowingly put her life in danger. When trouble did break out, he always told her to back off.

"Which one of his hundred or so family members is in trouble now?" I asked. Not sure if they took a vote or what, but the man had been made the family fixer. No problem was too big or small for the big guy to pawn off on Fab.

"This time, Gunz is the one with the problem. He bought a house—you know him, always sniffing out a great deal. Paid cash, escrow closed, and the previous owner not only didn't move out but told him in no uncertain terms that she wasn't moving anywhere—take it to court."

"Since the sale is a done deal, and assuming he has the paperwork, he should call the police," I said.

"You know Gunz has friends on the force. He

got hot on the phone, and they told him he'd have to go to court. Also warned against the previous owner disappearing." Fab laughed.

The man did have a reputation, which he claimed to have shined up. I'd give him one thing—no one had gone missing in the time we'd been working for him.

"We're not the court, or lawyers, or a lot of other things—what are we supposed to do?" I asked.

"Broker a truce."

"More moola is the only way that's going to happen—either pay her off or pony up exorbitant court fees. There's no reason he wouldn't win, but still." The story irritated me, and I wasn't the one in the middle. "Gunz is screwed no matter which way he goes, and there doesn't appear to be a clear-cut shortcut through the drama."

"The one thing he didn't do—which shouldn't make a difference, legally anyway—is he didn't do a walk-through of the property to make sure the occupant had gotten out before signing the final docs."

"I'm sure he's not the first person to skip that step, because who'd expect to be held up this way?" I asked.

"His cop friends told him it's one of the latest scams."

"I know Gunz is a man who wants everything five minutes ago, but I'm not feeling my perkiest right now," I said, catching Xander's smirk. "There's a lot going on."

"No worries. Already told Gunz first thing tomorrow." Fab held out her phone, showing me a picture of a swanky property.

"Nice manse. The new purchase?" I caught Fab's nod. "Not the dumpy multiple units he generally goes for." I handed the phone to Xander.

"My guess is that the seller knew what they were doing and exactly what they could get away with," Fab said.

"I wouldn't tell Gunz that this advice is from me—that way he won't ignore it out of hand—but the fastest way to get rid of the scammer is probably court. It will cost him in lost income if he plans to rent, so he needs to request reimbursement for that and any other losses, as well as attorney fees. Or scam her by renting to someone and have them move in and hopefully expedite her move out."

"Gunz would like her set out on the curb. I told him that wasn't an option, so he wants us to find out what she does want and negotiate a deal," Fab said.

"How can you trust that this woman won't take more money and still not move?" Xander asked.

"Good point," I said. "A face-to-face with her might not be easy, as we probably won't be able to get past the housekeeper—I doubt anyone in *that* house will be answering their own door. But we might get lucky."

"I don't see where we've got a lot of options. Legal ones, anyway." Fab sighed out her frustration.

Tired of Gunz's problems, I changed the subject. "You want to do business together? I suggest that we buy up the rest of the block between here and Spoon's. Okay, not all at once, since they're not for sale, but they'll come up sooner or later." I waved off the objections that Fab was about to unleash. "We kick out the slackers and get new tenants that pay. The three other buildings that Creole and I own all pay their own way."

"What about my strip center?" Fab huffed.

"It's infested with criminals, with the exception of the dress designer." It screamed trouble to me, and Fab was overlooking way too much. "Have you considered that brooming out the storefronts isn't going to be easy and might involve gunshots? I can already tell you my husband is going to put his foot down. If you give yours the real skinny, he's also going to veto the idea."

"I'm still hoping to do a straight-up deal with the owner."

Oh brother. With the number of criminals hanging out, he was probably the least of the problems. "He still ducking your calls?" I asked. Fab nodded. "What's his name again? Never mind. See if you can find the owner of this strip mall," I said to Xander, then picked up my phone and messaged him the address. "When you get a name, run a criminal background check."

Xander opened his laptop.

"Where's your friend Bertie?" I asked.

"It's Bert, just Bert."

"Whatever. He clear the county line yet? Kind of hoping he hopped a bus out of town."

"*Bert* is up in Miami, lying low and selling off assets to get himself off the hook with his investors. You'll be happy to know that I told him my good will was tapped out as far as his problems were concerned, that I wasn't going to let him take me down with him, and not to call again," Fab said, a *so there* look on her face.

"Now that Bertie's got your number, I'd be surprised—no make that shocked—if this is the last you hear from him." I winked at Xander, who laughed. Fab ignored us both.

"Just filled up your inbox," Xander said as he continued to click away on his laptop. "You need follow-up on anything, let me know."

"Are you okay with Kyle moving in?" Fab asked him.

"I'm fine with it as long as Kyle doesn't intentionally bring trouble around. Though I realize it could happen anyway. I remember when I didn't have any place to go and all the people that helped me." Xander nodded at Fab and me. "It surprised me that Billy offered to foster Kyle, but he'll let him know, like he did me, not to screw up the opportunity.

"If anything goes south, get hot on the phone," I said.

"I've been taking self-defense classes." Xander air-boxed with a grin.

Fab nodded her approval. "I'm ready to go home." She stood and walked back to her desk.

I lowered my voice. "Check out the rest of the properties on this block and tell me what you find out. But ssh." I crossed my finger over my lips. "Keep your eyes out and if you see someone you don't recognize, call the cops."

Xander gave me a thumbs up.

Chapter Fourteen

The next day, Fab and I got a late start on her job for Gunz. As she pulled out of my crushed-shell driveway—a surprise from Creole and I still didn't like anyone driving on it, but I told myself to calm down, it was my car and I wasn't parking on the street—she did a double-take.

"What's going on?" Fab tipped her head towards Casio's house.

"Looks like Marcus's backside is hanging out the window of that Porsche. Appears to be a newer model than yours." She snorted, which made me smile. Back when she worked exclusively for Brick, who owned a car lot, one of the perks was that she could change cars as often as she did shoes.

Fab stopped in the middle of the road, which caught the two guys' attention. Marcus stood and waved an envelope at her. The driver of the sports car rolled up the window and sped off, but not before Fab got a picture of the license plate. Marcus turned his back and walked inside the house. She glared through the windshield as the security gate opened and the car blew through without having to slow down and sped off without waiting for it to close, which was a longstanding edict to keep outsiders from sneaking in. "How did he get the gate open so fast?"

"Marcus hit the inside keypad?" But he didn't have time.

Fab accelerated, with the intention of following the Porsche, and had to make a hard right to avoid a Lexus making a last-minute dash inside before the gate closed.

Oops, tire marks on the grass! I wouldn't be the one to point it out—why stoke the fire coming out of her ears?

Fab backed up and easily caught up with the spendy sports car as it turned into Casio's driveway. She parked a smidge away from the bumper and jumped out.

"No guns," I yelled before she slammed the door.

I was hot on her tennis shoes, not about to miss a minute. We'd both dressed for a quick getaway day.

Fab walked up to the car and knocked on the window of the pristine, sleek Lexus with dark-tinted windows. No response. The driver, a male, stared straight ahead.

The front door flew open, and Marcus bounded down the steps. "You're on private property," he barked.

I almost laughed at his audacity. Fab could hold her own with his overbearing father; the kid would be a piece of cake.

"This is *my* private property," Fab barked back. "There are rules here. One of them is guests don't rush the gate when it's about to close. There are others, which we'll be going over. You disagree with a one of them, and you can move."

Whoever was in the car had decided to stay put, not even rolling down the window.

"Yeah, got it." Marcus exuded as much anger as Fab and moved to stand in front of the driver's window. "Won't happen again." It was clear he didn't like being told what to do, as he struggled to control his anger.

"How did the gate open for the other car?" Fab sneered at the hundred-thousand-dollar Lexus as though it was a beater.

Marcus stood mute and engaged in a staredown with Fab, taking his sweet time to answer. "I used the inside keypad."

"We don't want strangers wandering around," Fab said.

"Got it." Marcus stepped sideways and turned his back on Fab, still blocking even a glimpse of the driver.

Fab scanned the driveway, then the house, before she walked back to the Hummer and slid behind the wheel.

I wanted to walk backwards but took one last look and followed her. Marcus hadn't moved, but when the driver rolled down the window, he leaned down.

"There's something about that kid that sets off warning bells," Fab grouched, staring over the steering wheel. Marcus turned and glared over his shoulder.

"Neither Marcus nor the driver of the pricey auto is making a move until you're gone."

"It's been a while since I've checked the security feeds around the compound. I'll be doing that tonight." Fab took her time backing out of the driveway.

"If Marcus thinks he's calling the shots, he's in for a rude awakening." I flipped down the visor and used the mirror to keep an eye glued on them until they were out of sight. "Here's my advice: don't grouch out Casio unless you have something solid on the kid, and not just that he's arrogant and you'd like him to lose his 'I'll do what I want' attitude. It's in his DNA."

"Are your neck hairs crawling around or whatever they do?"

I laughed and shook my head. His actions made it look like he was up to something illegal, but I hoped I was wrong about that. The explosion that would set off made me cringe.

"Mine are." Fab pulled out of the compound, waiting for the gate to close.

"That means that instead of writing off your reservations as you being cray-cray, we need to pay attention." My phone rang, and I checked the screen before answering. Mother. "We got a late start and are on the way," I said on answering. "Haven't sprung the surprise on you-know-who yet. You can call back and do it."

Mother laughed. "You're on your own. But don't keep me waiting; I'm ready for the fun to begin."

"On our way to where? Do I even want to know?" Fab asked when I dropped the phone in my lap as she gunned it out to the highway.

"You need to hustle over to Mother's; she's waiting on us. Don't think I won't blame you if you bail." Without a word, Fab turned in the right direction, which didn't surprise me, as she'd never disappoint Mother.

"You've got a few minutes to unwrap the so-called surprise. Can't believe you agreed to one, knowing that I hate them."

"I thought it was better to say that than tell you Mother's gunned up and ready to ride along with her favorite PI."

"How did that come about?" Fab demanded.

"She called earlier and got all teary — not sure if they were real, but on the off chance... Anyway, she was feeling neglected and left out of all the fun. The invitation to include her in today's festivities just popped out."

"Does Spoon know about his wife's field trip? And that it's a Gunz job?"

"Are you making this a wager?"

"Heck no." Fab snorted.

"If you were, my cash would be on her springing the details of the day during kissy face time tonight."

"We need to make it a rule that if Madeline wants to ride along, that's fine, but she has to be upfront with Spoon."

I laughed. Mother did what she wanted. At Fab's disgruntled expression, I laughed again.

Fab made good time despite there being no shortcuts involved. She turned onto Mother's street and groaned. "I hate it when she stands out in the street with her thumb out."

"Either unleash a long, laborious lecture on how that kind of fun isn't acceptable or tattle to her husband."

"I'm going to threaten the latter." Fab pulled up alongside her.

I jumped out, holding the door. Pointing to her tennis shoes, I gave her a thumbs up. We were all shoe-matchy today. Mother kissed my check as she slid into the front, then leaned over the console and kissed Fab as I hopped in the back.

"What are we doing?" She rubbed her hands together.

"Gunz has an issue with a new property." Fab gave her the details.

"That's really nervy. If the seller's willing to take it that far, I doubt she's going anywhere," Mother said. "Kind of surprised that Gunz didn't just go scare the you-know-what out of her. If I could kick someone to the curb with one big ole foot, that would be my option."

"We're open to suggestions. I don't have anything, and I'm willing to bet Fab doesn't either. Unless 'play it by ear' is a plan."

"It sometimes works," Fab insisted as she turned off the main highway in the middle of town.

She made another turn onto a dead-end street—half built-out, with overgrown empty lots scattered between the houses—and stopped at the end in front of a three-story white stucco home that sat on an inlet. The house appeared to be new construction, but the landscaping had been allowed to die and weeds had taken over. There was a four-foot fence that ran across the front, with the section in front of the driveway left standing open and a white Mercedes parked up next to the garage.

I scooted up and stared out the window at the single green weathered door with an awning overhead. "This must be the back of the house, with the front facing the water?"

"Once we get someone to open the door, then what?" Fab eyed Mother and me.

"We're the new girls." Mother pointed to herself and me. "You're showing us the ropes on what to do. That's as far as I got. The rest is for you to figure out."

"The previous owner's name is Eva Milson, and this is her picture." Fab held out her phone to Mother, who checked it out and handed it over the seat to me.

The three of us got out and tromped across the gravel. Fab paused to get a picture of the license plate of the Mercedes. No doorbell, and Fab actually knocked like a normal person.

Surprisingly, a female voice called out, "Coming." A moment later, a leggy blonde opened the door. "Yes?" Definitely Eva Milson asked with a questioning look.

I gave Mother a slight shove forward, but she held her ground, shooting me an *Oh no you don't* glare.

Fab pasted on one of her practiced friendly expressions. "Are you the previous owner?" she asked, even though she knew the answer.

The woman gave her a thorough once-over before hesitantly nodding.

"I'm here on behalf of the new owner to find out what it would take to get you to move."

Eva's eyes sparked with anger. "I was wondering when that bastard was going to make a move. Figured he'd be the one to show his face and do his own strong-arming. What does he do? Sends a woman—three of them, no less." She gave me a disgusted laugh. "Which of you is he banging? You, I'd guess." She stared down her nose at Fab.

Fab's jaw tightened, but to her credit, she didn't pull her Walther and shoot the smirk off the woman's face.

Hearing Mother's growl, Eva turned her attention to her for a brief moment. "Nice that you bring your mother to work; must make her feel special."

Fab ignored her dig. "It's in your best interest to make a deal instead of racking up attorney's fees by going to court."

Eva held up a finger and disappeared from sight, leaving the door open, but was back in short order. "I'm going for the option that gives me the most time to stay put, and that would be court. You can tell Gunz that I'm not going anywhere, and whatever he comes up with, I'll counter."

Mother took a step forward. "What did Gunz do to you?"

Ignoring her, Eva pulled her hand from behind the door and pointed a gun at us. "If you come back, I'll shoot all three of you. I have the right to protect my property from trespassers."

"No need to get trigger-happy. Given that we're here at the owner's invitation, you'd be the one to end up in prison." Fab stared her down.

I fisted Mother's shirt and jerked her back, stepping in front of her.

"This is going to end with the sheriff putting you out on the road." Fab didn't back down, though her fingers twitched.

"There's a lot of court maneuvering before that happens." Eva wiggled her gun at us. "Don't make me use this." She fired several shots into the nearby trees before slamming the door.

Fab pulled her gun. "Good thing she went back inside after that stupid move or I'd have exercised my legal right and shot back."

I slung my arm around Mother. "You've had enough excitement for one day."

She leaned into me with a half-hug. "I'm guessing that Gunz didn't mention there was a scorned woman involved."

Fab kicked at the gravel, sending it flying. "Nope."

We walked back to the car, me with one eye on the door.

"So that Mother doesn't write this off as a snore bore of a job, get Gunz on the phone and have him meet us at the office," I suggested. "When he complains about Eva's lack of cooperation as though it's our fault, we'll sic Mother on him."

"I'm telling you now, Gunz isn't going to be happy with waiting for a judge to decide and will expect me to come up with a way to short-circuit her plans." Fab let loose a disgruntled sigh as she u-turned and went back to the highway.

"I did some research after hearing that Eva's not the first person to pull this scam." I scooted up and stuck my head between the seats. "Most fought it out in court, and in one case, it dragged out for over a year. But that case wasn't here in Florida. Another buyer moved the seller's stuff into the garage and their own belongings inside and had the locks changed while the seller was out of the house. My suggestion is to lure Eva away and have her stuff moved to storage. Then hire a couple of thugs to house-sit until someone takes residence."

Mother turned to face me. "Not a bad idea, but is it even legal? I don't want either of you going to jail."

"We don't want that happening to you either, and you know we'd be bringing you along," I teased. "I couldn't find any follow-up on what happened after the cops showed up when that one couple claimed their house, but probably both parties were told it's an issue for a judge."

Fab turned to Mother. "We dropping you off at home or the body shop? Your choice."

"Oh no you don't," Mother hissed. "If you're going to meet with Gunz today, I want to be there."

"You call him and set it up." Fab handed Mother her phone.

Mother didn't hesitate, just scrolled across the screen and made the call. Whatever Gunz said when he answered, she giggled, and then introduced herself and told him why she was calling. "The meeting with Eva wasn't successful, and though she didn't elaborate, it's clear it stems from a grudge she has against you. If you'd like to come to the office, you can talk over options with Fab." After a pause, she said, "See you soon." She put the phone in the cup holder. "That went well. I could tell from his tone that he wasn't happy the problem hadn't been taken care of, but he wants to talk solutions and the sooner the better."

Chapter Fifteen

Fab took a shortcut to the office and parked in the almost-empty parking lot, Xander's car the only exception. We got out, strode across the parking lot, and rode the elevator to the third floor.

"You might not want to be part of the meeting with Gunz, since you're not one of his favorite people," Mother said to me as we entered the office.

That's because he's a dick and knows what I think of him. But I refrained from voicing my thoughts, as I wasn't up to listening to a lecture on bad language. "That saddens me, but I'm well aware." I wiped away a non-existent tear. "I'll be in my office." About to skate, I added, "Be sure to let Gunz know that you have a new partner." I inclined my head towards Fab and pointed to Mother, then took off. I turned the corner into my office, setting down my briefcase and settling in my chair. "Where's our new underage friend?"

"Kyle went to work with Billy. Spoon offered him a job—all he has to do is what he's told." Xander grinned.

"Hanging out with reformed thugs may

encourage Kyle to get his act together." If anyone could convince him that the criminal life was a suck choice, it was that group. "Just so you know, Gunz-o is about to tromp his way into the building. He's most likely feeling crotchety since we couldn't negotiate squat for him this morning. One of us needs to eavesdrop." I pointed at him, in case he thought I was going to press my ear to the wall.

"Good time to test this baby out…" Xander pulled a small white speaker with a miniscule screen out of his briefcase and set it on the table. "I can see you're not impressed, but give it a chance. Paid a whole dollar for it." He grinned at my snort. "Yard sale treasure, and the woman assured me that it still works. Even offered a one-week warranty."

"Whatever it is is beneath your talents." I gave it a closer look.

"One has to be flexible." Xander chuckled. "Planned to test this earlier, so I set the other half on the shelf unit by Fab's desk."

"I'll be sure to order a tricked-out send-off from our funeral friends, because you're dead when she finds out."

"I'll be spared because I'll blame you." Xander put a finger across his lips and turned it on. The screen lit up with a view of Fab's office.

Gunz hadn't arrived yet, but Mother's and Fab's voices came through loud and clear as they talked shopping at overpriced stores, one of their favorite activities.

I took out a notepad and scribbled: *Can they hear us?*

He pushed one of the buttons on the side. "I just disabled that feature."

The door opened and slammed shut. Clump, clump.

"Guess who's arrived," I whispered.

"Hello, ladies." Gunz pulled back a chair and settled his massive bulk, not an ounce of fat on his muscled, big-boy physique. "Here's the deal: I'm going to lure Eva away from the property for a few hours while you pack up and move all her belongings."

"That was my idea," I snapped at Xander.

"A friend suggested it. He also assured me that though it's not entirely legal, neither of us would be looking at jail time, as it would be a civil issue. I'll take the chance; knowing the aversion Eva's got to law enforcement, she won't be making that call. Told her once that if she toed the legal line, they wouldn't have cause to seek her out. She didn't like that advice." Gunz barked a laugh. "Since I was fond of her at one time... I just want this over with."

Xander and I turned to each other and rolled our eyes.

"Just so you know, Eva shot up the trees while we were there. Didn't hear any screaming, so she didn't hit anyone... unless they're dead and haven't been discovered yet," Fab said, her annoyance ratcheting up.

"She was never a good shot." Gunz shook his head.

"She was close enough that wouldn't have mattered whether she was good or not," Fab gritted.

"How are you going to get her out of the house? Kidnapping?" Mother asked. "Not to be mean, but she didn't sound like she had any fond memories of you. You wouldn't hurt her?"

"I don't rough up women for any reason. In this case, I'm going to have to get a little creative, turn on the charm. For the kind of money I shelled out for that property, I'm not being screwed over one more day," Gunz grouched.

"When you brokered this deal, did you know Ms. Disgruntled was the owner?" Fab asked.

Good question.

"Eva came to me, knowing that I purchase properties all the time. Being a nice guy, I didn't dicker over the price, though it was a bit high, because I knew she needed the money. Look where that got me."

"I planned to sign on as Fab's backup, but my husband will flip if I get into any kind of legal trouble. Spoon wouldn't hesitate to kill you. And then he'd rough me up a bit." Mother's moony smile said she'd enjoy every minute. "You should hurry up and mend bridges with Madison before her husband finds out about this job, because you can bet Didier will hear two seconds later. Then you'll be hiring a new crew."

Why me?

"Whatever you do to divert Eva's attention, it has to be legal," Fab said. "You have to know she's not going to be happy, and you better have proof that your time together is consensual."

"Don't get romantic." Mother shook her head.

"Make the arrangements, give me a couple of dates, and I'll do my part. Once Eva agrees to meet with me, I'll give you a call and let you know it's a go," Gunz said.

"I understand your frustration, but you need to make sure you don't do anything to get in trouble," Mother said in a conciliatory tone.

"You've got my word." Gunz's stubby finger made an X across his chest. "I'm thinking that maybe Eva and I can get back to being friends."

"Friends?" I lowered my voice, shaking my head. "Not happening, at least not from the look I saw on her face."

"Doesn't he have a kid?" Xander asked. "What about that woman? I'm not suggesting that you ask, since he'd probably flip and then tell you, 'None of your business.'"

"You ask."

Xander shook his head.

"What days are good for you?" Fab asked. Gunz mumbled an answer. "I'll get everything set up and get back to you."

"How's your little family doing?" Mother asked cheerfully.

I raised my brows at Xander. "Here comes your answer."

I knew she was inquiring after his son, but with Gunz, it was a coin flip if he thought she meant his kid or one of his many relationships. I tuned out the conversation as he launched into a saga that didn't sound true but kept Mother laughing… and also kept her from asking any more questions.

Chapter Sixteen

The scraping of Gunz's chair on the floor caught my attention. "You should hide that before *you* get caught." I pointed to the monitor.

Xander picked it up and threw it in his briefcase, then flipped his laptop around to show me an image of a warehouse filling the screen. "This building is just down the street and available for a fast sale. The owner's willing to take a discount but doesn't want to be completely screwed."

"Why the urgency?"

"Dude has owned the property for years and, in the past, came under the scrutiny of law enforcement for rumored drug running. He claims to have gotten out of the business years back, when he got caught in an ambush and almost died."

"Seriously." I sighed. "How the heck did you hook up with *Dude*?"

"You asked me to keep a lookout, and when I come up with something, you cop a 'tude?"

"You want to see a 'tude?" I snarked. "Getting involved with someone like that could get you hurt."

"One night, when having a beer at a local bar—trying out your competition—I met Dude, aka Mike, through a friend of a friend. Once I heard the location of his warehouse, I tuned into the conversation. The old guy's worn out—he looks it anyway—and is ready to cash out and go. Where, I didn't ask."

"Quick sale, hmm..." I mused.

Xander nodded and flipped his laptop around, turning it back after a few clicks. "Here's some inside shots. A friend and I got the grand tour. I'm warning you now: It's smelly and bug-infested, though most appeared dead. There's plenty of dirt, but it's otherwise empty. Some would consider the loading dock a perk."

"You got a price for me?" I asked.

"Just forwarded you the email Mike sent with the asking price. He wants cash, and the sooner the better."

"My answer is yes. But I need to go downstairs and sell my husband on it. Forward the pics to Creole and CC me, subject line: 'For Sale.' Tell your pal Mike that this has to be a straight-up deal, meaning a title company will be involved."

"I warned him that if he was trying to pull a fast one, he'd get his brains rearranged." Xander flexed his muscles. "But not by me." He laughed. "Also, he warned me that he's had numerous break-ins over the last year. There wasn't any sign of suspicious activity the day I took the pictures, but based on the trash left behind, someone or several someones had been there recently."

"Speaking of suspicious activity, I'd rather get this deal than Fab's, because with hers, there are too many unanswered questions." I filled him in on meeting Bertie.

Xander chuckled when I mentioned money-laundering. "Reminds me of a few interesting jobs I've seen on the dark web. Don't have the stomach for a job where something could easily go wrong and leave me having to run for my life." He continued to click away on his laptop. "I just sent you a property report on that strip mall."

He'd screwed up his nose, and I knew the report would be fraught with problems. "Give me a quick rundown."

"The property is owned by Feld Huntman."

"So he lied—he's the owner as well as being a bogus real estate agent?"

"A rap sheet a mile long, and all drug-related." Xander tapped the screen. "Feld did a couple of short stints in jail. A couple of the cases, the witnesses couldn't recall or were no-shows, and the charges got dropped. He hasn't been arrested in five years. That might suggest that he cleaned up his act, but he's probably just gotten savvier about covering up his activities. I say that because businesses have come and gone from the mall, but none stuck around very long.

Not sure how he hangs onto the property if he can't show a profit, unless..."

How involved is Bertie with the dealers, and no heads up for Fab? "The dressmaker?"

"She's lasted the longest—been there a year."

"Personally, I think it was a poor location choice, but maybe the price was right," I said.

"Feld hung the bogus real estate sign out not long after he bought the property. It's not a legit business, in that there's no license and I couldn't find a broker associated with it. I checked for police reports, knowing you'd want to know, and couldn't find any on the property."

"The more I hear about the strip mall, the more I think it would bring more trouble than it's worth. Fab's not going to want hear my assessment, no matter how many reports back me up."

"If this is just about the dress business, find another location. If the woman stays there, what's to stop this guy or someone else from continuing to strong-arm her for cash? If the con's successful once, those kinds of people don't usually just go away."

Fab flounced into the office and threw herself into a chair. From the sounds of the voices, Mother was escorting Gunz to the door.

"If my mother has one hair out of place, I'm coming after you." I pointed to Fab.

"You need to talk to your mother and leave me out of it. She's in full-on excitement mode and reeling her in is impossible." Fab sighed. "I suppose you want a recap of the meeting?"

"No need; we listened in."

"What are you talking about?" Fab looked around my office. "How?"

"I put one over on Fabiana Merceau, hotshot PI? Not telling you anything; you'll have to figure it out." I grinned at her.

"When I do…" Fab sliced her finger across her neck.

"Good luck explaining that to Mother."

"Are you ready to go?" Fab asked.

"I'll get a ride home from my husband. I'm not available tomorrow for any ride-alongs; I'm going to be home catching up on my files. I'd like to reserve your services for tracking down Cook's friend's Porsche the following day."

Mother came in and sat down. "Gunz can be very charming."

I groaned and banged my head on the desk.

"I told him I'd smooth the waters between you and him and mend your relationship." Mother smiled at me.

"We've never had a relationship. Gunz's got the hots for Frenchy over there and always has. And there's a couple of other men whose names I can tick off that would like to get lucky too."

"Madison, really," Fab growled.

Xander needed to be a fraction faster to hide his grin.

"Just promise that you'll make an effort."

Mother held out her pinkie.

"Where did you learn that?" I asked and didn't get an answer. "Not sure what you're getting out of brokering this truce, but whatever it is, it better not get you into any trouble or, worse, your butt kicked."

"You're so dramatic."

"Thank you, Pot. If I were standing, I'd curtsey."

Fab laughed at us.

"Knowing that you like to be the first to know, or close anyway," I said to Fab, "there's a warehouse for sale down the street, and I'm putting in an offer unless Creole threatens to bail on the marriage."

"What about my deal?" she demanded.

"Your deal is fraught with big problems, and you need to admit it and move along to the next big deal. There's plenty out there. Be grateful I'm telling you now. I could've waited for Didier to find out, and then I wouldn't have to come up with a nice way to weasel out."

"Bert warned me that even if I got the owner to name a price, and there was a way to screw me, he would," Fab said, annoyed. "I suppose it's time to find something else."

"Can I trust you to get my mother home safely?" I asked, stuffing my briefcase.

"Same question her husband asked when he got home early as a surprise and no clue where wifey had gone." Fab smirked at her. "But he tracked her down in short order."

"I'm in big trouble," Mother said with a satisfied grin. She'd tuned us out and had been texting.

I headed out behind Mother and Fab, and the three of us rode down in the elevator together.

"You two behave yourselves," I admonished, then kissed Mother and headed into the Boardwalk offices. I waved to Lark, who was busy on the phone, and stuck my head into the large office that Creole, Didier, and Brad shared. They were kicked back in their chairs, laughing and throwing wadded up paper at one another. "I need a ride home," I said with a wink. "If it's a problem, I'll walk."

Creole laughed and motioned me over to him. When I got close enough, he reached out and pulled me down on his knee. I looked at his laptop, and he had the pictures of the warehouse pulled up.

"Hear you're looking into buying more trouble," Brad said.

"I suppose that depends on which property you're talking about." I faux glared at him. "What do you think?" I tapped the screen.

"Sold. I admit that I wasn't on board with owning the whole block, but what the heck."

"I'm thinking it won't take much to get it ready for long-term tenants." I leaned back into Creole.

"What did Gunz want?" Didier asked. Neither

he nor Creole thought much of the man; they'd warned him that they'd retaliate if either of us got hurt on one of his jobs.

"I wasn't in on the meeting by choice, but I did eavesdrop," I said, then gave him the gist of the new plan.

"What does he do to these women?" Didier asked. "She's not the first to want revenge, though others have wanted a body part."

"Gunz claims to be a chick magnet—and I admit he has the ability to bring them in—but it doesn't take long before they figure out that he's a turd." I pasted on a phony smile that garnered laughs. "He's got a one-hundred-percent track record when it comes to long-term dissatisfaction from his women. Fab is an exception. Probably because they're not and never have been lovey-dovey, thank goodness."

"How about letting Gunz take care of his own problems for a change?" Brad said. "Not that I think you'd end up in jail on this job, but it'd be a pain to visit you there."

"Fab's organizing the crew. Once the packing begins, I'm going to suggest that she sit in the car, which is where I'm going to be. I won't step one foot inside the house. I wouldn't mind a peek around, but not at the expense of breaking and entering charges."

"In case of legal trouble, Gunz needs to be the one onsite, since he's the one on the title and the woman has no paperwork to suggest otherwise," Creole advised.

"Don't say I can't learn from someone else's problems," Brad said. "If this is the newest real estate scam, which it sounds like it is, next closing, we'll be doing a walkthrough right before the signing. If there's any indication that there's someone living on the premises, the deal's cancelled. In fact, I'll make it part of the agreement that there's a deadline for when they have to be out."

"Sounds like this is primarily a residential scam, so it shouldn't be a problem with the closings we have coming up for the Boardwalk," Didier said.

"Is there a meeting in the offing to bring the rest of the board members up to date, so they know what you're up to now?" I asked.

"We're going to do like you and Fab and let you know after the fact," Brad said, straight-faced.

"You're hilarious today." I made a face.

Chapter Seventeen

After our foursome met for morning coffee—at my house this time—I had the rest of the day to myself because Fab was jetting off to get her moving crew together. Before I could issue an edict that I wouldn't be toting a single box, Creole stepped in and barked about personal safety. Fab rolled her eyes and, catching her, Didier glared. She stomped out the deck doors, but Didier easily caught up to her. I peeked out the door, and the two were walking up the beach. All was good between them, as Didier had his arm around her and she was leaning into him.

Xander had sent over a slew of reports that I now sifted through. Top priority was finding the Porsche belonging to Charlie Miller, Cook's friend. Cart Anders story as to what happened to the car had changed several times, the latest that it had been stolen. If so, why not file a police report? "Cart no longer lived where Charlie had dropped off the car, but Xander had found two other addresses. His search also uncovered no record of the car having been registered by a new party.

My recently concocted plan was to talk to Cart, which might go the same way it had when Charlie confronted him—with Cart calling the cops. That time, instead of the stolen story, Cart had told the cops he didn't have a clue what his friend was talking about and whispered PTSD to one of the officers.

The cops were sympathetic, and Cart offered to open his garage door to show them the car wasn't there. They'd told Charlie there wasn't much they could do, as it was a he said/he said situation. Unfortunately, he didn't have anything in writing to show that he'd stored the car with his so-called friend.

It was mid-afternoon when Fab showed up and plunked down next to me on the deck, setting a bottle of water on the side table. "I've been thinking—"

"Now what? As though we don't have enough going on," I reminded her in exasperation. "Whatever you're up to now, it may take us a few days to get to it."

"We're the clients." Fab flicked her finger between us.

"Okay, I'll play along, since it's not often that you don't make any sense."

"Check your email. I attached several snippets of video, enough that you'll get the gist."

I watched what Fab had sent over—twice. "Hate to point out when you're in error..." I smiled. "Since you own most of the property in this enclave, I need to correct you and point out that you're the client. Your mistake was using the plural, since basically I'm being roped in."

Fab expressed her exasperation with an unidentifiable noise.

"Based on the timestamp…" I tapped the screen. "When Casio's kids are in school and top dog is off wherever, Mr. Abrasive Attitude appears to have a never-ending stream of guests coming and going, all in spendy rides and not staying long. Question you probably can't answer: why isn't he in school?"

"You're right. Is that what you wanted to hear?"

I grinned. Her lips quirked. I was certain, much to her annoyance. "I find it interesting that for someone new to the neighborhood, Marcus has a boatload of friends. Unless they drove down here from Miami, and it's a long drive for a five-minute visit. Thinking now that the first time he tripped our radar, we should've looked at him a little closer."

"That's why we need to find out what he's up to. Whatever's going on smells illegal, but I can't make accusations without proof."

"You could turn the video over to Casio," I suggested.

"And if there's an innocent explanation?"

I wouldn't count on it, but maybe. Plus, that was a weak-ass reason not to. "Based on experience, if we were staking out the house and seeing the cars come and go, I'd agree with you on illegal. If the teens were hanging out, I'd say party house, since there's no adult around." If Marcus was engaged in illegal activity, I wasn't going to be the one to tell Casio. "Any traffic while Casio or the kids are at home?"

Fab shook her head. "Marcus's guests always start showing up shortly after Casio and the kids leave in the morning. The traffic stops an hour before the kids get out of school. Couldn't find where anyone stopped by at night or on the weekends."

"Be interesting to know what kind of trouble Marcus got into that sent him down here. Especially since his mother hates Casio, and after she tried to snatch his kids, there's absolute loathing on his part. His face pinches if her name gets mentioned." Those were tense times; I'd even testified at the custody hearing.

"My first thought when I heard that Marcus was staying with his uncle was that he's a teenager, how much trouble could he have gotten into?" Fab half-laughed, with a shake of her head. "But if anyone's read a headline of late, it could be anything. I called Brick, and having rehearsed six ways to beat around the bush, I ended up going for the direct approach and asked if there was anything I should know about his son."

My eyebrows shot up. "That was nervy. But based on your friendship, I imagine he didn't give a thought to you getting to the point."

"Knowing Brick is easy to set off and we're talking family here, I was careful to tiptoe around it, so as not to ignite a fire. If there was anything I could do to help, blah, blah. Brick confided that Marcus was hanging out with the wrong people and didn't elaborate. He wanted to send the kid to military school, but the wife had a fit. They got into it when the only other option on the table was sending him to stay with Casio. He's hoping that Marcus gets his act together so he can bring him back home and the wife will stop glaring at him."

"Casio's protective of his kids. If Marcus turns out to be a hotbed of trouble, I'd be surprised if he let him stay at his house, even as a favor to his brother. How did you leave it with Brick?"

"Before hanging up, he asked me to keep an eye on Marcus, though I could tell he wasn't expecting anything to come of it."

"Before you have a chat with Casio, you're going to need more information, and I'm not sure how you go about getting it," I said.

"The cameras that are currently installed only show traffic in and out of the respective driveways. Thinking of—" Fab grimaced. "— sneaking over in the middle of the night and installing a couple more."

"Bad news. Even if you're willing to pay me a premium, I can't get away with sneaking out in the middle of the night anymore." I laughed at her glare. "I'm surprised you can still get away with it."

Fab humphed. "Once I tell Didier what I'm doing and why, he won't like it, but he'll be my backup. He's going to agree about not wanting to stir up something over what might be nothing."

"Once Creole and Didier find out what you're up to, it'll put them in an awkward situation with Casio."

"Another option is that I pull Marcus aside and share my observations. Tell him to knock it off and no one else has to know. Maybe that will put a stop to whatever he's up to. Motivate him to get his act together and go home."

"You might want to think about that one before acting on it." I could see that she agreed. I thought that tactic was a longshot since Marcus had barely tolerated either one of us. He reminded me of his father, and I doubted he would back down for anyone. "You need to be careful when you go do your trickery tonight. Tomorrow morning, I'm expecting you to help me find that car." I'd emailed her the files Xander sent over.

"What are we going to do once we find this Cart character and he sticks to the same story? And he probably will."

"First, we swing by his previous residence, talk to a couple of his old neighbors, and see what they know. Then we track him down, and I'll stand back while you go gangster on him, shooting one body part at a time until we get the truth."

"Now you're talking." Fab crazy-girl grinned.

Chapter Eighteen

Fab and I wanted to get an early start, but before leaving, we convened a meeting with the husbands over coffee. Fab updated Creole and me on the installation of several more cameras around the compound, all had gone off without a hitch.

"And I never let her out of my sight." Didier smirked at his wife, who beamed back at him.

"I'm missing something here." Creole eyed me. "It's amazing that you pulled off creeping around an ex-detective's house. Even if it was outside."

"While you're in a chatty mood, would you mind backing up and going over a few details, as I didn't enlighten him? Not that I wasn't planning on it, but we got sidetracked." I leaned into his shoulder.

"No details." Fab stuck her fingers in her ears.

The guys laughed.

Fab relayed everything she'd told me, including her idea to install the cameras, then picked up her phone, handing it to Creole.

Creole watched the videos. "There's no one that would look at these and not think Marcus is up to something illegal," he growled. "Do not confront him about anything on your own, you can't predict how he will react. I want to know what you find out, and don't come up with some excuse for delaying the information."

Didier nodded in agreement. "One of the rare times I have an update. Had a short conversation with Casio not long after Marcus moved in, and at that time, all was well. Casio did say that Alex didn't like not being the oldest and was lukewarm about his cousin's arrival. The younger ones were all about the new dog."

"The dog fiasco." Creole chuckled. "My own update: Marcus's mother sent the dog down here with her son. The kid had no idea the dog was staying, since it wasn't his—belonged to his sister, but the mother didn't want it around. Casio was irked, but the kids and Larry took a vote, and it was unanimous for Melba to join the family."

"From what I've seen of Melba, she's a happy dog, so it worked out good for her," I said. "Now Fab needs a pet. Something exotic. I could score you an alligator."

Fab shook her head. Not happening. The guys laughed.

* * *

The house where Charlie had stored his Porsche was a modest, elevated two-story with an enclosed garage underneath, the door open, and an oversized pickup inside.

Fab pulled up and parked in front. "Now what? You do know that questioning the new owner is probably a waste of time?"

"You never know. How many steps to the door? That's enough time for you to come up with something."

"Hate to throw your words back at you, but this isn't my case." Fab grinned.

"We're investigators…" I tapped my cheek. "You, anyway. We'll go with the truth—, we're looking for the Porsche. I'll do all the talking, since I know how you love to watch me in action while you stand there and look pretty."

"Get out." Fab pointed to the door.

I swallowed my laugh and climbed out, meeting her on the sidewalk. The two of us gave the exterior a once-over, and then I led the way across the driveway and up the stairs and knocked politely. A thirty-something opened the door. "What?" he barked, then glared past me, checking out Fab like she was a delicious morsel and continuing to make eye contact with her.

"We're looking for this car." I held up a printout of the pristine vehicle. "There's a reward for any useful information."

He barely gave it a glance, then went back to ogling Fab, who'd yet to acknowledge the man. "Don't know what you're talking about. Whatever went down with the previous owner has nothing to do with me." He shut the door in my face. Then just as quickly opened it again and made eye contact with Fab. "Come back anytime. By yourself."

Fab ignored him and turned, leading the way down the steps.

"If you'd done the talking, we'd have been invited inside." I ignored Fab's grin. "Why was he so 'tudey if he's not involved?"

"According to the records, the guy hasn't been the owner long, and who wants to move into a new home and have anyone come knocking, asking questions about a situation you weren't involved in? We're probably not the first to show up to ask about the car."

Good point. I stopped on the sidewalk and looked up and down the street. "Hold up. Don't even think about getting in the car just yet. The neighbor across the street might be able to answer a couple of questions, or the house on either side. Forget the one with four cars in the driveway—one person cops an attitude and they'll all pile out the door."

"My vote, which is the only one that matters: we hit up the house directly across the street." Fab smirked. "Let's hope they're nosey."

"You could step up and show me how it's done," I said as we walked across the street.

"You did such a good job with this last guy."

We both laughed.

I knocked on the door. A grey-haired man

opened it and poked his head out, giving us both an appreciative glance. "If you're selling something, I'm not going to waste your time — not interested."

Before he could get the door closed, I stuck my foot inside.

He stared down. "Good way to get your foot smooshed."

I jerked my foot back. "Just need a minute of your time. Looking for information." I whipped out the picture of the Porsche and held it up. "You know anything about this car?"

"The cops showed up on my doorstep and asked the same question. I'll tell you what I told them — the previous owner, not a friendly guy, had a parade of cars coming and going. After a while, they all looked alike. For a couple of weeks, stories made their way around the block about what was going on and whether it was legal or not, and the story changed every time, so who knows the truth."

"Anyone on the block you'd find credible?" I asked.

He shook his head. "I do know that the cops went door-to-door and very few opened up, though I know they were home, since there were cars parked in the driveways. From what I could tell, no one knew anything. The cops didn't come back, and I was good with that, as I'd made up my mind I wasn't getting further involved."

"I promise I won't bug you again."

He gave me a toothy smile. "A little good advice, if you're prone to take it: the new owner is... let's say high-strung, easily cops an attitude. Hasn't made any friends that I'm aware of."

"If he gives you any trouble, call this number." I handed him our business card. "It won't be me showing up but someone hulky who'll rearrange his face."

He laughed and took the card. After a glance, he waved it and shut the door.

"No need to stir up any trouble on this block," I said as we walked back to the car. "Uh-oh, we're slipping. We should've parked out of sight." The first guy was standing on his deck, glaring down at us. I waved and got back in the car, not looking his way again, and entered the next address in the GPS. The third address Xander found was a mailbox drop and a waste of time.

We slid up in front of the next address a number of miles down the Overseas. It was a worn mobile home on cement blocks, and the answer to *Is the Porsche here?* was easily answered, as there was no garage and an SUV parked in the one rock-filled space.

"Appears Mr. Cart is home." I scrolled through my phone and matched up the license tag on the SUV with the one Xander sent as currently registered to the man. "This place is nothing like his last one; wonder what the appeal is? Not sure if Cart owns the home or what; the land is in someone else's name." It fit in with the rest of the street, which appeared to be lots where the owner put on it what they wanted — most were houses in varying degrees of disrepair.

"The price must've been right," Fab said.

"I'm tired and hungry, and if Cart opens the door, I'm going for the direct approach." I got out, leaving Fab to trail after me.

We walked up a set of makeshift wooden steps to the front door, every one of which wobbled under our feet. I knocked, and Cart Anders answered the door. I easily recognized him from the pictures Xander had sent.

I pulled my Glock and walked him backwards into his ratty living room, where he dropped on a couch with springs poking up and a missing cushion. "I have a few questions for you." I'd already decided this was as close as I was getting to the man. "Answer concisely, and we'll be out of here. If not, I'll shoot you and have someone come dispose of the body."

"Oh guns," Fab chirped, stepping out from behind me. "This is going to be fun." She pulled hers and pointed it at Cart.

"Get out of here before I call the cops." His confident show was belied by the fear in his eyes.

"You're not calling the shots. I am. Now don't move your backside or you're going to have a painful problem."

"My friend's hungry, makes her finger

twitchy." Fab shook her head in my direction. "I'd get cooperative if I were you."

"Eyes this way." I waved my gun around like someone who didn't know one end from the other, which ramped up his fear. "Where's Charlie Miller's car? Skip the stupid story you gave the cops."

Cart groaned and put his head in his hands. "That's what this is about."

I waved my gun again and pointed it at the middle of his forehead. "Not interested in your histrionics."

Cart straightened up and sucked in a ragged breath. "Sold it." He held up his hand. "Hear me out. I borrowed money from a guy who got tired of waiting for repayment and threatened to cut off a body part, one I'd miss a lot."

"How did you transfer the title when you weren't the owner?" I asked.

"Forged the signature. Before you bitch me out about legalities, the buyer knew and bought it at a reduced price. It's gone already. Heard the buyer flipped it to another party that didn't care about title issues because they had a way of changing the VIN number."

"How do you screw not only a friend but someone serving in the military?" I asked in disgust. "Why not tell the truth when he asked, instead of sending Charlie running around trying to figure out what happened while you painted him as crazy?"

"It wasn't personal. At the time, so much was coming down on my head that I had to make a snap decision, and he was the least lethal person to screw over. Tell the truth? And go to jail? Not choosing that option."

"I want the name and contact information for both men." I grabbed a pen and a store receipt off a side table and threw them at him.

"No way," Cart stuttered. "I'll end up dead."

"If you don't give me what I want, you're going to be dead now." I glared. "Stop sniveling and I won't tell them where I got the information." I cocked my gun. "The numbers better not be bogus."

"I only have the one number." Cart picked up his phone. His hand shaking, he wrote down the number and handed it to me.

After a glance—George Dent, never heard of him—I shoved the receipt in my pocket. According to Cook, Charlie and Cart had been friends since high school. So much for friendship. "How does a man with money issues afford the car in the driveway?"

"A favor—guy needed it out of his name and quick."

A number of scenarios came to mind, and I didn't want to ask. "You're a piece. Let me make this clear: I don't want to see your face anywhere in the Cove. Charlie has a lot of friends, and I can promise if you don't get out now, you won't leave in one piece." I nodded to Fab, and we backed out the door. As soon as it closed, I said, "We better hustle, in case Cart owns a gun and decides he wants retribution."

"Cart might want to change his pants first, since they're soaked." Fab laughed. "The way his hands shook, I doubt he owns a gun. But just in case…" We ran back to the car. She hit the gas and shot down the street, only slowing as she rounded the corner. She clapped her hand down on the steering wheel. "That was very tough-girl of you."

"I learned from the best." I winked at her.

"You're not one to walk away from a problem, so now what?" Fab asked as she headed back to the Cove. "Pretty sure you're not going to want to tell Charlie you weren't able to recover the car."

"I'm going to text this number to Xander to find out what he can. Then track this guy down."

"That's stepping knee-deep into trouble, and illegal trouble from the sounds of it. You won't go in looking for a fight, but that's what you'll get and most likely still won't recover the car," Fab warned.

I sighed, not wanting to agree with her, even though I did.

Fab's phone rang; she looked at the screen and chuckled, then answered, giving brief responses.

I poked her arm to put the call on speaker, which she ignored.

"We're on our way." She hung up.

"Tell me that was Didier, and I'll give you a pass for not letting me eavesdrop. If not, in the future, I'm cutting you off from listening in, since this isn't the first time you've done that of late."

"It was Raul, and our funeral friends would like to talk to us about a job."

"We haven't been to the funeral of someone we don't know lately... so sad if we got out of practice."

Chapter Nineteen

"Drop me off at home and go by yourself." I knew the chance was zero that Fab would turn around, and as tempting as it was, I wasn't jumping out at the next signal. "Tell our funeral friends that I'll drop by when I get back from Antarctica."

"Not happening." Fab snorted. "Besides, who's going to believe that lame story when you're grabbing a sweater whenever the temp dips below seventy?" She hit the gas and turned off the highway, taking a side street.

Tropical Slumber Funeral Home was an old drive-thru hot dog stand that had undergone several incarnations and now offered an array of final send-off options from the sedate to the outrageous. So far, nothing had been deemed too extreme.

Fab slowed going into the parking lot and stopped as we checked out the new renovations to the side of the main building. The large grassy area had been turned into a park-like setting with a covered gazebo in the middle, the entire area surrounded by decking. There were two triple fountains and upgraded landscaping all around, with a variety of colorful flowers everywhere. Since there were no other cars, she stopped just short of the red carpet that ran to the entrance.

Raul, one of the two owners, opened the front door and leaned against the frame, smiling patiently as we bumped hips up the carpet.

I slid by him with a smile and went inside, claiming my chair next to the door while he and Fab air-kissed.

Dickie, the other owner, looked tired, his lanky frame kicked back in a chair on the opposite side of the entry area, a rare spot of color in his pale cheeks. Looks-wise, the two men couldn't be more opposite. Where Raul was ripped and muscled, Dickie tall and gaunt.

I waved to Dickie. "Been keeping busy?" Now why did I ask that, since the last thing I wanted to hear about was anyone requiring his dressing-the-dead skills?

"I just finished up a client for whom it took quite a bit of patience to get everything just right. The family's pleased, so that makes me happy." Dickie preened.

Fab skipped her usual trek through the main room and the hallway with the visiting rooms to see how many people had been tricked out for impending services. Nothing made the woman squeamish. "Love what you did with the outdoor additions," she said, taking a seat.

I nodded in agreement.

"We're always looking for ways to expand our

business." Raul smiled. "After hosting a couple of weddings and getting great feedback, we decided to make it one of the services we regularly offer. We sat down with a landscape designer and the project turned out to be more than we envisioned, but we're happy with how it came out."

"We got our first booking, and that's why we called," Dickie said. "The groom had a last-minute request that we provide security."

"Isn't it unusual to hire security for a wedding?" Fab asked.

"The client wants everything to run smoothly, and you know we do our best to accommodate every request," Raul said.

I had never known them to say no to anything. "Did your client happen to give you a reason? Perhaps he's just paranoid in general… or possibly he's expecting a fight to break out?" That happened at funerals, why not weddings?

"I take it you want Madison and me to provide security?" Fab directed to both men.

They nodded expectantly.

Fab turned to me. What was she expecting me to say? No? Yes? What? We rarely said no to anyone, and if she wanted me to be the one to tell them that, Ha! I stared back.

She glared, then looked at Raul. "Should anything get out of hand, does the groom object to the use of firearms? It can quickly calm a situation."

"I did mention it to him, making it clear that you wouldn't shoot anyone," Raul said, pleased with himself. "What I suggest is that you blend in with the guests, so as not to stand out in any way. That way, if something goes awry, which we're not expecting, you'll be the first to notice and quiet everything down."

How would we do that? Tackle the offender?

"The fountain is going to be the backdrop for the ceremony, and there will be plenty of seating on both sides of the aisle," Raul continued. "I can show you where to sit so you have the best view of the property."

"You want us to be pretend wedding guests on the lookout for trouble?" I asked.

Raul beamed. "I knew you'd understand. We realize that it's an odd request, but since we've worked so well together in the past, you were our first choice."

"You know we make every effort to accommodate any request from you," Fab said. "We have some flexibility in our schedule, and there shouldn't be a problem."

I pasted on a smile.

"If you can be here early, I'm happy to do your hair and makeup," Dickie offered.

No way. I bit my lip to keep from laughing and nodded at Fab. *Another question for you, babes.*

She glared at me before turning a smile on the two men. "Nice of you to offer, but that wouldn't be professional of us. We'll want to time our arrival to make it appear that we're guests, which will make it easy for us to mingle."

Good one. I listened as Fab and Raul talked about the details of the wedding. Once they agreed on a time, I jumped to my feet and was out the door ahead of Fab, waving to the men.

"I'm thinking basic black will make us look like mourners," I said once we were in the car. "If you could pokey on over to my house and ransack my closet to choose something appropriate, that would be appreciated."

"You always complain when I do that."

"I'm making an exception this time."

Chapter Twenty

Fab stopped short of leaving tire marks as she flew out of the parking lot of the funeral home. "I need to stop at The Cottages and check on the boat," I said.

"Mac would know the answer."

"It's a shock, I know, but I've already called her a couple of times. All I get are vague responses, and then she has to hang up because there's a crisis that needs her attention."

"That's because she hasn't figured out a way to keep it yet." Fab chuckled. "She did ask me where I would park it if it were mine."

"And you're just now telling me this?"

"Before you go up in smoke, I told her I'd sell it and offer a few bucks off if it got moved the same day. She sniffed at me, and her nose went higher than I'd ever seen. So I growled, and she stomped off." Fab cruised around the corner, slowed and turned into the driveway, and parked in front of the office.

The nude male mannequin beside the door caught my eye. He was holding a sign that covered his lower half and read, *ML Property Management*. "What's his name again?"

Fab snorted. "As if I'd remember. I only half-listen to conversations I'm not interested in, and he qualifies."

I snapped my fingers. "Harry. He needs shorts, a skirt, something to cover his lower half. You chat it up with Crum and have him take care of it. A dish towel would work."

Fab stuck her fingers in her ears. "Can't hear you."

I was about to argue the point, then realized the boat had been moved to the far end of the driveway. A brief flash of someone disappearing around the back caught my attention. "How is it that a bunch of oldsters can get a mammoth boat moved off the street and then up and down the driveway?"

"Connections," Fab sing-songed.

I made sure she was looking and rolled my eyes, then reached for the door handle. She grabbed my shirt and jerked me back.

"What are you planning to do?"

I twisted out of her hold and jumped out of the SUV. Turning back, I said, "Need to know," and slammed the door.

Fab easily caught up and slung her arm around my shoulders. "Don't be 'tudey, or I'll tell your mother on you."

I laughed, then skidded to a stop, staring down the driveway. "What the heck is Crum up to now?"

We both watched as he cut across the

driveway from his cottage, a large box in hand; at the steps of the boat, he set it down before scrambling up. Mac, who'd come from the pool area, ran over and lifted the box, handing it up to him.

Fab unleashed a whistle loud enough to be heard in Orlando. Crum clutched his chest and dipped down out of sight. Mac turned on her heel and ran to greet us... or head us off.

"Oh good, you're here, saves me a call," she said, sounding insincere. "Lots going on." She spit on her finger and leaned down to clean one of the black eyeballs on her bright-orange lobster slides, the tops augmented with clear crystals.

"You forgot an eye," Fab said when she straightened up.

I bit my lip hard and stared down at the poor things, which weren't looking back like some of her shoes did—these were cross-eyed.

Mac bent down and spit-cleaned the other one. She straightened and shook her foot. "They weren't a bargain, but too cute to pass up."

"Cute." Fab managed to sound sincere, which had Mac beaming. "When's the boat pulling out?"

A loud bell rang.

A woman yanked on the rope hanging over the side of the pontoon, unleashing the loud noise twice more before mercifully stopping. Crum's head popped up. He leaned over the side, the woman handed him something, and he laid on an obscenely long, smoochy kiss on her. The woman bowed and, with a wave, walked back to her cottage.

"What the heck was that all about?" I demanded.

Mac unleashed a beleaguered sigh that I was certain could be heard down the street. "Since the boat's being picked up tomorrow, we're setting up for a good-bye shindig. That's unless someone shuts down my plans." She eyed me warily.

"What does that have to do with Squishy Lips licking on that woman? Guest, I assume?" Mac nodded, and I struggled not to roll my eyes. "From now on, all guests have to sign a sex release when checking in, because I don't want to deal with fallout from Crum jiggling around here sharing his treats."

"Another thing I've got covered. I sat Crum down for the sex talk, and he now understands that the guests are off-limits. Licking their faces—as long as there's no touching—is all the leeway I gave him."

I'm not often speechless, but…

"All the stress you're under is frizzing your hair." Mac eyed my head.

I was about to launch myself on her and hope not to be pummeled to death when Fab jumped between us. "Don't make me have to beat you up," she threatened Mac, who grinned.

"I could fire you," I snapped.

"Calm down; you have a decent enough sense of humor." Mac hopped up and down on her lobsters.

Before I could unleash a sarcastic retort, yells of "Help, help" echoed across the driveway. "He's dead!" Miss January tripped into sight, barely managing to catch herself before tumbling to the pavement.

The three of us ran over. Miss January whimpered unintelligibly, pointing to her cottage.

"Dead people are your forte." I nudged Fab.

"You calm her down," Fab said to Mac. "You're coming with me." She grabbed my arm and headed into Miss January's cottage.

I stalled on the doorstep. It was hard to keep track of Miss January's beaus, who had a tendency to either die or end up in jail. If Captain was indeed dead, I had every confidence that it wouldn't take long before she went for one of her infamous walks, came home with another boyfriend, and moved him right in. The forty-year-old, who looked double her age, found her solace in the bottom of a vodka bottle, only sticking her head out for a smoke, and let nothing interfere with her lifestyle.

"Call 911—" Fab yelled. "—we need an ambulance. Captain's still breathing. He reeks of alcohol, but it could be something more serious than drunkenness."

I stepped back onto the porch to make the call.

Fab joined me. "I tried to get him to open his eyes, but he didn't move."

It didn't take long for an ambulance to fly into the driveway. I left it to Fab to deal with the two paramedics as they rolled a gurney inside.

Kevin pulled up and parked, and I met him in the driveway.

Mac corralled Miss January into the barbecue area and settled her on one of the benches. She produced a pack of cigarettes from between her breasts and a pack of matches.

"Miss January going to be looking for a new boyfriend?" Kevin asked.

"Are you available? I'm telling you, she'd hop you in a second."

He snorted, shaking his head.

"There's a party tonight, and if you tramp all over Mac's plans for fun, you can forget her loading you up on snacks and such."

"Not to be a pooper—a Mac-ism—but I suggested to the guests that they calm down and relax. I've gotten glares that should've leveled me. Also a few grumbles of 'Mind your own business.' So much for being a nice guy." Kevin chuckled. "I've been assured the boat will get hauled away tomorrow, and good riddance."

We stepped back as the medics hauled the gurney down the steps and rolled Captain past us. Kevin followed.

Fab joined me.

"You tell the paramedics that Captain was

your beloved grandfather or some such?" I smirked at her.

"I told them what little I knew of him and Miss January, answered a couple of questions, and stood out of the way." There was a *so there* in her tone. "They're thinking he was drunk as a skunk and took a tumble, based on the sizeable lump on the back of his head, so he's off to the hospital for further testing."

"Does he have family or something?"

"Something?"

"Miss January can barely be responsible for herself. You're ballsy enough to sort through his belongings and get the information."

"I'll have Mac question her, and then we—no, make that you—will figure out anything else we need." Fab stomped over to the two women still cooling their heels in the barbecue area.

Miss January had a cigarette between her lips, but it wasn't lit. Kevin bent down at her side and said something to her, patting her hand the whole time, then backed away and went back to his car. She looked up at me with watery eyes. "Cap's going to get better."

"That's great news." I motioned to Mac, making it clear I wanted to talk to her. We moved into the middle of the driveway.

"I've got someone who'll stay with Miss January until we figure out what's happening with Captain. It'll cost, but I didn't figure you'd cheap out," Mac said.

"Whatever she needs, we'll cover," I said. "The party will keep her entertained. Speaking of, you need to assure Kevin that he won't be getting any nuisance calls."

"Got that covered."

A truck backed into the driveway and stopped at the pontoon boat. Two men jumped out and unloaded tables and umbrellas.

"Now what?" I asked.

"Another of my good ideas. You have to pass a sobriety test to go up the ladder of the boat; if you fail, there's plenty of chairs stacked at the back. Don't want anyone falling over the side." Mac's eyes darted around the driveway. She caught sight of Miss January slinking off, and easily caught up to the woman, who was headed back to her cottage.

Where the heck did Fab go? "She was here a second ago," I grumbled as I headed down the driveway toward the boat. Crum looked my way as he climbed down the ladder. Both feet on the ground, he was about to cut and run when I wiggled my finger at him. He glared. "It was my index, not middle finger," I said as he got closer.

"Just spit out whatever you want. Can't be good."

"I didn't come over here to crab at you, but that could change," I said, matching his growly tone. Fab suddenly appeared at my side. "I want you to assist Mac in whatever she needs to make sure the party doesn't get out of hand."

"Got it." He stepped back, ready to run.

"Hold up. What's with the kissy stuff?"

"I'm selling them as part of the entertainment. Did it once before, and it was a money-maker. Keeps me out of the trash, which should make you happy."

Probably not for long. Trash-picking was a favorite hobby of his.

Fab made an indecipherable noise, which had Crum staring her down.

"Just know that if your services get more… involved, it's a felony."

Crum grinned. "Yeah, yeah. Can I go now?"

"Fun talking to you."

He shot off like his pants were on fire, not that he was wearing any.

"Would you—?"

"No," I cut Fab off. "That's my answer for whatever gross question you were about to ask."

Fab laughed. "Ready to get out of here?"

Chapter Twenty-One

"You could step on it, and I wouldn't complain. For once," I said as Fab shot out to the highway. Not sure about her, but I was eager to get home, kick my feet up on the deck, and stare at the rippling blue-green water. Now, to decide what kind of drink to take outside with me...

"And when I do, you clutch the door handle until your knuckles turn white." Fab took our exit off the highway.

"Pull over, that's Melba," I yelled. "Slow down. Don't scare her."

"Who the heck is Melba?" Fab eased to the side of the road and craned her neck to look out the passenger window.

"If you're going to rule over a compound, you need to get to know your subjects," I said, throwing the door open and jumping out. "Melba." I clucked, hand out, and slowly approached the shivering, frightened dog. "What in the Sam hell are you doing out here?" I asked her in a calm voice as I bent down. "It's me, Madison."

Melba slowly inched closer, then licked my hand.

"A dog?" Fab sniffed from behind me.

"Not sure if we officially met or not—possibly just a picture—but that will have to count." I continued to talk quietly to the Border Collie and, at the same time, reached out and scratched her head. Melba whimpered.

"You don't even know if you have the right dog?" Annoyance laced Fab's tone.

I ignored Fab and lifted Melba's bloody paw. She yelped. "Don't worry, girl, we're going to get you help." Over my shoulder, I said, "I'm going to need your help lifting her into the car."

Fab opened the lift gate. She tossed me a roll of paper towels, and I wrapped Melba's paw. We each lifted one end of her and carried her over to the SUV, putting her in the back. I climbed in and sat next to her, stroking her head.

Fab stared between me and the dog. "What are you going to do with her?"

I pulled my phone out of my pocket and called my regular vet. I gave the receptionist my name and told her that I had an injured dog in the car. "Can you see her now?" I was told to bring her right in, and we hung up.

Fab closed the door, got back behind the wheel, and headed out to the highway. "Are you certain you have the right dog?"

"It doesn't matter. I'm not leaving an animal to suffer on the road when I can help." I picked my phone back up, scanned the images until I found the one Casio had forwarded of Melba, and held it up next to her head. "If it's not you, then you have a twin." I patted the dog's head, then called Casio. It went to voicemail.

The veterinarian was located just down the road in the middle of town. Fab parked in front of the door. The two of us lifted out Melba, who cried, and carried her into the small reception area. The woman behind the front desk ran around and opened a side door, beckoning us into an exam room. Dr. Kate, the vet, walked into the room at the same time.

She had questions for me as she examined Melba. "Looks to me like she was probably hit by a car. She's lucky that her paw can easily be stitched up and the other lacerations are minor. Barring any complications, she'll be ready to go home in a few hours."

I kissed Melba and went out to the reception area, where I filled out paperwork and assured the girl that I would pay, no matter who the owner was.

"You've got blood on you," Fab pointed out as we walked back to the car.

"Doesn't matter as long as the dog is alive." I looked down at my shirt and wadded up my skirt as I got in. "You can drop me off at Casio's, because I'm going to find out how the dog got out of a secured area."

"That's if—"

I cut her off. "I'm certain. But I'll know as soon as I walk in the door. If Melba is lying on the floor, then we know this is her twin. Or we'll know as soon as we pull into the compound and see the Famosa kids running around looking for her. Especially Lili, since she's joined at the hip with the dog."

"If it is indeed Melba, I'd like to know how she got out of the security gates and ended up getting hit by a car. Which didn't stop. They had to know what they'd done and kept going," Fab said in disgust.

"Chances are that it was someone visiting the compound, as who else takes that exit? There's occasionally a wrong turn, but they slow down to figure out how they're going to get turned around."

It didn't take us long to get back to the compound. Alex, Casio's oldest, was standing at the end of the driveway, glaring first one way and then the other. Fab coasted to the side of the road and parked.

"Have you seen Melba?" Alex yelled. He didn't wait for an answer. "That turd let the dog out of the house, although he says he didn't. I don't believe him, because who else would do it? Where is she? No way could she get out." He stared at the security gate. "Lili's crying. I overheard Marcus tell her to just get another dog." Angry, he looked a lot like his dad.

"Calm down. That's why we're here." I drew in a deep breath.

"Oh good, she's at your house."

"Melba's at the vet, and she's going to be fine. She needs a few stitches; the vet made it sound like an easy procedure. She'll be home in a few hours."

"What happened?" Alex demanded in a snarly tone.

More and more like his dad. "Can you go get your dad? That way, I only need to tell the story once." Casio's car was in the driveway, so I knew he was home.

Alex nodded and ran into the house.

"Sounds like Alex doesn't think much of his cousin," Fab said.

"That makes three of us," I reminded her. "The list of people who think Marcus is a *turd* is growing."

The front door flew back open, and Casio and Alex ran out. Marcus wandered out after them, stood in the doorway a moment, glaring at Fab and me, then went back inside.

"The vet? What happened?" Casio demanded.

"Dr. Kate says Melba's going to be fine." I told them both how we'd found the dog. "So there's not an issue, I'll go back with you when it's time to pick her up."

"We use the same vet, so not a problem, but probably a good idea," Casio said.

"With everything going on, I didn't mention you're the owner. Probably a good thing, if they have you marked down as a deadbeat. They know I'm good for the bill," I teased.

Casio chuckled. "Lili's going to be happy to hear that Melba's coming home. No need to get into any details," he said to Alex. "Any clue how she got out the gate and down to the road?"

"I was wondering the same thing." I met and held his stare. "Alex didn't know either. Maybe you should find out, so it doesn't happen again."

He nodded. "Thank you for jumping into action."

Chapter Twenty-Two

Creole and I had nothing planned for the weekend, so he decided on a quick trip to our favorite resort. He reserved a bungalow on the sand, and we spent the majority of our time in the water, making use of every water toy available to us. We didn't make an effort to get dressed and go to one of the restaurants, instead opting for room service. It was three days of bliss, and to guarantee it, we'd turned off our phones.

The morning after we got back, minutes after Creole left the house, Fab showed up, coffee mug in hand. She waltzed in the deck doors like she lived there and took a seat at the island. "How was the getaway?" She made kissy noises.

"It was..." I unleashed a big sigh and mimicked her kissy noises. "What brings you by so early?"

"I've got a case for you."

"No thanks. If it was even halfway decent, you'd have already taken care of it. Three days of free time—no telling what you got done."

"Pretty much the same as you." Fab flashed

me a moony smile. "Didier and I had dinner in South Beach one night... and that's why I'm here."

"The food was terrible, and you want me to... demand a refund?" I scrunched up my nose.

She slapped her hand on the counter. "This is serious business."

"Uh-huh."

"Sarcasm is so unattractive."

I laughed. "I need more coffee."

"You done?" she asked. I nodded and adopted a serious face. "This is about Xander."

"He better be okay."

"Xander's fine. Now can I finish my story?"

I nodded and got up to refill my mug. I held out the pot, and she shook her head like I was offering her poison.

"His girlfriend... what's her name?"

"Krista." *Good thing one of us remembers names. Some of the time anyway.*

"Anyway, she's not pregnant."

"What happened? She have a miscarriage?" I sank back down on the stool.

Fab jumped up and grabbed a water out of the refrigerator before sitting back down. "When Didier and I were out to dinner, we ran into her at a bar, tossing down one drink after another. She didn't recognize me because we've never met."

I threw out my hands. "And?"

"Krista was shimming around on the dance

floor in a dress molded to her curves, and no baby bump, not even a smidge. You'd think if she'd had a miscarriage, she wouldn't feel up to drinking and dancing."

"Xander was getting into the idea of fatherhood, researching everything he could get his hands on. Wonder how he's taking the news?"

"There's more." Fab made a face. "The bartender was chatty, knew everybody and their business. I slid him some cash and asked, 'What do you know about her?' with a nod to Krista."

"That must've made Didier happy."

"Didier said I was sexy in action." *So there* in Fab's tone. "Back to the bartender. He told me emphatically that she was big trouble, always running one scam or another. The place we were at was one of the few places she hadn't started trouble yet; turns out she's been banned from most of the bars around the beach area. He then asked why I wanted to know. Told him about the baby without mentioning names. He laughed and said, 'She running that scam again?'"

"Scam? How do you pull that off when at some point, you're going to have to produce a tiny human?"

"Bar dude wanted more cash, which I handed over, but only after warning him that I'd come back and shoot him if he was full of it. He laughed and said, 'I can't guarantee that's what Krista's doing now, but she's done it in the past.

Besides, does she look pregnant?'"

"I know where this is going, and you want me to tell Xander." I put my face in my hands and groaned. "We need to be absolutely sure."

"Told Bartender Ben that I was a PI and got his number, in case he could be helpful in the future. You never know," she said to my raised eyebrows. "According to him, Krista hooks up with a guy who's got the money to pay her bills, tells him she's pregnant, and when the guy starts getting demanding, asking too many questions, she 'has a miscarriage.' It's an old scam according to him, and he was surprised I didn't know it."

"Krista's baby bump?" I'd seen Xander running his hand over his soon-to-be baby.

"Asked the same question. Ben told me that a fake baby bump is easy to buy. Only half believing him, I did some research once I got home, and they come in various sizes, strap on, and easily fit under clothes. If you don't cheap out, you can buy ones that feel real."

"You just typed in fake… and a variety of options popped up?" I asked. Fab nodded. "What a…"

"Ben gave me an address for her."

"How much did that cost you?"

"It was worth it," Fab assured me. "When Krista's got a mark, she has several different addresses she uses—friends that are willing to cover for her. Ben was able to give me the address where she actually lives because once, when he was visiting a friend, he saw her go into a condo high-rise. He asked his friend and found out that Krista's lived there for a while. She's not friendly and keeps to herself, and he didn't know much about her. The one thing Ben didn't know was the unit number, but there's an office and you can probably get the info out of them with a little cash. That was Ben's suggestion; he even gave me a name, which I have in my phone."

"Ben's a helpful chap. As long as he doesn't turn out to be full of it."

"What are you going to do?" Fab demanded.

"You only want the sister title when you're bossing Xander around, but when stuff hits the fan, it's on me." I stared out the sliders at the baby blue skies. "You're certain?"

"I guess bring it up to Xander and see if anything's changed in the last couple of days. Maybe she's told him she had a miscarriage."

"I'm not telling Xander that Krista isn't pregnant; she can do it," I said in disgust.

"How are you going to make that happen?" Fab demanded.

"You kidnap her, bring her to the Cove, and when she's done confessing, put her in an Uber and send her back to wherever you picked her up. Or she can walk."

"That's got jail time written all over it," Fab snapped.

"Then figure out a way to lure her down here,

and before Xander makes another money transfer."

"Before we do anything, we ask Xander 'How's the baby?' in a roundabout way."

"We've got the wedding coming up, so we need to make this top priority," I said.

Chapter Twenty-Three

The next morning, Fab and Didier showed up early, coming in the front door without knocking. She had a pink bakery box in one hand and I'd bet a lockpick in one of her pockets. Creole had made two pots of coffee.

"How is it that I'm the last to know about this impromptu meeting?" I asked.

Fab slid onto a stool across from me at the island. "Have a cinnamon roll—they were fresh out of the oven. You'll be much perkier."

I barely stopped myself from licking my lips.

Didier placed breakfast pastries on a platter and set them in the middle of the island, then passed out plates while Creole poured coffee.

It didn't take long for the food to disappear and the coffee mugs to be refilled.

"Did you tell Creole about Didier and me seeing Krista at the bar?" Fab asked.

"Knowing my hub's not going to like my idea of how to deal with that woman, I thought I'd wait and shuffle the telling onto you. If I manage to stay out of jail, why mention old news?" I could feel Creole's glare without looking his way.

Didier shook his head at me.

"Who's Krista?" Creole asked.

"Xander's... you might not know this part." I motioned to Fab. "Knowing you love a good story, be sure to start at the beginning."

"Xander's girlfriend. She's pregnant... sort of," Fab said.

"You don't look very surprised by this announcement," Creole said to Didier.

"Sworn to secrecy." Didier smirked and nudged Fab. "Be sure to throw in a timeline."

Fab relayed the events of the night she and Didier had seen Krista in the bar. Nothing varied from what she'd told me.

"I take it that Xander doesn't know what you found out?" Creole asked.

"The reason for this morning's meeting," Fab said. "Told Didier your idea, and he thinks it needs to be revised. But only in parts."

"What were you thinking of doing?" Creole asked. "I'm sure you both know that this is one of those situations where there's no good way to break the news."

"Kidnap Krista at gunpoint, drag her ass down here, and make her tell on herself," I said.

Creole laughed. "That was Fab's idea, and she's letting you take credit."

I glared at him. "I can come up with thug ideas of my own."

"The part I don't like is that you could go to jail," Didier said.

Creole put his hand over mine. "There's not going to be a good way to tell Xander that he was conned. I do like your idea of making Krista do it herself, minus the illegal parts."

"Unless she's forced, she's not going to fess up to anything," I insisted.

"I've come up with an amendment to the plan." Fab waved wildly.

"No more coffee for you," I said.

She ignored me, which I'd expected. "We invite her down here for a birthday lunch for Xander. I know it's not his birthday, but maybe she doesn't know that."

"Better yet, invite her to celebrate Xander getting a big bonus," Didier said.

"If she's as greedy as it's been suggested, she'll show," Creole said.

"As long as we're clear that once we get her into the office, I get to pull my gun." Judging by the groans, I'd have to bring them around to my idea.

"Maybe," Creole hedged. "You're going to need to line up witnesses that will swear it never happened."

"Once Krista's been outed, my guess is she'll cut her loses and move on to her next mark," Fab said. "Especially since this isn't her first time—it's how she lives her life."

"Then we need to come up with a way to stop her," I seethed.

"Put the word out to your bartender buddy

that you'll purchase any good tips." Didier grinned at Fab. "The man was eager to earn an easy buck."

"Boy is that an understatement," Fab grumbled.

"Two good ideas from Didier." I clapped. "Next time we're stuck for one, you can expect to get a phone call."

"Both Didier and I would like it if you called more often. Makes it easier to know what the hell you two are up to," Creole grumped.

"I solemnly swear—" I crossed my heart. "—I would've told you sooner... maybe... but it's all your fault."

Didier and Creole laughed.

"One more item. You extend the invitation to Krista." I waved off Fab's refusal. "Go all snooty girl on her. Make her feel like a special guest, which she basically is, and insist she needs to be there."

"That sounds fun." Fab rubbed her hands together.

"It also saves us a trip to Miami," I said.

* * *

Fab got hot on the phone and called Krista, inviting her to a surprise party in two days. "Sorry for the short notice, but I had to get the number from Xander without him knowing." Fab laughed.

Krista politely refused, saying, "I have other plans."

Not deterred, Fab poured it on about the new job opportunity Xander had been offered and the *huge* signing bonus. As we suspected, at the mention of money, Krista decided that she could change her plans.

When she hung up, I asked, "How did you get her number?"

"The bartender. Surprised me with a freebie. But considering what I'd already handed over…"

We got to the office early, each of us riding in with our husbands. It had been decided that Fab would be the welcoming committee. She waited downstairs for Krista to arrive, and I went upstairs. I wasn't surprised to find Xander already in the office, as he claimed there was more room to spread out here than at home.

I nodded at him where he was sitting at one end of the desk. "Want to give you a heads up that you're in for a surprise, and that's about all I can say at the moment. Be prepared for anything and try to roll with it. Know that Fab and I have your back."

"I'm guessing that you want me to hold off on questions?" Xander asked, brows raised.

"Just know that after… you can ask away." I hoped that after he found out, he took into consideration there was no good way to tell him and didn't hold it against us.

"Now we're having an awkward moment, and

I'm not sure what to say except that I don't care much for surprises." Xander half-laughed.

My phone alerted with a message. I picked it up and glanced at the screen. "Let's move out to the couch."

The door opened, and Fab and Krista came in. Krista had on a dress with a fitted bodice that draped over her baby bump, which was larger than the last time I'd seen her. I wasn't going to offer her anything to drink—one less thing to throw at me. Xander and Krista hugged, and he ran his hand over her stomach. Fab glared.

I stood off to the side and stared at the woman as she sat down next to Xander. I decided to get straight to the point of this get-together, since the sooner it was over, the better. "Krista has something to tell you. Fab and I already know but thought it was more fitting coming from her."

"I don't know what you're talking about." Krista's eyes flitted between Fab and me. "I'm here to celebrate the new job that Xander's been offered."

"Don't forget the huge bonus." I gritted my teeth.

"So happy for you, hon." Krista leaned over and kissed his cheek, not appearing to notice his poorly hidden surprise.

"To move this little gathering along, I'm going to turn the floor over to Fab, who can get it started by telling us what she witnessed when she was out with her husband the other night," I said.

Fab leaned against the front edge of her desk and related the same story she'd told me, leaving out all mention of the bartender and instead saying that it was friend of Krista's who said it wasn't the first time she'd run the baby scam.

"You liar." Krista jumped up, red in the face, and turned to Xander. "I'm not listening to this and neither should you."

"If we're wrong, then I'll apologize." I gritted my teeth. "It's easy enough to prove—lift your dress."

Xander's eyes darted between us, and he looked torn, unsure what to believe.

"You've lost your mind," Krista practically spit, then grabbed her purse and headed for the door.

I scurried around and stepped in front of her, gun drawn. "I really, really want to shoot you. I promised my husband not to go off and empty a clip into you, but I'm sure he'd understand. I do know that he'd help me dispose of your body."

Krista stepped back, sheer terror on her face.

"Hold on." Xander jumped up and stepped to Krista's side. "The only one you need to show is me, and we can go into the other office. Then I'll assure these two that you're not scamming me, and we can all go home with no bloodshed." He shot me a side-eye: *Have you gone nuts?*

"Make sure you get a good look at the fake

pregnancy belly—state of the art according to the product description," I said.

"You bitches." Krista brushed off Xander's hands and stepped around him.

"You're not going anywhere until Xander knows the truth," I said and turned to Fab. "You got the cuffs?"

Fab held them up, twirling them around on her finger. "You want to take Krista down or do you want me to do it?"

Xander reached out and turned Krista's face to his. "You're not pregnant, are you?"

"Your sisters are crazy, Xander! Don't you know that kind of thing runs in families?"

"Whatever. Good thing you figured it out, so you know I'm not kidding about shooting you," I said and got an *I can handle this* look from Xander.

"Tell them that they're wrong. Better yet, show me that they're wrong." Xander stared at her, and she looked away. "Show me."

Krista turned away, arms crossed, and was silent for so long, it wasn't clear if she planned to answer. "I can't," she murmured finally.

Xander unleashed a sigh of disgust. "Was it just about the money?"

"You don't know what it takes to maintain a lifestyle in Brickell." Krista swept her arm around. "It's expensive. A girl's got to come up with creative ways to make ends meet."

"That's why you wouldn't tell me the dates of

your doctor's appointments? Because there weren't any?" Hurt was etched on Xander's face. "And when you were due to deliver? Then what were you going to do?"

Krista glared at him for a long moment with no sign of remorse. "I'd—"

Xander cut her off. "The sonogram? You buy that too?"

"I'd have miscarried." Krista turned to me. "Happy now?"

"No. I'm not," I yelled and was pleased when she took a step back. "Listen up, sweets. We're going to have eyes on you, and if you run this scam again, we'll shut you down. I've got friends in the Miami PD. That'll be my first call, and hopefully you'll end up in jail for a long time." I knew it was a long shot, but her face paled and that pleased me.

"I say we call the police now," Fab said, locking eyes with Xander. "It's up to you."

Krista hissed.

"Show me your baby stomach, and I'll call them off," Xander said, shifting his gaze to her stomach. "I want to see what you used to put one over on me."

Krista sucked in a breath, dropped her purse, and stood up straight. A militant look on her face, she lifted her dress and short slip, showing a silicone pregnancy belly that fastened around the back. "Satisfied?" She jerked down her dress.

Xander locked angry eyes on her and stepped back.

"Say the word, and I'll shoot her," I said to him. He shook his head. I pointed to the door with the muzzle of my gun. "The only reason you're walking out of here is because of Xander. If I ever see you again, all bets are off."

"Run your scam again, and we'll hear about it. If you don't end up in jail, we'll take care of you," Fab promised.

I walked to the door and held it open.

Krista scooped up her purse and ran out of the office.

I kicked the door closed with a resounding bang and approached Xander from behind and gave him a quick hug. "I thought Krista should be the one to tell you. Honestly, I didn't want to do it myself, but I would've if getting her to show up didn't work. Please don't hate me."

"Never." Xander turned and leaned against the desk. "I wanted to be a dad someday, though not this young, and then all of a sudden, I was going to be one. Just because I didn't know anything about kids didn't mean I couldn't learn. I researched, read, and figured I could do it. I knew I'd make mistakes, but what parent doesn't? I wanted to be a Girl Dad." The sadness oozed out of him.

"No doubt you'd have been great." My heart broke for him.

Fab reached out and squeezed his hand.

"That fake baby bump felt like the real thing. More than a couple of times, I thought something was off… but not that. Then told myself not to be a dick, that it was just my inexperience."

"You're not the first to be conned this way," Fab told him. "I did some research, then checked out a couple of websites that showed that pregnancy bellies are big sellers."

"Just great." Xander sighed. "Hope I never run into Krista again."

"Now that you're available," I said with a teasing smile, "my mother would love to fix you up."

"Please no," he groaned.

"You're in luck," Fab said. "Madeline told me herself that she's out of the matchmaking business."

The three of us laughed, and that broke the tension.

"I—"

Xander cut me off. "No more apologies. There was no good way to tell me. Better that you made her to do it, and to my face. Not sure I would've believed it otherwise." He went back to our office and gathered up his paperwork and shoved everything in his briefcase. "Taking the rest of the day off. I need a beer."

"Jake's and it's on the house."

Xander had almost cleared the office when he stopped and turned. "Thank you seems weird, but I appreciate that you didn't let it go on."

Then he was gone, the door closing behind him.

I buried my face in my hands.

"Hey, we all agreed that there was no good way to tell him," Fab said. "I know the guys are going to corner him and give him a pep talk—remind him he has friends."

Chapter Twenty-Four

The weekend arrived, and it was time to get ready for the wedding. Fab and I both chose black sleeveless dresses and heels, and decided that we needed to arrive at the funeral home before the guests. However, when Fab pulled into the parking lot, it already held several cars — the wedding party had arrived. We got out and headed over to the garden, taking the walkway that ran along a wrought iron fence flanked with a hedge of bright-pink roses that blocked the view of the cars. We entered through a side entrance that led into the main room where funeral services took place and heard voices in the entry. Our appearance interrupted a conversation between Raul and another man, who both looked up.

"Todd Melon," Raul introduced the groom.

"Women?" Melon muttered. His appraising look and surly tone made it clear he'd expected a couple of burly men. "Under no circumstances does my bride need to know that I hired security." He glared as he issued his edict.

Fab's growl stopped me from saying, *We can leave now if you'd like.* I was ready to hotfoot it back to the car.

Raul stepped between Fab and Melon and assured the man that he'd seen to all his last-minute requests. Melon begrudgingly nodded, glaring at us one last time, and Raul was able to steer him out the front door.

I grabbed a handful of Fab's dress, tugged, and with a toss of my head, headed us back in the direction we came in, outside to the bar that had originally been built for those who needed a drink to get through a funeral. The bartender hadn't arrived, and I slid behind the bar and filled two glasses with soda, setting Fab's in front of her as she slid onto a stool.

"Try not to beat up the groom, even if he is dickish. It might be wedding jitters." I'd left the details of this wedding gig to Fab, caught up in Xander's drama, and now wished I'd paid more attention. "How long are we here for?"

"Couple of hours, max." Fab checked her watch. "Once the ceremony's over, there's pictures, and then the guests will be headed to a local restaurant where they reserved the outside deck."

"Are we on restaurant duty?"

Fab shook her head. "Even after questioning Raul, I still don't have a clear understanding of why our services are needed."

"If you should decide to branch out, be sure and add it to your resume — guard duty at festive occasions on the off-chance that... you'll think of something. Do a splashy ad campaign that targets funerals and weddings to get the word out and show your versatility."

"Done yet?" Fab's mouth was set in a stern line, the only giveaway her eyes, which sparkled with humor. "Sometimes, your ideas are—"

"So great that you're overwhelmed by my brilliance." I grinned.

"If that's what you want to believe." Fab's lips quirked. "Now that the guests are arriving, I'm going to go find Raul—hopefully he's done chatting with Melon—and suggest that he speed things along."

"You might want to calm down. Weddings tend to happen at their own pace." Her glare told me she wanted me to be more supportive. "I'll wait here and check out the guests while you go strong-arm whoever." It could be an excuse to creep around the funeral home and check out the dead guests, and no thanks, happy to wait here.

Not one to sit around, Fab disappeared back inside.

I turned my attention to the guests as they arrived and greeted one another, laughing and joking. They were directed up the walkway by one of the groomsmen, who'd come out the front door and had been waiting for their arrival. This job was a bore. Like Fab, I wasn't sure what I should be on the lookout for, but not wanting to mingle with the guests, I switched to a seat at the far end of the bar. From that vantage point, I could keep my eyes on the parking lot and guests for anything out of the ordinary. The chairs on both sides of the aisle filled up quickly.

Minutes later, another car pulled into the parking lot and chose a space at the far end, away from where the rest of the guests had parked. Was the straggler here to make funeral arrangements? A lone man got out, dressed in jeans and tennis shoes, and cut straight across the parking lot, headed around the back of the funeral home in the direction of Dickie and Raul's living quarters. Friend possibly? But why not use the front entrance?

Where the hell are you? I sent off the text, tapping my finger as I waited for a response. Nothing. I slid off the stool. It was almost time for the ceremony to start, and Fab and I needed to claim the seats in the back that had been saved for us. She was nowhere in sight.

I waited for the man to reappear, and thus far, he hadn't shown back up. Maybe I should take a quick peek around the front to make sure all was still quiet. I quietly opened the front door and slid inside. In the book of firsts, this would be one: lurking around a funeral home. I was getting to be too much like Fab, I thought, closing the door behind me. The entry was deserted. I pulled out my phone and texted Fab: *911.*

"What?" She appeared in the doorway across the room.

I almost jumped out of my skin and stopped

short of squealing. "How long does it take to check out dead people? As often as you do it, one would think you'd be a whole lot faster."

The sound of breaking glass interrupted what I was sure was her about to tell me off. We both turned in the direction of Dickie and Raul's personal residence.

"That's what—"

Fab put her finger across her lips and disappeared back the way she came.

She doesn't need my help. I'll wait right here. I sank down on one of the plastic-slipcovered chairs in the entry. It didn't take long for the man from outside to creep down the hallway, not a glance my way. Where the heck was Fab? How did he get past her? I'd missed the bag over his shoulder when he got out of the car and wondered why he needed it. Once he was out of sight, I jumped up and tiptoed after him.

For the second time in minutes, Fab stole up on me out of nowhere. I bit back a scream and pointed after the man, and she nodded. I gave her the thumb to go after him herself, and she took a militant stance and shook her head. "I do everything," she said in a whisper.

I answered with an exaggerated eye-roll and held my ground.

She jerked on my arm, tugging me along with her as she started after him.

The man tried the doors of the visitation rooms, all of which were kept locked when there were no visitors... unless you came with a lockpick. He examined the name plaques and continued on to the far end of the hall, where the door to the bridal changing room stood open. Fab pulled her weapon, and I drew my Glock. From the doorway, we watched as the man stood in the middle of the large room and scanned every corner. He headed over to several pieces of luggage stacked up against the wall, choosing a designer train case to paw through. He pulled out a several items, setting them aside, and slipped several pieces of jewelry into his bag.

"What the hell are you doing?" Fab barked.

The man jerked upright and gave us a cursory glance, apparently missing the guns pointed at him. "I'll be out of here in a minute," he said dismissively, grabbing a travel bag and dumping the contents on the floor.

Fab stepped forward and planted her foot in the middle of his butt, and he ended up on all fours. "Don't make me shoot you," she barked. "If you didn't know, you can die from a bullet to your posterior."

"Don't know what your game is and don't care; just go away." He straightened up. "A watch interest you?" He held one up. "Not sure it's worth much, but it's pretty. Probably worth something, knowing the groom's net worth."

"Are you calling the cops?" I asked Fab, not taking my eyes off the man.

"Go ahead." He smirked. "The groom won't

be happy, that's for sure; he'll hate the headlines. Yeah, I'll go to jail, but Melon will be sharing the ride once I tell my story. Squaring off in court would be worth the humiliation of getting locked up. I've already suffered a lot of embarrassment and found out that I'll get over it."

"If it's your plan to steal from the groom, you're in the wrong room. Melon's changing room is around the corner at the end." I jabbed my finger in the general direction.

"I'm fine with what I've found." He reached into the bag and held up a fistful of jewelry, shoving everything into the bag he brought.

"If this is your idea of retribution of some sort, you're going about it the wrong way," Fab said.

"Cops on the way? Or do you need me to make the call?" I asked, knowing Fab wouldn't call. Wasn't this the kind of activity we'd been hired to stop? Instead, we were having a basically friendly chat with the man.

He stood, grabbing a large jewelry case. "Turn around and I'll be out the door, and no one will be the wiser until after the ceremony."

"Here's how this is going to go." Fab stepped up. "Drop your bag and the case, empty your pockets, and you're free to go. No one needs to know you were here."

"Hell no." Spit flew. Lucky him, it didn't hit either of us. But close. "This doesn't make a dent in what Melon stole off me. Don't you worry none—I'll be letting him know that I was the one to appropriate these sparkly items and if he wants any of it back, he can pay up. If not, I'll pawn everything."

I turned to Fab. *Now what?* I'd be telling her later that a smirk was not an answer.

"You're telling us that you crashed a wedding to steal in retaliation for whatever Melon stole from you?" Fab asked.

"You're a quick one." He nodded.

"What did he steal?"

"He managed my money, and then one day, he cleaned out the accounts. Clever bastard made it look like I was the one to do it. I've got a forensic accountant going over the books, but who knows how long that will take. In the meantime, he needs to feel some pain, if his greedy, larcenous heart is capable of such an emotion."

"This isn't the way to go about replenishing your coffers," Fab told him. "Regardless of what Melon's done, you'll end up in a jail cell alongside him." She moved around me, put her foot in his gut and wrestled him around, then cuffed one wrist to a chair leg and left him lying on the floor.

Finally, she's out of patience. Took her long enough. Where did she hide a pair of cuffs under that sexy off-the-shoulder black dress?

Fab pulled out her phone and made a call. "Come to the bride's dressing room," she said and hung up.

The mystery of who she'd called was solved when Raul poked his head through the door and surveyed the mess. His eyes landed on the man on the floor, who hadn't moved but now rolled over on his back and stared at the ceiling. "What's going on?"

Fab hit the highlights. "Why don't you go get Mr. Melon? He can decide if he wants this man arrested."

"The ceremony's over, and pictures are about to get underway. You need to take this man to the office before anyone from the wedding party shows up." Raul, usually calm under pressure, now looked anything but.

"Go fetch Melon. I'd enjoy a little face-to-face." The man laughed, a dry, disturbing sound.

"How about a name to give him?" Fab asked the man. "It might make him eager to see you."

"Jeff Push," he grunted.

"You go get Mr. Melon, and I'll take care of Mr. Push," Fab said to Raul.

"You won't have to cuff me; I'll come willingly." Push shook his wrist.

Fab uncuffed him and pointed him down the hall, giving him ample opportunity to run, but he plodded along until he got to the office. Fab motioned him through the open door, he entered and plopped down in a chair.

I leaned over and whispered, "I'm going home now."

Fab grasped the side of my dress and tugged hard, then stepped back, standing guard at the door.

We didn't have to wait long before an angry voice could be heard coming down the hall. When Raul showed Mr. Melon into the office, he caught sight of Push and bellowed, "You have to ruin my wedding for your petty-mindedness? You were a stupid ass and lost your money; get over it. Or I know, make it back, if you're smart enough."

"Lost it? You stole it," Push shouted back.

Dickie barely poked his head through the door before backing up. "I'll let you handle this," Raul said to Fab and followed Dickie back into the hall.

Everything happened at once. Both men brandished guns and pulled the triggers, the shots going wild. One grazed the back of my calf, ripping off the skin. I hissed and looked down to see blood trickling into my shoe. That bullet lodged in the wall behind me. Who knew what the other one hit. No one was screaming, so not a person. Or they were dead. I grimaced at the thought.

Both men had dived to the floor, landing in a heap. For now, there wouldn't be any more shots fired, as they'd both dropped their guns. Push leveraged himself forward, his hand out, and pulled one of the guns towards him.

Fab jumped between the two men, shooting

Push in the hand. He howled and rolled over as she kicked the gun out of reach. Melon held up his hands in surrender. "Either of you moves and you're dead," she roared.

The hallway was filled with screams that seemed to echo all around.

Fab stepped back and blocked the already closed door. "You okay?" she asked me.

"Swell." I limped over and hung onto the back of a chair. "Bullet grazed the back of my leg, and it burns like the devil."

A male voice in the hall yelled, "Cops are on the way."

Fab and I looked at one another and silently agreed, *No avoiding that one.*

Push stopped mewling and rolling from side-to-side and went completely still, his head turned away.

Is he dead? I telegraphed to Fab.

Fab crossed to him and bent over, checking for a pulse. "He's out but still breathing."

I let out a huge sigh of relief.

Melon, who was sitting with his knees to his chest, looked ready to be sick on his tux pants.

The door flew open, and two cops stepped in, Kevin in the lead. One look at the two of us and his face filled with anger. He attempted to stomp in our direction but got cut off by paramedics rolling a gurney into the office.

Fab slung her arm around me and, after a word to one of the medics, eased me out of the office and into one of the closest chairs inside the entry.

I stared down. "My shoes are ruined. Hopefully, I didn't leave a trail of blood." I winced from the pain. "What if one of those two gets away?"

"The cops are here; they can handle it. The last thing they want is our interference, and that's the way they'd see it." Fab, who'd sat next to me, pulled me to her side. "Remember that day we practiced fainting?" she whispered.

Out of the corner of my eye, I caught Kevin's rapid approach. I closed my eyes and slid to the floor.

"What in the…" he snapped.

"Madison was only grazed, but she's squeamish when it comes to blood, especially her own." Kevin turned on his heel, and before he disappeared, she asked, "Did Push die?"

"There's your answer." He stood aside for a gurney making an exit, then said something to one of the medics and followed them to the front door.

"Keep your eyes closed. Kevin's got eyes in the back of his head and might see that you're on the road to recovery, and then he'll have a zillion questions."

"You're not going to hold him off for long."

"You need to go to the hospital," Fab said sternly. "I call dibs on telling this story at the next family dinner."

I tried not to laugh, but it escaped anyway.

A paramedic rolled a gurney in my direction, and I pretended to come around, figuring he'd spot a faker in a second. He bent down and checked my leg. In minutes, I was loaded onto the gurney and taken to the hospital. I felt sort of bad leaving Fab to answer questions. I'd have to make it up to her.

My stay in the emergency room was the shortest ever; it didn't take long to clean up and bandage my leg. It didn't surprise me that Creole blew into the room like he owned the joint while I was waiting to be released.

With a big smile, he pulled me into his arms and kissed me. "You're in so much trouble," he grumbled.

"Promise me, when we get home, that you'll send me to our room. You're going to have to stay by my side to make sure I don't go anywhere."

A nurse, who'd walked in with the discharge papers, overheard me and laughed.

"That can be arranged." Creole gave me a squinty half-smile. "Once you can answer a couple of questions coherently, you're out of here."

The nurse laughed again. "You're good to go. Follow these instructions, which are pretty simple." She handed me the paperwork.

Chapter Twenty-Five

I'd woken up early and made my way out to the deck with a mug of coffee. I kicked back in the chair and watched as the cloudless sky turned a baby blue. The back of my leg pinched, but nothing that Tylenol couldn't handle.

Creole came out with another mug and traded me for my current one, which was empty. "Our weekly meeting is here this morning, and I texted Fab that she better bring food." He chuckled as he sat down.

"She coughed it up last time—two in a row would be a record."

Creole made a face at my choice of words. "Figured, since she's going to burst through the door to check up on you, or whatever excuse she comes up with, that she might as well bring something to eat."

"At least she knows what we like, so we don't have to worry about her showing up with something weird."

It didn't take long for Fab and Didier to show up. Didier brought the bakery boxes out to the deck, and Creole got up to meet them. He dragged over a table and set down a tray of food, plates, and silverware.

Didier leaned down and kissed my cheek. "How are you feeling?"

"I was able to limp out here hanging onto my hunky nurse, although he did grouch all the way, wanting to carry me."

It didn't take long for us to devour the food. Creole refilled the coffee mugs.

"You so owe me." Fab had claimed a seat next to me.

"It's always something. What now?"

The two men laughed.

"I was dragged to the police station to make a statement. Since I saw that coming, I got hot on the phone to Tank, and he met me there."

Fab had met Tank, AKA Patrick Cannon, during a jail visit when he'd had a short stay behind bars. He said he was innocent, and it turned out he wasn't lying. Actually, he was a criminal lawyer, which we were in need of more often than we liked.

"I'm guessing that Madison and I are the only ones who don't know what happened after she was carted off in the ambulance," Creole said.

"I've got an update." Fab finished off the last of her coffee. "Mr. Melon—the groom, for the one of you that doesn't know—got irate with the cops, thinking he was off the hook since Mr. Push pulled his weapon first and it was therefore self-defense. He got a rude awakening when he was cuffed and taken away in the back of a patrol car. Mr. Push was taken to the hospital, where he got his hand sewn up, and was then booked."

"Turns out there was a warrant for Melon on some previous theft charges," Didier told us.

"How did you find that out?" I asked.

"Kevin told—"

"Kevin!" I didn't screech but it was close, cutting off Didier. "He never tells us anything."

"You were saying…?" Creole laughed.

"Just that Melon has a track record of fleecing his clients, and it's finally caught up to him." Didier shook his head.

"Tried to eavesdrop on the questioning in Raul's office, wanting to know why the couple chose a funeral home for the wedding, but didn't get anything… except almost caught," Fab said. "Talked to Raul this morning and hinted around, and he seemed to think it was the park setting, though he wasn't all that sure. Once the screams had stopped and the guests were under control, they were given a vague version of what happened and were effusive in their compliments about the service and the venue. Raul was ecstatic."

"You made that up." I made a face at her. "Next you're going to tell us the bride was happy the groom got carted off to the cooler."

"Could be the guests thought it was staged for their entertainment. Who knows? Raul told me that the bride didn't have much of a reaction—not to her groom being shot at or to him being taken into custody." Fab snapped her fingers. "I know, we could stop by for lunch—I bet they have those little sandwiches you like—and get an update. With their connections, they'll know the latest."

"So sad I'm going to be missing out on that fun because I have some of my own planned. There's a Boardwalk meeting at the office, and then I need to go to Jake's."

"You need to stay off your feet," Creole grouched.

"The doc said I probably wouldn't be able to run a marathon this weekend but other than that, no restrictions." *So there!* I smirked at Creole. "But if my bestest friend offered to drive me…"

"Yeah!" Didier nudged her.

Fab rolled her eyes at me. "Maybe."

Chapter Twenty-Six

The investors' meeting for the Boardwalk got shuffled aside—Billy and Spoon were concerned because another thug had attempted to snatch Kyle while he was in the middle of devouring a hamburger at a local drive-thru, and they wanted a sit-down with the Chief and Casio. Since everyone was downstairs, where the food was, they grabbed plates and took a seat at the conference table.

I amped up the drama and dragged my leg as I shuffled over to take a seat. Brad glared at the bandage on my leg and growled, while Fab stood behind him with a smirk, shaking her head.

"Just be happy the guy was a terrible shot." I leaned in and brushed a kiss over Brad's cheek. "You can be the one to tell Mother." I wondered why she was a no-show, then figured that Spoon had told her the discussion would be about Kyle. I winked at the kid, who was busy cleaning his plate.

"I'm feigning ignorance. Last to know is fine with me on this one." He made a face.

"Madison, got a message for you," Casio said

from the other end of the table, where he was sitting next to the Chief and Xander. "From a friend that wishes to remain anonymous."

I groaned. "Don't want to know." His flinty stare told me it wasn't going to be good, entirely aside from the anonymous business.

"I want to hear." Fab set down a bottle of water and sat next to me.

"As the owner of a certain black Hummer that's hardly an inconspicuous vehicle—"

"Message is for me, dude." Fab returned Casio's intense stare. "Since I'm almost always the driver. What? Someone saying I hit them? They're full of it."

He grunted at her. "That strip mall you have your eye on? Find something else to buy. The dressmaker babe? Find her a new location. The sooner the better."

Fine with me.

"Don't think you can get away with issuing an order without ponying up a few more details, and not some vague rambling." Fab glared back at him.

"Do you want to get yourself in the middle of something and end up dead? Or how about in jail, would that be fun?" Casio snapped.

Didier hooked his arm around her and pulled her to his side. "No to both. You can tell your friend that the deal's dead and he won't be seeing either of them at that property again." He turned his stare on Fab until she nodded. Took her long enough.

"Don't go all frowny." I smiled at her. "After the meeting, I've got an idea to share with you."

Creole leaned in and whispered, "Do I know what you're up to?"

I nodded and winked at him, mouthing *warehouse*.

Now that the food had been consumed and the plates taken away, it was time to get the meeting started.

Billy slapped his hand on the table. "Our young friend Kyle was involved with criminals, who made him an errand boy making deliveries and pickups." Kyle nodded but stayed focused on his soda. "Word is that there's a reward being offered to anyone that turns over the kid's current location."

"Has anyone showed up at your house?" Creole asked.

Billy shook his head. "Plus, he's never there by himself. During the day, he goes to the body shop, and we put him to work."

"No one will get to him at either place," Spoon growled. "Thus far, no one's come sniffing around the business, so I'm assuming his exact whereabouts are still unknown. Billy and I have assured him that it's safe and we'll do everything we can to make sure it stays that way."

"So kid, what were you delivering?" the Chief asked.

"Drugs, guns, cash," Kyle answered with

forthrightness. "Sometimes I knew what was in the package I was delivering. The first time I didn't know, I asked and was told none of my business. I didn't ask again."

"Same for pickups?" the Chief asked.

Kyle nodded. "The pickups were mostly money and always packaged, so I had to take a guess but could figure it out based on who I was dealing with."

"This has been going on for a while — recruiting kids to do the illegal work, knowing they'll do less jail time than an adult," Casio said, disgusted.

"Kyle told me he was threatened constantly if he talked to anyone, even the other boys, and told that if he screwed up or went against orders, he'd be dealt with harshly. Running away is a death sentence." Billy encouraged Kyle to take a deep breath; his face had taken on a sickly pallor.

"There was this kid — one day he was gone. I never saw him again, and we were told to never mention his name," Kyle barely squeaked out.

"How did you end up with this group?" the Chief asked.

"Lived on the street for what seemed like forever, maybe a couple of months, and one day while panhandling, I was forced into a car. Kicked and screamed the whole way, but no one looked my way." Kyle reached for a bottled water and gulped it down, causing himself to go into a coughing fit. Billy clapped his back. "I was taken to a house and locked in a room. After a couple of days, a guy sat me down and explained the rules, which amounted to 'Do as I tell you.' I agreed to everything, not wanting to get my butt kicked, and bided my time, thinking it wouldn't be forever. It didn't take long to figure out I was wrong about that one."

"Two months ago, Kyle was coming back from making a delivery, and a man cornered him, claiming to be a cop," Billy told us. "He wanted to know details about everything that went on in the house and every delivery and didn't want to hear any excuses. Told Kyle if he didn't do as he was told, he'd be arrested and sent to jail, where his safety couldn't be guaranteed once his bosses found out he'd snitched."

"I kept giving the cop one excuse after another until he'd had enough. His patience snapped, and he told me the next time we met up, I'd better have something useful." Kyle's hands shook as he recalled the events. "The next day, I picked up an envelope of cash, and on the way back, the cop came out of nowhere and tried to take me down. More afraid of going back empty-handed, I launched myself into oncoming traffic and got clipped by someone's front bumper. The car squealed to a stop, traffic stacked up, and I heard sirens and took off. Not sure where the cop went, but I didn't look back."

"How long after that did you decide to make your break?" Casio asked him.

Kyle held up three fingers. "Stupid of me. They were on my tail from the start. They could've had me but made a game out of it." He shuddered.

"Then a fancy ride pulls over, two women inside, and Kyle jumped in. He was out of options and figured what the heck," Billy said. "Claims Fab knows how to get around." *Imagine that* in his tone. "Thought she was nuts when she directed him to make a getaway behind a dumpster."

"The hole was just where you said it would be," Kyle said, awe in his voice. "The street was nice, with a bunch of houses, and I crawled under a hedge and stayed put until it got dark. Did my best to stick to side roads, grabbed a burger, and found a couple boulders to hide between at the beach. Not terrible as long as it's not high tide."

"Time to bring this operation down." Casio clapped his hand on the table. "We don't want a criminal operation like that getting bigger in the Cove."

"Too bad that when you round up one bunch of criminals and shut down their business, another group immediately takes over," Creole said.

"I'm friends with the sheriff, and I say we bring him in and share what's going on," the Chief said. "Since none of us are in law enforcement anymore, we're out of the loop.

They might already have an open investigation, and if it turns out it's news to him, we owe him the courtesy."

"If you need to hand over a name for who tipped you off, use mine," Billy offered. "Do your best to leave Kyle out of it."

"No names would be better. Just say a street snitch that needed a few bucks," Creole advised. "If Billy's name surfaces, he'll be looking over his shoulder for who knows how long. Getting even is a sport for these kinds of people."

"Better me than a kid," Billy said in a resigned tone. He turned to Kyle, and the two traded some kind of silent communication. Kyle nodded. "Got an address for you." Billy took a sticky note out of his pocket and passed it to the Chief. "Nice house, by the way."

"Is this where you were living?" Casio asked Kyle. He nodded. Casio leaned over the Chief's shoulder and entered the information in his phone. The Chief handed the note to Xander, who did the same as Casio and handed it back.

"There's no one better to run someone down than Xander." I smiled at him.

"We know that, don't we?" The Chief nodded at Xander, who grinned.

"You better not have threatened him in some way." I leveled a stare at the Chief.

"After all the time we've known each other? My feelings are hurt. Most people find me quite charming." He smirked.

Fab laughed. All eyes turned to her, but she didn't flinch.

"Who'd have thought that after all the time you spent wanting to lock Fab and I up in the big house, now we're all friends." I shook my finger at the Chief. "No rolling your eyes—according to Mother, they'll get stuck and then what will you do?"

Everyone laughed.

"Mother has all kinds of dire warnings," Brad said. "I can't prove this, but I think she makes them up as she goes."

"If you need my help in any way, let me know," Fab offered.

"I'd prefer you didn't," Didier said. "We don't need trouble coming to our neighborhood when we have kids to look out for."

Fab nodded reluctantly.

"About your wedding job..." the Chief said. "It wasn't the bride's first choice of location, but wanting to maintain a low profile because of the people he's screwed, the groom insisted, thinking no one would find the venue and crash the party."

"Turns out he was wrong," I mumbled.

"If we get another job that makes no sense, we'll have Xander run a check. If we'd done that this time, we'd have known about Melon's criminal activities," Fab said.

If? I wanted to laugh at her. I'd remind her that having Xander run background checks would be at the top of our list from now on.

"What happens to those men now?" Didier asked.

"Both have pending gun charges. Push got bail, but Melon's behind bars awaiting another bail hearing for fraud," the Chief told us.

"A honeymoon at the local jail—bet that was special," I said.

"Not happening in this case." The Chief chuckled. "There is no Mrs. Melon, as she paid the preacher not to file the marriage certificate, ripped up the paperwork, and lit out."

"Does Melon know he's been dumped?" Fab asked.

"I'm sure he does, since news like that travels fast. Also, he might have figured something was off when his supposed wife didn't show for a visit," Casio said. "I say we adjourn upstairs and discuss how we're going to keep Kyle safe." He turned to Fab and me. "Since you two are the ones that originally picked him up, keep your eyes peeled for anyone following you."

"If that happens, you get hot on the phone," Creole growled.

"Or engage them in a chase, which Fab is good at, and I'll lean out the window and shoot the tires out." I attempted to imitate gunshots, which sounded like puffs of air. Fab and Kyle were the only ones amused by my display.

"Call. The. Police," the Chief said sternly.

"Gotcha." Somehow, I refrained from saluting.

"This was fun." Fab stood. "I've got another appointment." She motioned for me to stand.

Ready for fresh air and sunshine, it was all I could do not to jump up and run for the door. I leaned into Creole. "Thought I'd invite Mother and Spoon for dinner so she doesn't get all attitudinal about my leg injury. No, I'm not asking you to pick anything up; I'll have it delivered. I'm doing the cooking, in the same vein as Mother does." It was a long-running family joke that Mother let people believe the takeout she ordered was homemade.

Chapter Twenty-Seven

"What appointment?" I asked, getting in the car. "If you're going to make something up, you need to be quicker." I caught her grin. "I've got a possible solution for your dressmaker friend." I pulled out my phone and double-checked the address. "It's just down the road, so don't drive like the cops are after you."

"This area?" Fab scrunched up her nose and waited for the security gate to close, then turned in the direction I was jabbing my finger. "Lucia's designs are upscale. How's she going to get clients back in here?"

"The strip mall isn't exactly upscale." Duh! "Keep an open mind. Slow down." I held up my phone to compare the picture. "It's that building."

Fab turned into the parking lot, her nose stuck in the air. "Lucia belongs in Miami Beach."

"So, make it happen. But while we're here, let's check this warehouse out." It was a two-story and on the rundown side, but nothing that couldn't be fixed. "Did you bring your lockpick?" I asked as she pulled around the back. I guess a snort's an answer.

"I talked to Lucia. A couple of different men came around, and that scared her so badly, she finished packing up and is officially working from home. I arranged with Doodad to send over a couple of heavy lifters to get everything moved."

"Same guys that are working Gunz's job?"

Fab nodded. "It might be tomorrow. No grumbling about last-minute—it happens."

"Fess up—you didn't give advance notice so I wouldn't be tempted to skip town."

We got out of the SUV and stared at the building. I had my phone out, taking pictures.

"It needs work." Fab opened the lift gate and rummaged around in the toolbox she kept in the back, pulling out a flashlight. "How much depends on who you're leasing it to." She threw her arm in front of me, stopping us both in our tracks. "Door's open. That's not a good sign."

"Maybe we should backtrack and bring the guys." I took a step back.

"It's probably nothing." Fab drew her Walther.

"Yeah sure. Let's go look for trouble." I drew my Glock and caught up to her, as she'd gotten several steps ahead. At the door, she motioned for me to stay behind her and snapped on the flashlight, stepping inside.

The light startled two guys snorting up in the corner, who checked us out then went back to what they were doing. Another man lay on his back, staring at the ceiling. The smell suggested he was dead.

"This is private property," Fab called out.

After another brief glance, the guys finished up and wiped their hands on their dirty pants, then stood and leaned against the wall.

"Your friend?" Fab waved her gun in the direction of the man, who hadn't moved an inch.

Neither said a word as they made a run for the door.

We both stepped out of their way, not wanting to hinder their exit in any way.

"You need to go check on him." I tossed my head toward the corner. "Dead or whatever — that's your specialty."

"I'm sick of hearing that."

A bark caught my attention, and I turned, catching sight of a Golden Retriever staring pitifully at me. I stepped around Fab, doing my best to stay as far away from the probable corpse as possible.

"Needle sticking out of his arm," Fab called out.

My attention was focused on the bedraggled dog, who was nursing four kittens and a puppy, all hooked on her like she was a buffet. The lot of them were in sad shape. The puppy looked enough like her that they were probably related. "Are you friendly?" I asked the adult dog, who whined. I reached in my pocket and retrieved my phone.

"Who are you calling?" Fab demanded. "Not certain whether the man over there is dead. He smells so bad, I can't bring myself to get any closer."

"The cavalry." As soon as Creole answered, I said, "The warehouse I was interested in down the street, can you get here now? Bring a couple of blankets."

"What's going on?" he barked.

"Neither Fab nor I is hurt. Just hurry." The dog licked my leg, and I dropped my phone, which disconnected the call. I knelt and reached out, slowly extending my hand, and she took a sniff. I took that as a good sign and patted her head. "You're an amazing mom, taking in kitty orphans… I'm assuming since I don't see a cat mom around." She licked my hand.

Fab appeared at my side. "We need to get out of here, and don't tell me no. That was an edict issued by Didier and seconded by Creole, based on his yelling in the background."

I didn't have to ask who made the call. "Do you suppose this dog family belongs to him?" I inclined my head towards the man, then mimicked Fab, pulling my top up to cover my nose.

"We need to wait outside." She tugged on my arm.

We turned our heads at the squeal of tires outside. I'd bet money on Creole being behind the wheel. Doors slammed, and the two men stormed through the door, both with their guns out. Seeing us safe, they reholstered their weapons.

Creole stomped toward me, then veered off to the guy, bent down, and checked his pulse. "Call 911," he barked.

Behind him, Didier made a groaning noise.

"Was that your first sniff of what might be a dead person?" I asked Didier, who uttered a noncommittal response. I crooked my finger at Creole. "We need to get this little family out of here before they get scared and run. Not sure they're able to get far on their own, so they probably need to be carried."

He waved Didier over. "Going to need some help here."

"I'll open the back of the car." Fab ran outside.

Didier scooped up two kittens, as did I. Creole grabbed the puppy, and the mom dog got shakily to her feet and followed. Fab had the lift gate open and grabbed the blankets out of the back of the truck to spread them out. We'd just got them settled when cop cars and an ambulance blew into the parking lot.

Kevin was the first to get out of his car, followed by another officer. Creole and Didier intercepted them. The four talked as they walked back into the building. The paramedics grabbed their bags and a gurney and were hot on their heels.

Fab cleared her throat, staring at the animals

as she softy petted the dog. The babies were curled up against her stomach, asleep.

I pulled out my phone, called the vet, and explained the situation. "They need to come in for an exam."

Suddenly, Fab hopped down and ran across the parking lot.

Not another body, I hoped.

"That's no problem. Bring them in as soon as you can," the vet tech told me, and we hung up.

I watched as a cop crossed the parking lot in my direction, Cooper on his name tag. He bent down and ran his hands over the sides of the dog's body. "They all need to be looked at by a vet."

"That was my plan. Not to be rude, but can we hurry up with the questioning so I can be excused to take Pooch and her family to the vet?"

"You've named the dog already?" His eyebrows went up.

"A quirk of mine. I'm happy to come to the sheriff's department… or I can come right back, since it's only about five minutes from here. If you think I'd skip…" I listed off several ways he could find me, ending with that Kevin was a tenant of mine.

"Kevin has a few stories about where he lives; they're hard to believe."

"They're a crazy bunch. He's a favorite with the ladies." Wait until he heard I said that.

"Come back here as soon as you've dropped them off."

Surprised and relieved that he was letting me leave, I ran and jumped behind the wheel. Thankfully, it was a short drive. I parked in front of the door, got out, and hustled inside, asking for help. A tech came out with a gurney, and we got all the animals inside. After a brief explanation of what happened, I assured them I'd be responsible for all the bills.

"We'll call as soon as we've checked them over," the tech assured me.

"I have to go back and answer questions," I told her, then took off, knowing that I was leaving the animals in capable hands.

I raced back to the warehouse and turned into the parking lot. Fab, who was leaning against the side of Creole's truck, stared as I approached and parked. I got out, disappointed that I wouldn't have the opportunity to ask her what had happened in my absence, as Kevin was beelining straight for me. Didier and Creole were laughing with Officer Cooper.

"What's your story?" Kevin barked as he got closer.

"Interested in buying the building, I had Fab do a drive-by..." I launched into the rest of what had happened, my version of events having more to do with the animals.

"I know the owner, and he won't be pressing charges for trespassing. He doesn't care to deal with my 'ilk,' as he's told me a time or two." Kevin sort of smiled. "You're free to go. I know where to find you if I have more questions."

I walked into Creole's arms, and he hugged me hard, which I needed. Out of the corner of my eye, I saw my SUV cruising around the side of the building.

"Told those two to go ahead and go, I'd make sure you got a ride." Creole swept me up and put me in his truck.

Chapter Twenty-Eight

I had a couple of days to myself, as Fab needed time to finalize the details on the Gunz job. The primary holdup was that Eva hadn't been willing to spend five minutes in the man's presence, but she finally relented and agreed to meet with him.

"Not knowing how much furniture and belongings we're talking about, this could be an all-day job, and there's a chance that Eva might show back up before it's finished. If that happens, you can expect the cops to be called." I made a face. Fab's mulish expression let me know she didn't want to hear any naysaying.

I'd been to the vet's office to visit Pooch and her children. All were doing better than when they first arrived, as they were all getting food now. Poor Pooch barely had enough milk to feed one baby, let alone five. Dr. Kate informed me they'd be ready to go home in a couple of days but would need full-time attention. Even though they were being bottle-fed now, she thought it was best for the kittens to stay with Pooch along with Pooch Jr. The doctor had laughed at my name choices, much to her disgust, I was sure.

"Have you named the kittens?" Dr. Kate asked.

"One through four." We both laughed. "I've got an in with an animal rescue, and I'm going to call them about full-time care."

I'd gone home and got hot on the phone to Blanche, the owner of Sanctuary Woods, which was primarily a dog rescue but had been known to take in a variety of other animals, and explained the situation.

"You know I'd never say no to you," Blanche gushed. "It's been too long since we've had babies around; we'd love it."

I promised to keep her updated on their progress and when they were ready to be discharged.

* * *

If Fab had asked me ahead of time, I'd have said an early start would have been better than mid-morning. Telling her just that got me a grouchy, mumbly response. It was one of the few times I'd found myself sitting in the SUV, ready and waiting for her to slide behind the wheel. "About time."

Fab revved the engine in response and shot out of the driveway.

"Just a reminder, in case you weren't listening the other six times I told you—don't expect me to get out of the car. Capiche?" I asked with a raise of my eyebrows.

"I had to super swear to Didier—and no waffley excuses under the threat of divorce—that my only role was to organize the move... and to also not get out of the car. And if I couldn't resist a closeup of events, to take my binoculars."

It would take more than going off half-cocked for Didier to divorce her, but good threat. Even better if it worked.

Fab cruised over to the main highway, and I knew from our previous trip to the mansion that it wouldn't take long to get there. Mean as it was, I hoped for red lights all the way.

"Once I got the call from Gunz that he'd picked up Eva, I alerted the moving crew to meet me at the house. The man I hired promised that he could get the job done fast with no damage to her belongings."

"How did Gunz get a woman who loathes him to agree to spend several hours with him?" I asked.

"I've heard that he exudes a certain amount of charm." Fab wrinkled her nose.

Hard to believe. "Everything gets packed up, and then what?"

"Gunz is paying for six months of storage."

"Let's make sure we're nowhere around when Eva finds out that their get-together today was nothing more than a con to get her moved out."

We pulled up to the house at the same time that the moving van arrived. Fab u-turned and parked on the opposite side of the road. I stayed put while she got out and talked with the guys. She unlocked the front door and followed them inside, which didn't surprise me.

A small unmarked van pulled up and parked in the front. A man I recognized as one of Fab's compatriots got out, opened the back, and hauled out a rolling tool case that he picked up and carried up the driveway. The man wasn't known for idle chit-chat, but I remembered him from a couple of security system jobs that Fab had needed his expertise on.

A few minutes later, she came out and crossed the street, giving the house one last glance before getting in the SUV.

"That didn't take you long. So did you perchance find time to look around, knowing Eva was otherwise occupied?"

"I wanted to, but Didier, reading my mind or something, wrangled another promise out of me. Rather than argue, I just agreed." Fab sighed.

"You just gave in?" My tone was laced with humor.

"I told him that he was going to have to give me my way some of the time. Then he kissed me, which led to other stuff, and… here we are."

I bit my lip to keep from laughing.

"Happy I didn't renege on my promise. It wouldn't have been worth it, since I'd be surprised if Eva even lives there. In my quick walk around, I counted three pieces of furniture, and the dining room is stacked with boxes to the ceiling."

"Since I highly doubt that Eva would live in a mansion that's barely furnished, why not just take her boxes and go instead of all this drama?"

Fab shrugged.

"Did Gunz ever tell you why she was screwing him on a million-dollar transaction?"

"Gunz claims that he's always upfront with the women in his life about being all about sex and not happily ever after. Eva wanted the latter and didn't take the rejection well. She went to him with a sad story about needing to sell her property, having run out of cash. After he'd been screwed, he had Xander run a financial check and found out he'd been played, but it was too late by then."

A woman out walking her dog was headed our way, shifting her gaze between the Hummer and the house.

"What's she up to?" Fab asked as the woman peered through the windshield and then knocked on the passenger window.

"I don't see a gun."

Fab rolled the window down halfway.

"Eva moving?" The grey-haired woman gestured.

Fab leaned across me and peered out the window. "An offer was made a while back, and everything's been finalized."

"Now, now, Base, none of that," the woman

clucked at her dog. "It wasn't polite of him to pee on your tire, but it washes off."

I chuckled. Fab straightened up and shot me a glare.

"I saw a moving van loading up about a month ago and thought Eva was moving out then. But then I saw her a couple of times while walking my dog, and the last time, I asked if she'd moved. Told me it was none of my business." The woman laughed. "We were never that friendly, but when I saw her after that, she didn't even make eye contact. Most of the time when someone on foot was headed in her direction, she turned around."

Fab rolled the window down all the way and leaned across me as she and the woman chatted.

"Why are you sitting in your car?" the woman finally asked.

"I'm here to rate the service provided by the movers." The woman nodded. Fab then asked a couple of generic questions about the neighborhood, which she answered.

"Base is ready to get moving." The woman cooed at her dog. They ended the conversation with a wave, and she continued up the street.

"That was unusually chatty of you."

"Remind me to bill Gunz extra."

Two hours later and the movers had the truck loaded. After a cold drink sitting on the bumper, they pulled out of the driveway at the same moment as a nondescript white sedan pulled up.

Eva leaped from the back seat, reaching back in to grab her purse. She stood at the end of the driveway, staring at the disappearing truck, and began screaming. She didn't bother to close the door, but the driver squealed off anyway.

Fab scooted down in her seat, and I followed suit. We both kept our eyes peeled over the top of the dashboard. I hoped that if she turned our way, she wouldn't remember the SUV from our previous visit.

Eva moved to the middle of the street, her yells turning to shrieks, and continued to wave her arms. If she thought the truck was going to stop, she needed to think again; they were already at the corner and ready to turn.

"Wonder who she's got on the phone?" Fab shook her head at the display Eva continued to unleash.

"Guessing the get-together between them didn't go well, since she showed up without him. Did he pick her up?" I interpreted Fab's shrug to mean that she didn't know or care. I watched as Eva, who'd finally calmed down, started pivoting in circles, her phone still to her ear. "Let's hope she's not calling the cops because they're certain to notice us and we don't have a good reason for lurking."

Eva pocketed her phone and ran toward the house, her keys out. When she couldn't get the door open, she kicked the bottom several times, then hopped up and down, shaking her foot.

"We need to get out of here," I said as she raced around the side of the house. She didn't have a car, so unless she called for a ride, wherever she chose to go would be a long walk. "Did you hear me?" I barely got the words out before Eva rounded the corner.

She stood in the middle of the driveway, kicking the gravel, and jerked her phone back out of her pocket.

"Roll down your window," Fab ordered.

"N. O." I nodded up the street as a black Escalade flew into view. "Gunz is stupid, showing up now. And this is about to get even more interesting. Please… let's get the heck out of here."

The SUV squealed to a stop, blocking the driveway, and Gunz hopped out, hands up in a conciliatory gesture as he tromped towards Eva.

"If they get into a brawl, do I jump out?" Fab asked in a hushed tone, as if they might hear her.

"Great idea, getting in the middle of two fighting ex-lovers. I'll wait here and let you know if I'm able to get any good pictures. Scratch that…" I waved my finger. "Leave the keys in the ignition, and you can get a ride home with Gunz."

"Fat chance," Fab whispered.

Eva pocketed her phone and turned on Gunz, anger radiated off her. She marched up to him, tipped her head back, and yelled in his face. He appeared to be trying to quiet her down, but that only infuriated her more. Eva turned away, reached in her purse, and whirled back around, gun in hand. She pulled the trigger, and Gunz dropped to the ground.

"What the..." Fab screeched. She threw the door open and hopped out, drawing her weapon. "Drop it, or I'll shoot," she yelled.

"I'm calling 911," I called out before she slammed the door. I inched the window down as I made the call.

Eva stepped forward and stood over Gunz, raising her gun again.

"I'm not going to tell you again," Fab roared.

Eva turned and stared down Fab's weapon, then dropped her gun to her side. She looked between Gunz and Fab, then bent down and scooped a set of keys off the ground. She ran for the Escalade, jumped inside, and burned rubber down the street.

I got out and joined Fab, who knelt down next to Gunz.

"Don't die, damn you," she ordered Gunz, checking his pulse, and then ripped open his shirt and applied pressure to the wound.

"If you need me to do anything, I'll be standing right over here, out of the way." I moved into the street, ready to flag down the first set of flashing lights, and here they came.

The first squad car pulled up, and I was hoping for anybody but Kevin, but no such luck. He jumped out, a *Now what?* glare directed my way, and stormed over to Gunz and Fab.

Eva better be headed for the Georgia border, because when Gunz's sisters found out that she'd shot him... well, they were a mean duo, and after a slow death, she'd disappear.

Another squad car pulled up, and Officer Cooper, the sheriff's deputy from the other day, got out. He looked my way, and his eyebrows went up. Behind him came an ambulance. The paramedics leaped out and were quickly all over Gunz, getting him stabilized and loaded into the back.

Fab and I hadn't talked about what our story would be if the cops converged.

After talking to Kevin, the deputy approached me, and I waved. "How's Gunz?"

"Getting shot in the chest isn't good, but he was still breathing when the ambulance rolled out," Cooper said. "What happened here?"

I told him Gunz was a client of Fab's and that he'd hired her to move out the old owner of the house, avoiding any mention of the legal issue. "It's my understanding that Gunz and Eva are ex-lovers and were out together this morning. She returned by herself as the job was winding up. Shortly after that, Gunz showed up, and after what looked like angry words on her part, she shot him."

"You happen to know what they were arguing about?"

"No clue." I could probably speculate and get

close, but I wasn't going there. "Based on his previous track record with his exes, the break-ups are messy and the women try to leave with a body part."

It was a toss-up whether Cooper believed me or not, based on his expression. If he stuck around longer than Kevin's other partners, he'd find out that I wouldn't feed him a line of bull. A little vague maybe, but no bull.

"Where were you when all this went down?"

I pointed to the Hummer. "The moving truck had just left, and Fab and I were about to follow when Eva arrived in a white sedan. Didn't get a good look at the driver, as he didn't stick around long. Then it seemed like everything happened at once."

"Where's Eva now?"

"She jumped in Gunz's Escalade and took off." I glanced across the street and saw that Kevin was still questioning Fab. "Free tip: If notifying next of kin is the sheriff's deputies' job, don't let Kev shove it off on you." His lips quirked. "Gunz's got two whack-job sisters, and that's being nice."

"Thanks for the tip. How's the dog and her brood?"

I smiled, pleased that he asked. "Poochy?" He grunted a laugh. "All they need is food and love, and they're getting both. If you're wanting to adopt…" My eyebrows went up.

"I've got a Great Dane that likes being an only

child." Another laugh and Cooper shook his head. "Kevin warned me you'd be at most of the calls, and I laughed. Guess I owe him an apology, which he's not getting."

"Your partner's headed this way," I warned.

Fab beelined for the car and got back inside.

Kevin stormed over with a tight-lipped expression. "You know where we can find Eva Milson?"

I shook my head. "No clue. Didn't know her before this job and don't want to now. I told what little I knew to your partner."

"Don't leave town," Kevin snapped.

"Everyone behaving at The Cottages? If not, I expect you went all meanie on them and told them to hop in line or else off to the clink they go. There might be a song there."

That finally got a smile out of him. "As many times as I've told them the party's over, I'm still a favorite."

"That's because when you shuck that uniform of yours and go all boy next door, you're fun. And the ladies think you're hot." I made a sizzling sound. Cooper chuckled. "I'm always happy to cooperate with law enforcement."

Kevin snorted, and the two deputies walked back to the scene.

I was tempted to run the couple of feet and jump in the SUV but managed a sedate walk and slid inside.

"What did you tell them?" Fab asked as I hit

the door locks.

"Kept it short and to the point and didn't go off into the weeds, like my lawyer would've instructed had he been standing here." I eyed her stained shirt. "You need to change."

Fab looked down, jumped out, and grabbed one of the go bags we kept in the back for emergencies. "I'm perturbed that you got the new guy and I got the grouch," she said as she swapped out her top and got back behind the wheel.

"It was refreshing that Officer Cooper didn't jump all crab-assy from the start." I was relieved when she headed to the corner. "He said Gunz was still breathing when they rolled him off."

"Thankfully. The paramedics were tight-lipped about his condition, and with Kevin standing there, I could hardly pass myself off as his sister just to get info. I'm tempted to trot out that con when I call the hospital but also leery since the real deals might be in hearing range." Fab shuddered.

"Probably better not." I tugged on her arm. "Let's go home. Call Xander; maybe it's information he can get."

Chapter Twenty-Nine

"Let me know when you find out how Gunz is doing," I said, breaking the silence on the drive home.

"If I get another one of these kinds of cases, I'm going to recommend that my client go through the courts and have law enforcement serve the eviction notice." Fab blew out her exasperation. "When I talk to Xander, I'm going to have him put a news alert on Eva."

"With Gunz's sisters on the loose, she might want to think about the safety of being behind bars."

"Gunz can usually control them, but with him in the hospital, all bets are off," Fab said, turning into the grocery store parking lot. "I need to get a couple of things."

I nodded, making a mental list.

We shopped; the husbands cooked. Unless it was our turn to cook, and then we got out the takeout menus.

The two of us maneuvered through the aisles, got we wanted, and got out of there. Exiting, I engaged Fab in a game of bumper carts. I attempted to cut her off, and she rammed the side of the basket, forcing me to swerve away and skid to an abrupt halt. The two of us stood there laughing.

Then I did a double-take, not sure if what I was witnessing was really happening. A person with a slight build, their baseball cap pulled low, was pulling their arm back for a second strike at the driver's side window of the Hummer.

"Not my car, you don't," I yelled, rolling my cart toward Fab and running to stop the car thief. Ignoring Fab's "wait up" behind me, I barreled forward. The person with the hammer turned out to be a woman, who caught sight of me as she was about to take another swing. I wrenched her arm back and whirled her around, the hammer clattering to the ground.

Instead of running, which I expected her to do, she charged me. I jumped sideways and tripped her, and she crashed to the ground, landing on her hands and knees. She was about to get to her feet when I planted my foot on her butt, and she went back down, this time sprawled out on the pavement. I took a couple of steps sideways and kicked the hammer under the Hummer, then turned back, getting a good look at her, and realized the *woman* was a teenage girl.

"Thanks for your help," I grouched at Fab, who'd leisurely rolled up with the two carts under control.

"Hey, I got the groceries and your purse." Fab pointed inside the cart.

I blew her a kiss and rolled my eyes at her.

Fab laughed but sobered as two squad cars rolled into the parking lot and headed our way. "Didn't take someone long to call 911."

"Saves us from making the call." The girl inched away, about to stand, and I rested my foot on her backside. "You get up, and I'll put my foot up your butt."

Fab snorted. "More wisdom from your mother?"

I shook my head. "Grandmother didn't fool around. She was a do-it-now-or-else chick and didn't repeat herself."

The deputies cruised up, parked, and got out. One eyed my foot, and I removed it. "What's going on here?" he asked.

The other officer helped the girl to her feet. She eyed the two officers and ran. It didn't take long for him to overtake her and get her cuffed. The cop in front of me called out to his partner, who nodded, indicating he had everything under control.

Not waiting to be questioned, I launched into an account of events. "Kicked the hammer with her fingerprints under the Hummer." I pointed.

The officer examined the cracked window. "Surprised it didn't break."

"Bulletproof glass." At his raised eyebrows, I added, "Courtesy of JS Auto Body; my mother's married to Spoon. And I need to disclose that I have a Glock in my back waistband; my license to carry is in the car."

"Me too." Fab waved. "Mine's a Walther and strapped to my thigh. Same on the license, and I'm also a private investigator."

The officer pulled his weapon. "You both need to set your guns on the ground."

We nodded and complied.

"I'm happy to retrieve our licenses," Fab offered, and he nodded for her to go ahead.

I stayed put, noticing out of the corner of my eye that the girl was being put in the back of one of the patrol cars.

Fab handed the officer our licenses and a business card and came to stand next to me. "Both of our numbers are on the back."

"Do either of you know her?" the officer asked.

"When I first approached her, I thought it was a woman, not a teenager." I shook my head and turned to Fab.

"No," she said.

"Vehicle break-ins have been on the rise. Don't go anywhere," the cop said, then went to meet the other one at the patrol car. The two talked, and one came back with an evidence bag in hand. He had Fab pull the Hummer forward and bagged the hammer, then took pictures of the damaged window.

"If there were witnesses, they've scattered, so there's no one to verify what happened before the fight started," the cop said.

"The grocery store has outside cameras." Fab pointed to a camera and then another. "I'm betting that one or all of them picked up everything that happened here."

"I know where to reach you if I have any questions." The cop turned and went into the store.

"I'm assuming that the girl was arrested, since she was hauled off," I said and climbed into the passenger seat. "I'd like to know what she told the cops—that I attacked her? I felt brushed off."

"The fact that she ran makes her look guilty, although she could've concocted some excuse... she was afraid, it was our fault, or some such." Fab shook her head. "If she's out stealing cars, I'd guess the Hummer wasn't her first attempt, despite how clumsy it was, and she didn't appear the least bit embarrassed by her actions."

"She also didn't seem scared by being arrested."

Fab backed out and turned onto the main highway. "Thank goodness the store has cameras and we know they work. They'll verify our story, and we won't end up under scrutiny."

"Shouldn't the girl be doing high school things, worried about one boy or another?" I pulled out my phone. "I'm calling Spoon."

"I forgot," Fab blurted.

I moaned. Now what? She never forgot anything.

"Madeline called, and the conversation was

short because I told her I was with a client."

"When did she call?" I scrolled across the screen of my phone. "There's a missed call from her, and oh look, messages. Do I dare read them?"

"I can save you the time. Family dinner at the Crab Shack tonight."

"I'm tired," I whined. "All I want to do is put my feet up. Call her back and have her reschedule. Make up something really good."

"The husbands already RSVP'd, so good luck with that one. *You're* more than welcome to try. I'll just sit here and listen." Fab grinned.

"Husbands?" I groaned. "You do realize that we've had this action-packed day and haven't checked in… unless you did?" I asked in a hopeful tone.

She continued to grin, shaking her head.

"We're going to be in trouble. I need a drink."

Chapter Thirty

"You're always crabbing that I don't have a plan. Well, now I do, and a fun one," Fab said, pulling into my driveway. "You've got one hour—be dressed and ready."

I opened the door and stepped one leg out.

"One more thing," Fab admonished. "You can't ask questions, and no drinking."

"That's two things." I got out and shut the door on her laughter.

Fab didn't waste time blowing out of the driveway.

I sulked all the way into the house and down the hallway. I didn't dare glance toward the kitchen or I'd be mixing that drink—just the thought had me licking my lips. I put off calling my husband, knowing he'd ask, "How was your day, babe?" and I'd go off on a whine fest.

To improve my mood, I went to the closet and chose one of my favorite dresses—a knee-length tent-style seafoam dress—and reached for a pair of slides, throwing both on the bed. Then petted the cats. I got in the shower and drained most of the hot water. Then, feeling like a new woman, or improved anyway, I wrestled my red mane into a messy bun. Dressed, I grabbed my purse. A glance at the clock told me I had two minutes, and it wouldn't surprise me if her highness was waiting. I was coming down the hall when the door flew open.

"Hop, chop," Fab yelled at the top of her lungs. "Let's get going."

"If a piece of plaster falls down, you're getting the repair bill." I walked into the entry, covering my ears. "I'm sure that whatever your idea is, it's a good one…" I flicked a finger at her—*Don't interrupt*—and took a breath to ratchet down the sarcasm. "Where was I? Oh yes. Mine's better. Let's grab some ice, go outside, and I'll play bartender."

"You're too late with your idea, so maybe next time." Fab linked her arm through mine and about jerked me off my feet as she hauled me out the door. "Stop dawdling. Pick up your heels." She glanced down. "Flats. That should make it easy. My idea is a good one, and we're short on time."

I yanked my arm out of her hold. "I can walk."

She already had the passenger door open, and I slid inside. The door banged shut, and I noticed immediately that she'd hit the child lock.

Like I can't get out. "Whatever you're up to better be damn fun and quick," I said as she slid behind the wheel. "We've got to hustle back here, pick up the guys, and get to the restaurant on time."

"Took care of those two already. They're meeting us." Fab roared out of the compound and over to the highway.

Those two? Wait until they heard that. They'd laugh.

"Please promise me that this isn't some Gunz job, and how's he doing by the way? I'm certain you must have an update."

"Called Xander, who it turned out knew someone who knew…"

"He's the best, even without connections."

"Gunz is out of surgery and listed in serious condition."

It was too soon to tell where we were going. "Knowing that you're going to want to visit your dear friend in the hospital, my suggestion is to call instead. You run into one of his siblings and a fight will break out. The sounds of screams and such aren't good for the other patients."

"You really do need a drink."

It didn't take long before I knew right where we were going, and it was confirmed when she pulled into the parking lot of the Crab Shack. The tiki-style building sat off the main highway, overlooking the cool blue waters of the Atlantic.

"I thought why not get here early and have a drink," Fab said as she got out.

I threw my arms around her. "You're the bestest."

She smirked. *Of course I am.*

We walked into the restaurant with its low-key vibe—fake palm trees and fish mounted on the walls and rope lights strung everywhere—stopped at the bar, and placed our drink order. Since the rush hadn't begun yet, it was easy to snag a table out on the patio, not far from a table already set up for a large party.

It didn't take long for the server to deliver my pitcher of margaritas and Fab's martinis.

"This is a really bad idea," I said as we toasted.

"That's why we're going to sip slowly; no sucking them down."

"Uh-huh." I managed not to roll my eyes. "When Mother ramps up her lecture on being sauced at a family dinner, I'll be finger-pointing your way." I mimicked squealing brakes. "Is there an occasion? What if we need a gift?" I held up my empty hands.

"We'd have had advance notice if that was the case. If not, then we blame Madeline."

I'd finished my first glass, as had Fab. I refilled for both of us, and we toasted again.

"What do you suppose will happen to Eva?" I asked.

"If Gunz wants to protect her, like the others that have gone psycho on him in the past, it's not going to work this time—the cops are involved. Not thinking about what Gunz would want, when Kevin asked for a description of her, I went one better and texted him a photo."

"I'm assuming that the big dude is going to pull through, and when he does, you need to sit his big behind down and have *the talk* with him." At her horrified look, I almost laughed. "Not that talk. The one where he cleans up his act and stops choosing women half off their rocker and easy to push the rest of the way." She shook her head the whole time I dispensed my good advice. "Your other option is having Mother do it."

"Do you think your mother would wear a camera? I don't think I could sit through that talk, but I'd still want to hear every word."

We both laughed and tipped our glasses.

"We've had enough to drink," Fab lamented.

"Not yet—neither of our pitchers are empty." I held mine up as proof. "If we hurry and down these, we could order a second and pretend it's our first." I tipped my glass towards Fab's.

"That will work until we pass out, slip under the table, and have to be carried out." Fab raised her chin to look over my shoulder, then checked her watch. "Madeline and Spoon are early."

"Mother is never late." I followed Fab's finger to where they were standing by the reserved table. I'd discounted that one after counting the place settings—too many for the usual crew. "Coin toss." I flipped an imaginary one in the air. "Yell out her name? Wave wildly? Jump up and down? The missus won't think we're funny, but the mister will be amused, and one out of two isn't bad."

Before Fab could tell me that she didn't take sucky bets, little voices yelling "Gram" and "Grandpa" preceded Mila and Logan up the stairs from the beach. They ran straight for Mother and Spoon and wrapped themselves around the two. Brad and Emerson weren't far behind. After Mother lavished both kids with kisses, Spoon swung them off their feet, made airplanes out of them, and set them back down.

"Since kids are present, are you two going to be on your best behavior?" Brad asked as he stopped in front of our table.

I tipped my glass and deliberately slurred, "Sure." Then winked at Fab, who smirked.

"Behave." Emerson punched Brad playfully, then bent down and kissed Fab and me.

On their heels, Creole and Didier walked out onto the deck, both with beers in hand.

The kids called to Brad, wanting his attention, and with a wave, he and Emerson went to find out what had them laughing.

Creole picked up my half-empty pitcher. "How was your day?" He bent down and kissed my cheek.

Didier asked the same question.

"Where to start…" I smiled sweetly.

Mother called us over, cutting off a response.

Creole held out his hand, and I stood and kissed his cheek. He hooked his arm around me, and I shoved my drink into his hand. He took the pitcher in his other and led me over to the table, where he set everything down at the seat I'd chosen.

Mother had put out place cards, which I shuffled around while she kissed everyone's cheeks. "I had the seating all planned out," she grouched in my ear.

"You do a great job, but I'm just a tad better." I gave her a hard hug.

Mother laughed. "Have you two been behaving? Please don't forget that I'm on call for anything fun."

"Fab's got a job for you. Just know you'll have to wear a mic. I can get you one of these pin things…" I shaped it with my fingers. "That way, we have video and audio evidence." I didn't step away from Fab quick enough. "She pinched me."

"Both of you need to behave." Mother shook her finger at us. Shouts of "Gram" caught her attention and off she went to the far end of the table to sit next to Spoon and Brad's brood.

I'd put Fab, me, and our husbands at the opposite end. According to the place cards, the chairs in between were for Casio's family, with the kids all grouped together so they didn't need to shout to get each other's attention. Just as Creole nodded to the empty seats, wanting to know who was going to fill them, his answer came trooping up the steps from the beach led by Casio, Lark and his brood behind him, minus Marcus. Did that mean he was hanging out at the house, his friends coming and going?

Lily ran over, throwing herself at me. "Thank you for finding Melba." She hugged me.

"How's she doing?" I kissed her cheek.

"The vet says she's all better, and when I'm not home, Larry looks out for her." Lily beamed.

"You've got the best dogs."

She flung herself at Fab and thanked her, too. They exchanged nose bumps. Then she ran and sat with her brothers. I waved to Alex, who kept an eagle eye on his sister until she sat down.

"Nice to be included in a Spoon family shindig," Casio boomed.

I caught Lark's eye and raised my brows. *Well? What? Is she in a relationship with Casio?* She laughed. I felt a hard nudge from Fab; I better not have dirt from her shoe on my leg or I'd kick her butt.

"Are you growling?" Creole murmured in my ear, amusement in his tone.

"Who me?" I asked, wide-eyed.

"Don't make me throw you over my shoulder and carry you out of here."

"Please." I clapped my hands together. "You would so be my favorite husband if we could skate out now."

Creole laughed.

The server came over with a tray and served the kids the sodas Mother had ordered. Another one served the adults, so everyone had a drink in front of them.

Spoon stood, whiskey glass in hand. "To family and friends," he toasted.

The conversation was light and full of laughing banter, and the kids all got a chance to share what they'd been doing. Mother ordered a large platter of seafood choices, which was set in the middle of the table, along with a platter of hamburgers for the kids.

Before, during, and after dinner, Fab got up several times to take pictures, the kids eagerly posing. But once dinner was over and the food had disappeared, the kids weren't willing to sit at the table a minute longer.

After whispering in Casio's ear, Lark stood. "Okay kids, ready for the beach?"

A chorus of ayes went around the table.

"Everyone has to listen to Lark and no going near the water," Alex told them all, standing. Ready to run, the kids got up and headed for the stairs, disappearing down to the sand.

I reached for the pitcher, but Creole beat me to it and emptied it into my glass. "You're tipsy," he said, pointing out the obvious, even though I'd been on my best behavior.

"I don't want to waste a drop, and besides, it's been a long day."

"Do I even want to know?" He refilled my glass.

I leaned in and brushed his lips with mine. "You could make good on your earlier promise to haul me out of here."

"And risk the ire of Madeline...?" He chuckled.

Spoon caught my attention and tipped his glass toward me. "Now that the kids aren't in earshot, what the hell happened to your car window?"

Didier turned to Fab. "What's he talking about?" Apparently, her sexy smile wasn't an answer. "I didn't get a call, did you?" he asked Creole.

Creole nudged me.

"I'd be ever so appreciative if you could arrange a loaner car while your men are fixing the window. They do great work, but you know that." I wasn't sure who groaned. "I could drive the pickup, but I'm not in the mood to sweat around the Cove in a ride without air." All eyes turned to me, waiting for an answer to Spoon's question. Too bad.

"That beater-mobile of yours doesn't see much action," Fab said, her eyes gleaming with mischief.

"That's why it's your job to go out to the garage and start it once in a while. Don't tell me you don't have a key when we know that's never stopped you before."

I ignored her glare.

"I was about to suggest that Fab roll out her fancy-ass Porsche but then remembered it's at the shop for service." Spoon chuckled. "I'm sure I can fix you up with something. Can't guarantee dark-tinted windows, though."

"Madison Westin, what happened?" Mother demanded.

The amusement on the faces around the table was more than a little annoying. "You forgot my middle name."

Mother smacked her hand on the table.

Brad smirked, enjoying every minute. "We're all ears, sis. I'm sure it's going to be good."

"What's the question again? You have to be specific." I finished off the last of my drink. "The shooting in the street—technically the driveway? Or stopping the car thief mid-heist?"

Fab waited until I turned my gaze to her, then rolled her eyes.

"I'm assuming, since the two of you are sitting here, that you weren't hit during the exchange of gunfire?" Didier demanded.

Whatever Fab whispered in his ear, he relaxed slightly.

"You're in so much trouble," Creole grumbled in my ear at the same time as several questions were thrown at me at once. I fended them off, pointing my finger at Fab.

"A few of you are aware that I organized a move for Gunz on a real estate deal gone bad. If not, catch me later, and I'll share the details. To sum up today's job, the previous owner and ex-girlfriend didn't care for how he handled the situation and shot him in the chest." Fab made a couple of popping noises, then fell back in her chair, hand on her forehead.

I clapped. No one else was amused.

"Gunz's dead?" Mother gasped.

"Gunz's not dead," Fab assured everyone, mostly Mother. "The doctor expects him to make a full recovery."

"Always thought he was a big fat-ass, but that's a suck way to go," Casio said.

"You've been nominated to bring Lark up to speed; don't want her feeling left out," I told him. "And speaking of Lark, we'll be having a talk later."

"Can't wait." Casio rubbed his hands together.

"Waiter, I mean server… you, dude." Our server turned, a grin on his face. I held up my glass and one finger. Fab's glass shot in the air.

"Anyone else?" he asked.

The guys ordered another round of snooty beers.

"You've had enough," Mother said, a finger-shake in her tone.

I gave her an exaggerated eye-roll and flopped my head back. "My eyes are stuck," I yelped and didn't look up quick enough to see who laughed. "Hey Fabster, you might as well spill the rest of the day's fun and frolics," I said, which she ignored.

"And while we're talking about my biggest client, I have a job for you," Fab said to Mother. "Madison recommended you."

"Is this the one Madison mentioned earlier?

I'm more than happy to help; you know that." Mother preened.

"Since Gunz listens to you, perhaps you could point out that he needs to make a major change in his dating habits before he ends up dead."

"My wife is not getting involved," Spoon growled at Fab. "I also suggest that you mind your own business."

"You could be helpful and volunteer." I deduced that Spoon's snort meant no… probably hell no.

"Were you sitting in the car when this went down, like you promised?" Creole grumbled in my ear.

I patted his cheek. "You betcha, babe."

"And your excuse for not calling?"

"Before you get all grouched out, I suggest that you hear about the rest of the day… and then get worked up all at once." I gave him a cheeky smile.

The server delivered our drinks, and I sucked about half of mine down, as did Fab. We locked eyes and giggled.

"Your turn." Fab pointed.

"Not a chance." I zipped my lips.

Fab launched into the wannabe car thief story, with one slight change—in her version, she kicked the chick to the ground with a few well-placed hits. Where was I? Cooling my heels, watching the excitement.

"On the way home, panting for a drink, I

found out about the family dinner." I took another sip of my drink. "There went my plans to cook for you. What's a girl to do? Hustle and change quickly and get my butt here in time to guzzle a pitcher down."

"Was Fab telling the truth?" Creole asked.

"Close enough."

He snorted in my ear, and I made a face.

"Thought you were going to call me about the boat job." Casio flexed his muscles.

Finally, a change of subject. "Some tow service—not the one that got their truck ripped off—showed up and hauled it off, much to the distress of several guests, who wiped tears away. Owner dude dragged his feet, wanting to make sure insurance would cover everything. By that time, Mac had about claimed ownership and was busy making plans for it to be the next main attraction—another one sad to wave good-bye as it rolled down the street."

"Next time you need some muscle, you got my number." Casio shifted around in his seat, checking on his kids. "I know you're going to be looking for homes for those c-a-t-s—not one word in front of my kids."

"Rest assured I won't be outing you. Far be it from me to tell the dogs and kids that you deprived them of a puss friend."

"Given the no-pets rule instituted by the ruler of the compound, you're going to be busy finding new homes."

"Fab likes the title of queen," I told a smug Casio. "A friend, Blanche, took in the family of six and, after a day, called and announced that they'd found their forever home at her farmhouse. The more the merrier, apparently. They couldn't have gotten luckier."

"We should do another fundraiser to benefit Blanche's rescue," Mother suggested.

"Another good thing for you to organize, and one that will keep you out of trouble."

"You need to take your own staying-out-of-trouble advice." Brad snorted. "Happy to hear the cats have found a home, as I didn't want you mentioning them to my kids; we have enough going on."

"Yoohoo, listen up—I had no intention of mentioning squat to your kids." I pointed between Brad and Casio. "Know this: they're going to get older and ask all on their own."

"What happened to the drug addict you found in that warehouse?" Emerson asked.

"Near dead and totally dead is her job." I pointed to Fab. "She has connections to find out if he OD'd or not."

"Near-death was a wakeup call for the man. He agreed to a drug program, and once he's released from the hospital, he's off to rehab," Fab updated us.

"Are you still buying the place?" Casio asked.

"Need to talk to the hubby; plans might've changed."

"Knock off the updates; here come the kids," Mother said as they ran up the steps.

"Time for dessert," they yelled, almost in unison.

Chapter Thirty-One

The next morning, I was slow to get moving and only able to make it happen after two cups of coffee. I'd fallen asleep on the way home from the restaurant, but I did remember Creole carrying me inside and putting me in bed.

I'd sent Fab a text to be ready to go and threatened that if she bailed, I'd hunt her down, but got no response. I got in the Hummer, cruised to her house, laid on the horn, and didn't give it a rest until she opened the door. I rolled down the passenger window and said, "Hop in. I'm going to make you sick with my driving for a change."

Fab got in and slammed the door. "Good thing we have all day."

"Slow drivers get the worm, or however that saying goes."

"That doesn't even make sense."

"Sometimes that's life." I backed out of the driveway and, instead of beelining for the gate, cruised slowly past Casio's. Marcus was bent down, head in the driver's window of a sports car, entertaining one of his friends in the driveway. "Must be nice that Daddy's so rich, he can buy a spendy ride for his teenager to cruise around in."

"Got another camera installed, and now I'm able to get clear pictures of the license plates." Fab turned and looked over her shoulder as we cleared the gate. "Marcus knew we were inching by the house, and he never so much as glanced up."

"I thought you were going to have a chat with his old man, and I didn't hear how that went." I cruised out to the highway and straight to the Coffee Shack, a new cafe in town that boasted an impressive chalkboard of flavors.

"Brick brushed off my concerns, saying his son is a friendly guy and makes friends easily. Thinks that they must be new acquaintances, as he doesn't think anyone would drive down from Miami."

"When he's home all day?" I snorted. "Brick's got his head stuck in his... you-know-where and is believing what he wants to. Ignorance will come back to bite him in the posterior."

"Brick had his mind on other things and was in a hurry to get off the phone. He talked the little woman into a short romantic getaway, and they were getting ready to fly to the Turks. Relations have been chilly between the two since Marcus was re-homed."

I blew into the drive-thru, having to jerk the wheel to make the curve. I ignored Fab's snicker as I stuck my head out the window and ordered something stronger than usual. "Triple the whipped cream." I looked over my shoulder at slowpoke, who always knew what she wanted. "Make up your mind, or I'm doing it for you."

"Something that will beat down a hangover extraordinaire."

"Triple latte," I called out. "The strongest blend you've got. No sugar or anything like that. Might make it taste somewhat passable." I mumbled the latter to Fab and picked cash out of the ash tray. "My treat."

Back on the road, I headed straight to Spoon's. I'd texted while in the drive-thru, and the fence was already rolled back. I cruised past a black BMW SUV parked out front and stopped in the middle of the parking lot. I watched in the rearview mirror as one of the guys closed and locked the gate.

Spoon came out of the office as Fab and I hopped out. He crossed the lot and walked around the Hummer, giving the cracked window a close inspection. "This is a fairly easy fix; shouldn't be here too long."

"You're a great connection for all things cars." I leaned in and kissed his cheek. "The upside is that it wasn't bullets this time."

"You have the distinction of being our only repeat customer for window replacement." Spoon smirked.

"Swell. Probably your only repeat customer

for getting the you-know-what kicked out of their car way too many times. I'm just happy you've been able to patch it up and keep it running, as I rather like it." I handed him the key, which he tossed to one of his guys.

"Come to my office." Spoon motioned for us to follow and, once inside, pointed to the chairs. "Since I didn't know who knew what, I didn't think it appropriate to bring this up last night at dinner. After the sit-down with the Chief and Casio about Kyle, I got to thinking you should park the Hummer and ride around in something less conspicuous. At least until Kyle's case has been sorted out."

"That's not likely to happen anytime soon." Fab sniffed. "Pulled Casio off to the side and found out that the cops are investigating the criminal ring but need more evidence to make the charges stick. Turns out that they've been working the case for a while. It was made clear to me that I wasn't to go nosing around, as they want all the charges to stick."

"Kyle was in with some violent criminals. Thinking he didn't have any other options, he made bad choices," Spoon said. "From talking to him, I know he's scared witless that those men are going to find him. He's convinced they won't stop looking until he's dead."

"Kyle told me that there are a half-dozen other kids involved—all runners doing what they're told," Fab said. "The adults have figured out how to use the kids as shields. Be nice if they ended up getting long prison terms."

"You'd think it would be risky using a kid," I said. "The cops know how to pressure them into talking, and getting one to tell all they know would be fairly easy. It was that way with Kyle, although by that time, he trusted us."

"With Kyle's agreement, Casio arranged a meeting with the detectives working the case. Heard back that he answered all the questions put to him and named names where he could. When he didn't have an answer, he said so instead of making something up. They were impressed with how he handled himself." Spoon blew out a sigh. "Haven't had this conversation with Kyle, because it's not my place, but for his own safety, he might need to relocate… to the other side of the country."

"The kid has had so much upheaval," I said. "That's the last thing he's going to want to hear. It's easy to see he's already gotten attached to Billy and Xander, and he trusts both of them."

"If it's in Billy's power, he won't let anything happen to the kid," Spoon assured me.

"I hope for Kyle's sake that he gets a resolution that makes him happy," Fab said.

The door from the work area opened, and one of the mechanics walked in and crossed to Spoon's desk, handing him a piece of paper. "I've ordered the glass for the window." Spoon signed the paper, and the man left.

"The BMW out front, is that our loaner?" Fab asked. "Not exactly discreet but a fun ride."

"You'll need to ask Madison if you can drive it," Spoon said, the corners of his mouth turning up. "I'm still working on your Porsche, but if you need a ride, I'll bet your old man's Mercedes is in the garage."

Old man! I bit back a laugh.

Fab shot Spoon a growly look, complete with sound effects. Didn't faze him in the slightest.

"The majority of the SUVs on the road are black and similar enough in style that they blend in with the other models on the road." Spoon leaned forward and handed me the keys. "I'd appreciate it if it doesn't need body work or new windows when you bring it back. Keep in mind that the ones on this SUV aren't bulletproof."

"I don't suppose you want to have to send out the flatbed for it either," Fab said, amused with herself.

"Ha, ha." Spoon snorted. "When I asked you to invite your mother along on some tame jobs of yours, I didn't intend for her to be a substitute in dealing with Gunz. He's trouble, and while she loves to dispense free advice, I don't want her getting hurt."

"Tame? Despite what Fab says, she never gets jobs like that," I said.

"Hey, there might have been one or two," Fab protested. "It'll be a while before I see Gunz, since it's unclear when he's going to be discharged from the hospital."

"What we'll do is take Mother to lunch and shopping." I caught Fab's nod out of the corner of my eye. "Then hope the restaurant doesn't get shot up, like that one time. Though Mother wasn't with us or she'd still be talking about crawling for the exit."

"You're not one damn bit funny," Spoon growled.

"That's not true." I made a sad face. "I know you think I made up that particular shooting, but I didn't. Just ask..." I pointed to Fab. "It was her client. Thanks to her knowing every alley in town, we were able to get away without any bloodshed."

"You conveniently forgot about all those other shootings." Fab smiled sweetly. I shook my head at her. "I've come up with an idea that's way better than either of yours—locate a warehouse that sells discounted goods, and we'll wiggle our way inside. Madeline loves those kinds of places and always manages to leave behind a pile of cash."

I bit my lip and looked down.

"Since you're talking stolen merchandise, I'm not looking to bail my wife out of jail. Last time she came home with a bag of shoes, I couldn't get out of her how she found the place and she wouldn't give up the address, but I did get her to promise that she wouldn't go back," Spoon said with a shake of his head.

"Between Madison and me, we have more than a few shady friends. Makes sense that Madeline would have a few, considering how easily she chats up people. Her daughter does the same thing."

"No worries, Fab will come up with something that will have Mother talking about all the fun she had." I ignored her stink eye. "If she can't, then I vote for a flea market jaunt." I knew that would motivate her to come up with something.

Fab's phone beeped with a text. She pulled it out of her pocket and scrolled across the screen. "My *old man* wants to know why I'm not home."

"She's never going to forget you said that," I said to Spoon.

He laughed and walked us out to the BMW.

I handed Fab the keys. "I drove over here, and once we left the compound, she didn't make a single slow driver comment, so she can fly us home."

Chapter Thirty-Two

Fab headed back to the highway down a lightly trafficked back road.

"Nice ride." I leaned back and ran my hands over the leather seat. "I suppose I should keep my feet off the dashboard."

"Dare you. When I tell your mother, you'll get a lecture, and I'll enjoy every minute."

As I reached down to move the seat back and call her bluff, a truck swerved around the curve, headed straight at us. Somehow, they managed to stay in control and get back in their own lane despite their speed, another truck on their bumper. Fab eased out of the way of both and coasted to the far side of the lane.

"That was Billy," I said, turning in my seat. I'd barely gotten the words out when the bigger truck rammed Billy's rear bumper and he ended up nose-down in a ditch, tipped to one side.

The other truck slammed on the brakes and skidded to a stop in the middle of the street. The doors opened, and three men jumped out and ran to Billy's truck. Not to check on Billy's health, since they had their guns drawn as one tugged on the door handle.

Fab threw the car in reverse and squealed backward, closing the gap.

"What are we doing?" I pulled my Glock.

Fab u-turned and slammed on the brakes, unholstering her Walther.

One of the men turned our way, his weapon pointed at us.

Fab, who'd rolled down the window, threw her arm out and, without hesitation, took two shots. The man grabbed his shoulder and dropped his weapon, bending double.

The other two men, unable to get the door open, beat at the driver's window with the butts of their guns. At the sound of gunfire, they ducked and took cover. One crawled to the front of the truck and came up, weapon pointed. I shot him in the leg, and down he went. The one shot in the shoulder inched his hand toward his weapon. Fab shot him again, and he rolled over. The third one stumbled to his feet and ran to the truck, jumping across the seat to the driver's side.

"He's going to leave his friends," Fab said in disgust.

He threw it in reverse, burning rubber, and brought the truck to a stop at an angle, using it as cover as one injured man helped the other to his feet and they both managed to get in the truck. Hard to tell which one leaned out the door and shot out the front window of Billy's truck, but the door didn't get closed as the truck shot down the road.

Fab and I jumped out and raced over to Billy's truck. He was face down in the air bag, not moving. The door was locked. "You think Spoon's got a slim jim in that car?"

Doubtful. It was good we wouldn't have to report bullet holes in the Mercedes and would be better if Billy walked away from this. "I'm calling 911." I ran back to the car and grabbed my phone. Gun in one hand, in case the thugs came back, I made the call.

Fab hauled herself into the truck bed and banged on the back window. "Roll down the window," she yelled, making the motion. "Kyle's inside and appears to be fine," she called out to me.

I reported the ambush and answered the operator's questions.

Fab leaned over the side of the truck and, after a minute, climbed out of the back and ran around to the rear driver's side door, which had just opened. Kyle slid to the ground and put his head in his hands. Fab climbed inside and hung over the seat; after a minute, she jumped back out.

"Billy's unconscious but still breathing," she yelled. "Even if it were possible, I don't think trying to drag him out is a good idea."

I could hear sirens coming from the main highway. Figuring that I had less than a minute before their arrival, I called Spoon. When he answered, I briefly told him what happened. "We're less than a half-mile from your business, headed towards the Overseas."

"On my way." Before he disconnected, I heard a door slam.

I called Creole, and it went to voicemail. I hurriedly sent a text with a few details, including that Fab and I were fine. "How's Billy?"

"He hasn't come around." Fab stood on the running board, not taking her eyes off him.

I walked over to Kyle and smoothed his hair. "Come sit in the car. We'll leave the door open so you can see and hear everything." I extended my hand and helped him to his feet.

"That was Burrows and Cabot," Kyle murmured. "If anything happens to Billy, it'll be my fault."

"Billy's tough; he's going to be fine." I walked him over to the car and opened the passenger door.

Spoon roared up and parked on the opposite side of the street. At the same time, a police cruiser and an ambulance turned onto the street from the opposite direction.

"Is he all right?" Spoon demanded, running across the road, heading straight to Billy's pickup. Fab jumped down, and Spoon stuck his head in the window.

I got closer and heard him say, "This is what I was afraid would happen—the thugs found Kyle. If I find out who passed along that bit of information, I'll kick their teeth in. Where's the kid?"

"Sitting in the car." I cast a glance over my shoulder.

"He's pretty shaken up," Fab said. "This wreck could've been a lot worse; thank goodness the ditch is shallow."

The police cruiser and ambulance pulled up. Kevin was the first to get out.

He passed us, walking over to the truck. "You run him off the road?" he asked Fab, motioning the rest of us away from the truck.

"You're not funny," Fab crabbed back at him.

"I've heard that before." Kevin smirked.

We watched as the paramedics rolled up a gurney and went to work. They were able to get Billy out and strapped to the stretcher quickly and pulled away with the siren blasting.

Turning to Kevin, Fab told him what happened without him having to ask.

I glanced at the Mercedes with its open door but couldn't see Kyle. I made my way over and peered in the back, expecting to see him stretched out, but he wasn't there. I looked around the area, but if he was close by, he'd found a good hiding spot. But why? Scanning the area, I saw that the closest buildings were two warehouses a quarter of a block away. I was saved from having to decide what to say about Kyle because Spoon and Kevin were talking about the truck when I walked up.

"You towing this to impound or should I send one of my trucks?" Spoon asked.

"It's going to impound," Kevin said.

"Since I didn't witness anything, do you mind if I go to the hospital, check on Billy?" Spoon raised his eyebrows at me. "Where's Kyle?"

"Who's Kyle and does he need medical attention?" Kevin asked me.

"He's a kid that's living with Billy. He was riding in the truck, and I had him move to my car. I just went to check on him, but he's gone. Must've gotten scared."

"Just great." Kevin laughed, not amused. "You hiding him somewhere?"

"I have no clue where he is; he was there a minute ago." I looked at Fab with a *Help me* expression.

"Does he have a gun?" Kevin asked.

"Hardly." Fab sniffed. "I'm happy to check in the weeds for you."

Kevin ignored her and said to Spoon, "Go ahead to the hospital." He turned to me as Spoon took off in his car. "What's your side of the story?"

"The same as what Fab told you. I shot the one, who forgot to retrieve his weapon—stupid, if you ask me—it's over there." I pointed to it lying in ankle-high grass. "Fab shot the other one. Self-defense, by the way. If they weren't trying to kill Billy, they made a good show of doing just that."

Fab stepped up with descriptions of the three men—varying heights and hair color and nothing particularly remarkable about any of them. She also told Kevin the make of the handguns, then pulled out her phone and read off the license number of the truck.

"You didn't think to start with that piece of information?" Kevin grouched. He took out his phone and made a note of the number. "Don't go anywhere." He walked back to his cruiser and got inside, leaving the door open.

"You never fail to surprise me. I'm thinking we're going to get our heads blown off, and you're getting license numbers."

"If you're going to be a hoodlum and carry a gun, you might want to learn how to shoot. Both were terrible shots. They're lucky you've harped on it enough that I don't shoot to kill as often as I used to."

"Harped? I object."

"Where's Kyle?"

"I didn't know when Kev-o asked and I still don't."

"My guess is when he knew there was going to be cop action, he took a hike for fear of being hauled off to foster care." Fab slowly scanned the area. "Not sure what his status is with social services or if Billy's application has been approved."

"When Kevin asks for more info about Kyle, you better think of something."

"I'm thinking the men after Kyle wanted him alive or they'd have blown up the truck. Though

I suppose they might've if we hadn't proved that we'd return fire and were better aims than them," Fab said with disgust. "Now you can bet they're worrying about whether or not Kyle gave their names to the cops."

"We need to be really careful. We weren't in the Hummer, but they may have recognized us." I sucked in a deep breath.

Kevin came up on us, evidence bags in hand. "I'll take your weapons." He held out a bag to me and then Fab, and we dropped our guns inside. Then he got the one off the ground. "Any clue why someone wanted Billy dead? He's not known to go looking for trouble. Or does this have to do with his friend?"

"Tow truck." Fab pointed.

It made the curve and parked just ahead of Billy's truck.

Kevin made his way over to the wrecker as the driver got out.

"That was a timely arrival," I whispered to Fab.

"You think Kev would notice if we snuck away?"

"It would make his day to arrest us." I nodded. "He's headed this way."

"You got anything else to add?" Kevin asked as he approached.

I shook my head. "If you have any questions, you know where to find us."

The three of us watched as the tow driver

made short work of hooking up the truck and hauling it out of the ditch.

"I'm off to the hospital to see if Billy's come around and is able to answer a few questions," Kevin said. "You two are free to go. Like I always tell you, don't go anywhere." He walked over to the tow driver.

Fab and I didn't waste any time getting back in the car. She returned to Spoon's body shop and backed into the driveway.

"Not sure what you're doing, but no way Spoon's back from the hospital yet. Unless you're waiting for Kevin to leave, and you can't see him from here," I said, pointing out the obvious.

"I'll give him a few minutes, then go back and look for Kyle. If Kevin comes this way and sees the car, he'll think we're waiting for Spoon. In case you didn't notice, we passed several warehouses, most of them rundown; you putting in an offer?"

Now that's a good idea. "What's happening with Lucia?"

"Ignoring my question, are you? So the answer must be maybe," Fab said with a knowing smile. "Feld scared her so bad that she went to stay with a couple of family members until she's certain he's lost interest." She made a growling noise. "Told her that you had warehouse space available and gave her the address to have a look. Also told her that there was no need to get back to me if she wasn't interested. From her lack of enthusiasm, she's decided pretty much the way I figured she would—the same way I would if I were her."

"If you believe in the quality of her work, and it sounds like you do, get off your tuchus and find her a place in South Beach."

Fab leaned over the steering wheel as the tow truck passed us. She craned her neck, watching until they were out of sight, then inched her way out of the driveway and crept down the street. No sign of Kevin or Kyle.

"If you're planning on poking around that rundown warehouse, I'll wait right here," I said as she turned into the parking lot.

"He's not a stupid kid—he's probably keeping his eyes peeled. I'm hoping he sees us and comes out from wherever he's hiding."

"Then what?" I asked.

"They knew Billy's truck, unless they got lucky. Do they know where he lives and works? If only they'd shown up at the latter, then we wouldn't have to worry about ever seeing them again."

"They could still be lurking around. If they hung around the area, they know the cops left and Kyle wasn't in the back of the squad car. I'd think they'd be back, since they don't know you got the license number."

"They've got more pressing issues—patching up their bullet holes unless they want to die."

"That's all we need." I shuddered.

"My guess is that we'd never know. Whoever is in charge of the crime ring isn't going to want to bring any scrutiny their way, so the bodies would disappear. According to Kyle, they've done it before." Fab looped around the parking lot, honking the horn.

Kyle's head shot out of the trash area, and he waved. Fab cruised up next to him, and he hopped inside.

"How's Billy?" he asked.

"He's at the hospital, and Spoon followed the ambulance and is keeping an eye on him." Fab pulled back out onto the road and turned in the direction of the office. "First thing we need to do is hide you, and then run that plate. Once we get the info back, we'll do an investigation of our own, and a talk with Casio would be a good idea."

I pulled out my phone and texted Xander, getting back a quick response. "Xander's in the office."

"Tell us what happened," Fab prompted.

"We went to pick up a part for Spoon and were headed back; that's when Billy noticed we were being tailed. He told me to double-check my seatbelt, and then he tried to lose them. We got caught in a traffic jam, and he managed to swerve around it, but that didn't slow them a bit; they just kept on us." Kyle had a faraway look as he relayed what'd happened. "I offered to jump out and make a run for it, but he said no. It'll be my fault if he dies."

"Billy's tough," I reassured him. "My money is on him to pull through."

"Mine too," Fab added.

Chapter Thirty-Three

It was a short drive to the office. Fab opened the security gate and, like at the compound, pulled inside and waited for the gate to close. After today, we didn't want any surprises.

My phone rang, and it was Creole. I got out and walked over to a bench as I answered it. It was a short call. I reassured him I was okay, and he told me that he and Didier were on their way to the office.

By the time I hung up, Fab and Kyle had gone inside.

Lark came over, having left Arlo to sniff around in the grass. "What's going on? You know you can always tell me it's none of my business."

I told her what had happened and that we were trying to figure out what to do next. There was the issue of Kyle—he was a witness and hadn't stuck around to talk to the cops, and Kevin would be around asking more questions.

"Those men are going to keep coming back until they get what they want. You shot these guys, but someone else will take their place," Lark warned.

"Be on the lookout for any signs of trouble."

"If you want, I can try to get info on Billy's condition over the phone. I know there's a slim chance, but it's worth a shot. I'm also offering to go to the hospital and say I'm his sister or wife or something."

"I'd love to see Billy's face when he wakes up and a nurse tells him his wife visited." Arlo ran up with a frisbee in his mouth, and I scratched his head. "I should go upstairs and see if Fab's cornered Casio to get his help yet."

I headed to the elevator and was about to get on when Casio yelled my name and waved me into the Boardwalk offices. He was sitting at the conference table shooting questions at Kyle and Fab.

Before I could go in, Xander came down the stairs, laptop under his arm. "There's no problem with Kyle staying at the house while Billy's recovering. I'm going to reassure him so he doesn't freak out, and then I'll take him to the hospital for a quick visit."

"The fewer people that know his whereabouts—or anything else about Kyle—the better," I said. "The last place he needs to go is the hospital, as they'll probably look for him there."

The two of us went inside. I grabbed a cold water before sitting next to Xander at the conference table. He already had his laptop open.

"The truck was reported stolen last night," he

announced. "Out of Miami and from the owner's driveway."

Casio grunted.

Bet the owner will park it in the garage from now on… if he gets it back.

Creole and Didier walked under the roll-up door. Creole crooked his finger at me, and I jumped up and met him at the door. Didier winked as he passed me. I walked into Creole's arms for a hard hug.

"What the hell happened?" he growled in my ear as we stepped just outside the roll-up doors.

"It could've been so much worse." I gave him a full account of events.

"How's Billy doing?" he asked.

"His wife over there is going to find out." I nodded to Lark, who was chasing after Arlo.

Creole laughed. "We'll have to add wife to her job description for when we need one and you and Fab aren't available. Before you think she'd be put out by us asking, she never says no to anything."

A squatty sedan pulled into the parking lot at a snail's pace and maneuvered into a space. Two men got out, each with a few days' facial growth. They were dressed in jeans and t-shirts, and it wouldn't have surprised me if they'd spent the night in an alley.

"Friends of Casio's." Creole nodded and chuckled as the two approached.

"You should have a talk with them and tell

them it'll lend to their street cred if they go barefoot, like you used to do."

"That happened maybe once," Creole said with a smirk.

"Yeah, okay."

Creole acknowledged the two men and motioned them inside. "Casio's holding court at the conference table."

We followed the two. A shrill whistle was followed by Lark on our heels, Arlo at her side; she wasn't one to miss anything. She took drink orders and eyed the newcomers with a slight smile; one winked. When she came back to the table, she set down a bowl of snacks, which were eyed appreciatively.

Neither man introduced himself. One detective skipped the niceties and immediately began questioning Fab, and then Kyle. He finished up and the second one had a few questions, then turned to me.

"I don't have anything to add. It was Fab who jumped into action. I stayed out of the way and called 911."

"You need to lie low; I promise you we've got the situation covered," the first detective told Kyle.

Detective #2 let out a disgruntled huff of air. "We're going to have to speed up our timeline on this case. Hope to have the players behind bars in the next couple of days."

"You withdraw your offer to buy the strip

center?" the first one asked me.

I pointed to Fab. "That's her deal."

They both shot questions at Fab about Feld Huntman.

"I met the man once, and he wasn't forthcoming about the fact he was the owner. He made it clear he didn't know anything and that I wasn't to ask. Made several attempts to get him on the phone, and he neither answered nor called back."

Creole arched his eyebrows, and I gave a slight shake of my head, letting him know that I knew less than Fab did. Thank goodness. I noticed there wasn't one question about Bertie. Hopefully that meant he was long gone.

The meeting was finally adjourned, and Casio walked outside with his friends. On the way, Lark stopped them and handed the two detectives to-go bags. They looked inside and grinned at her.

"You hanging in there?" I asked Kyle.

"Yep. I'll be happy when I can see Billy and apologize." Sadness filled his face.

"It's not your fault," Didier assured him. "Show your appreciation by not doing anything reckless."

"Come on." Xander clapped him on the back, grabbed his laptop, and the two headed out.

"Where's Brad?" I asked. "If he were here, he'd have smoke coming out his ears." He hated drama.

"Logan's got a part in a school pageant. Brad and Emerson went to cheer the kids on, and because there was a limit to how many could be invited, they agreed to take pictures," Creole said.

"While you were talking, I called the hospital and found out that Billy's in stable condition," Lark told us. "I was outside on the phone, and as the others came out, I told them as well."

"That's great news," I said with a big sigh.

Everyone nodded.

Chapter Thirty-Four

It was exasperating how much time it had taken to dig up information on George Dent, the man who bought Charlie's car. Xander finally sent over a file, and I wasn't the only one frustrated. He noted that there were barely any online mentions of the man and wondered if he'd paid someone to scrub his name. What *had* made the news was the auto body shop the man owned, which had been raided several times, but no arrests made. Xander questioned if the man was tipped off ahead of the raids and whether Dent might be an alias.

He'd contacted a client of his that repoed autos for financial institutions. The man used Xander's services to track down individuals who'd stopped making their car payments and refused to return them. Xander scribbled in the notes that his client called Dent human scum and warned him to stay away from him. Then went on to tell him that the reason Dent hadn't been arrested yet was that when he took possession of stolen cars, he immediately disposed of them in a variety of ways. His favorite was to strip the car and sell the parts. Another rumor widely shared in the auto industry was that if you needed a car to disappear completely and fast, he was your man.

Swell, I thought. None of that boded well for Charlie getting his car back.

My phone jiggled on the island—another text, which I ignored. Fab had already sent a couple of messages wanting to know what was on tap for the day. I ignored her; maybe if she was on the receiving end, she'd stop doing it. Probably not. It didn't surprise me when she came barreling through the deck doors. To my disappointment, there was no food in her hands.

She slid onto a stool and picked up my phone, scrolling across the screen, then held it out to me. "Oh look, a couple of new text messages that you didn't read."

I held out my hand, and she slapped it into my palm. I made a call and put it on speaker. "Hey Mr. Spoon," I said when he answered. "You're on speaker."

Spoon groaned. "Now what are you two up to? And can't you stay out of trouble for longer than a day?"

"Not me," Fab yelled and made an obnoxious noise that vibrated through the phone.

"That's Fab pleading innocence, and you know she isn't." I grinned at her; she clearly had retribution on her mind but was sitting too far away. "Depending on how you answer my questions, we could be up to something as soon as we hang up." That got another groan. "What do you know about Dent's Body Shop? It's located on the outskirts of town on one of those side streets where shifty stuff goes on in almost every building."

"How did you get involved with a weaselly cretin like Dent?" Spoon demanded.

"Involved is a big reach." I ignored his snort and told him about Charlie's car. "I want to get it back."

"Not happening. I can tell you now that the car's long gone. Even though it would be stupid to break that auto up... But then, Dent's just that stupid. Possibly a piece or two is still sitting around, but I wouldn't count on that. He could've easily found a buyer, stolen or not."

"Sometime when you're bored, explain to me why anyone's willing to shell out money for something without a legal title." I'd never understood why that wasn't a red flag to any potential buyer to run, and fast, rather than take the chance of getting get caught and looking at felony charges.

"You listening? I'm telling you you're wasting your time with Dent."

"Spooner, you're a downer. That almost rhymes."

He chuckled. "What I can do is put out feelers for a comparable auto, but you can bet it will be a piece of — and need full restoration, and even then, it won't be cheap."

"Okay... maybe."

"Oh no you don't. That waffley response was too quick. I'm telling you to leave it alone and forget whatever cockamamie plan you've come up with in the last minute," Spoon demanded.

"I'm thinking confront said weasel and demand to know what happened to the Porsche. Charlie deserves to know the truth so he can stop dwelling and thinking one day it's going to show up."

"You going to bring your gun-toting friend along so she can shoot his butt cheeks off?"

Fab chuckled, nodding.

"I'm every bit as accurate as Fab and not sure why you didn't think of me shooting his butt off. It's been a day since we shot at someone; it's good not to get rusty. Don't worry, we won't kill him."

Spoon groaned. "How about a better idea?" He didn't wait for a response. "I'll send a couple of my guys over to Dent's place to get your questions answered and have a look around."

"Thinking—"

He cut me off. "If you don't say yes, I'm calling Madeline when I hang up."

"Go ahead and tattle to Mother. That will backfire when she insists on going along, and you can bet she'll be gunned up. That's a good idea; Mother would do a good job interrogating Dent."

"Not happening," Spoon growled.

"Hold up while I take a vote." I ignored his snort and looked at Fab, who shrugged, then nodded. "It's unanimous—you've got the job. Don't dawdle, and call me as soon as you know anything."

"It might be tomorrow, and either way, I'll call you. So don't go off half-cocked."

"Owe you."

"I'll be collecting. And one more thing: Billy might be getting released tomorrow if he can convince the doctor he'll follow orders. His brain scan showed that he has a very hard head and it's still intact."

"When he's released, I'll check with Xander and then take over some home cooking."

Spoon laughed. "You might want to hold off on that; your mother's got it covered."

I groaned. "I forgot to call and tell her that, though not involved, I was a witness to an accident and the cops got called."

Fab snorted.

"Don't complain when your nose gets giganto." I shook my finger at her.

"No need to sweat that one; I told her what I knew when I got home. She knows it's a police investigation, and we agreed that we didn't want to be involved, especially when neither of us knows anything. For once, I liked being the bearer of recent news, and she was pleased that I didn't leave her out of the loop."

Fab made kissy noises.

Spoon laughed. "Don't do anything until I get back to you."

We hung up.

"When Didier hears about the change of plans, he's going to be very happy with me. I plan to take all the credit. Although I was looking forward to threatening Dent," Fab said, with a grin.

"That makes two of us."

Chapter Thirty-Five

A couple of days had passed, and it was time for a weekly meeting, for which Fab and I had chosen the Bakery Café as the location. Creole and I arrived a smidge ahead of Fab and Didier, which I'm sure annoyed her; she'd been forced to stop for a red light. We grabbed our favorite sidewalk table, and breakfast went off without any drama since we didn't have anything explosive to report.

"You haven't mentioned Gunz's progress of late, so I'm assuming he's not dead. Besides, so far, I haven't heard about a funeral." I felt Creole nudge my leg.

"You're not going to believe this," Fab said.

"Let me guess—he's got a half-assed job he wants you to do, and we're leaving in the next minute." I caught Didier's smirk.

"Are you finished?" Fab snapped.

"Sure."

"Gunz is no longer at Tarpon Cove Hospital. He was transferred out yesterday to another facility, and I couldn't find out which one or any other details. Basically, he's disappeared."

"How do you know he didn't go home?" I asked.

"Since when do I pass along bad info? Never." Fab stared, challenging anyone to prove otherwise.

"Would be interesting to know who orchestrated the move and why," Creole said.

"It's fun to watch my wife get information out of people." Didier pulled her to his side and kissed the top of her head. "Fab thinks his sisters had something to do with his relocation."

"They may be meaner than stink, but they're very protective of their brother. I imagine they'll smother him with more attention than he can take," I said.

"It could also be that he went off the radar since the cops still don't have Eva in custody." Fab shook her head. "Surprises me that she's managed to elude them this long."

"That would be a good reason for the sisters to swoop Gunz into their protective custody," I said.

"Eva's looking at felony charges and won't be able to stay off the cops' radar indefinitely unless someone's helping her," Creole said. "If that's the case, then whoever it is will also be in big trouble."

"Even knowing she'd be arrested on the spot, she chanced going back to the house and breaking in to do damage." Fab shook her head. "Called the storage unit, and the kid, who didn't care who he was talking to, said she's never shown up. Told him that if she did, to call the cops because she's dangerous."

"Gunz knows how to pick his women," Didier grumbled. "I don't want to see him dead, but I'm happy you're not going to be working for him for a while."

"You could call the sister that hates you—inquire how he's doing and let her know you're available to be at his beck and call." I grinned.

"Not funny."

"Tell her it's not true." I banged my head on Creole's chest.

"Not true." Creole mimicked the same grouchy tone as Fab. That got a laugh out of Didier, and he got an elbow from Fab. "Casio called early this morning. Pretty sure he hadn't had any coffee, and I suggested that he might want to grab a cup or two."

"Bet he didn't appreciate the good advice." I laughed.

"Last night, the Feds raided the house where Kyle lived before he made a run for it," Creole told us. "There were a handful of boys in residence, all underage. One told the cops that a call had come in about an hour before they arrived and the two men who'd been left in charge scattered. Also said that they only leave a couple of adults in charge at any one time, but earlier, there'd been a half-dozen, who were all called away to a meeting."

"Sounds like they were tipped off that the cops were on the way," Fab said in disgust.

"Do you think that means they're leaving town?" Didier asked. "Don't want our wives and Kyle living with one eye over their shoulders."

"Everyone involved—" Creole shot Fab and me a stern eye. "—needs to lie low, see how this plays out. My guess is they're not going out of business, just moving to a new location. If they're smart, it won't be anywhere near the Cove."

"It must be frustrating to work a case and not be able to haul in the criminals." I put my hand over Creole's and squeezed.

"Especially when they're exploiting kids."

"What happens to the kids that were in residence? Please tell me they weren't carted off to jail." I sighed with exasperation.

"Emerson went to Casio and made her services and connections available to any kids they found, and the Feds readily agreed."

Good for her, I hoped one day she'd be my official sister-in-law.

The server came with the check and a refill on the coffee.

"What are you two up to today?" Didier eyed Fab.

"Don't know why you have to put it that way." Fab turned toward Didier, and after a stare-down, she relaxed. "No clients today."

"No worries. The day's young, plenty of time to find trouble," I told him with a smile. "If something does happen, you can be assured of getting a call."

Didier shook his head, conveying, *Not funny*.

Creole checked his watch. "We've got a meeting to get to, so we'll walk you out."

Fab eyed my cup and said, "We're going to finish our coffee."

"That way, we can have a little meeting of our own." I rubbed my hands together. "I haven't given up hope of roping you into the warehouse deal. I've got another pitch for you, and you could be nice and listen."

"Uh-huh."

The guys laughed and stood. Creole bent down and kissed me while Didier kissed Fab.

"Behave, you two." I finger-pointed. "You're supposed to be the good example."

That had them laughing again. We watched as they walked to Creole's truck.

Chapter Thirty-Six

"I should've told you sooner, but a warehouse isn't me. The kinds of businesses that would be interested in the location don't appeal to me," Fab said. "But I'm still open to us partnering on something else."

Before I could answer, a man rushed the table, threw himself in the chair Didier had vacated, leaned over, and slurped on Fab's cheek.

Bertie. I groaned silently.

"Fabbie, so happy to see you. It's fate—I was just on the way out of town, and this way, we get to promise to hook up again soon." He blew air kisses at her.

I was contemplating making a loud, obnoxious retching noise, but that thought was cut short.

Everything happened at once.

Bertie went airborne, the chair kicked out from under him, and lay sprawled on the sidewalk, kissing the concrete.

A wild-eyed man—worn jeans, his hair standing on end—standing not more than a foot away whipped out a gun. "You double-crossing son of a..." He pulled the trigger.

Bertie rolled away, yelping—couldn't tell if he was hit or not. He stopped moving.

Fab jerked back.

As another shot sounded, I leapt out of my chair, wrapped my arms around Fab, and threw us both to the ground.

The sound of people yelling from the surrounding tables filled the air.

The shooter ran to a waiting truck and hopped in, and it burned rubber.

When I shook off my daze, Creole and Didier stood over us. Creole picked me up and set me on my feet while Didier leaned down for Fab.

"You need to be careful; I don't know where she's bleeding." I couldn't take my eyes off Fab, looking for blood.

"I didn't get hit," she grouched. "Why did you tackle me?"

"You were in the line of fire." There was a *duh* in my tone.

"What the heck happened?" Didier demanded. "Some guy comes out of nowhere, manhandles you, and then bullets?"

Creole wrapped his arms around me, and I buried my face in his chest. "We were about to back out and witnessed the whole thing."

Sirens could be heard screaming nearby—must've already been in the neighborhood.

Before Fab could say anything, two cop cars screeched to a stop in front of the café. Of course, it would be Kevin that got the call.

"Did you know either of those men?" Creole whispered.

I shook my head. I was leaving it to Fab to tell them that one was Bertie. I'd tell Creole later.

"What happened here?" Kevin demanded as he closed the distance.

"A man approached the table, mistaking me for someone else, and before I could tell him otherwise, another guy came out of nowhere with a gun," Fab said.

That's the story we're going with?

"Where did they go?" Kevin looked around.

The shooter had already lit out, of course, but Bertie… We all looked around, but there was no sign of him. Sneaky guy must not have been seriously hurt and ran at the first opportunity, and no one noticed. I looked around for a blood trail and didn't see one.

"Can anyone corroborate your story?" Kevin asked in exasperation.

I waved my hand. "The tables around us were all full — you can get verification from any one of them. Most people jumped under their tables at the first shot, but once the excitement was over, they stuck their heads out, cameras in hand."

"This is a first for you two — mistaken identity." Kevin snorted.

Didier stepped up right in his face. "You calling my wife a liar?"

"Calm down. Nine out of ten calls I get, these two are involved. So give a cop a break." Kevin had his hand on the butt of his gun.

Creole pushed Didier back.

"You need an eyewitness? Well, you've got two." Didier pointed to himself and Creole. "We were in the truck right over there and saw it all go down. It happened fast and just like Fab said."

Kevin nodded. "Either of you need medical attention?"

Fab and I shook our heads.

"I'll need a description of both men." Kevin eyed Fab and me. "Unless one of you managed to get a picture."

"Not this time," Fab said and gave generic descriptions for both men.

"I don't have anything to add," I said.

Another deputy showed up, and the two talked.

Kevin came back. "You're free to go."

"I'm taking my wife home," Creole said and hooked his arm around me.

Fab stared at me with a slight head-shake.

I translated that as *keep your mouth shut*.

Creole helped me in the truck and got behind the wheel. "Did Fab tell the whole truth?"

"I have a headache."

"Oh no you don't."

I stared out the window and then turned back. "I'm going to need you to super swear that this is between you and me. Lips zipped." I held out my pinkie finger.

"I knew it." He hooked his finger around mine.

"Remember the squatter from the strip mall — a long-ago friend of Fab's?" He nodded. "That was Bert. What he's doing back in town, I'm not sure, as I heard he resides Miami way. He did tell Fab that he was on the way out of town, his return uncertain, if ever."

"Why not tell the cops?"

"I'm guessing it's because he saved her bacon a couple of times in the past; she's loyal like that."

"Didier thought she'd been shot."

"Him and me both. The shooter had a grudge on for Bertie. I've never seen him before. Thank goodness he was a poor shot."

"You know where this Bert fellow ran off to? Him not sticking around means he's up to his neck in something illegal."

"Didn't see Bertie disappear, and from the surprise on Fab's face when she realized he was gone, she didn't either."

"Let's hope he keeps his word and it's the last we see of him."

"This has made you late for your meeting," I said.

Creole glanced at the dash clock. "I'll call Brad; he can handle it."

Chapter Thirty-Seven

Word drifted back that Fab had fessed up to Didier about knowing the man who was the intended target and he put her on house arrest for a couple of days. But it was about time for her to resurface, since the guys had a meeting and I had it on good authority from Creole that Didier would be there.

My phone rang, breaking the silence of the quiet morning. I glanced down at the screen: *Spoon*.

"Can you come to the office?"

Barely got out "on my way" before I heard someone yelling his name in the background and he hung up. I hoped it was good news about Charlie's car. I was disappointed not to have confronted Dent myself and knew Fab felt the same way, but this saved us from a lengthy lecture on safety.

I grabbed my purse and briefcase and blew out of the house. In a minute, I'd cruised into Fab's driveway, parked, and ran around, hopping into the passenger seat. I leaned over and laid on the horn without letting up. I knew she couldn't ignore me forever, although it did take longer than I would've bet on before the front door opened.

Briefcase in hand, Fab stormed out and got behind the wheel. Gritting her teeth, she squealed out of the driveway. "This better be good." She slowed going by Casio's, but it was quiet.

"What's the latest on Marcus?"

"He's got more friends than anyone I know." She shot down to the gate. "Same old. His pattern doesn't deviate by much. Meets his friends in the driveway, chit-chats through the window for several minutes, and off they go. Somehow, he got the code app for the gate and put it on his phone; I've seen him pull it out, and seconds later, the gate opens."

"Casio would've had to have given it to him unless he has a hacker friend."

"Either way, it bugs me. Went over the schematics of the property and picked a couple of different locations to put more cameras, and I've already captured a couple of license numbers and sent them over to Xander."

Out on the highway, Fab had to stick to the speed limit thanks to a speed trap.

"Since you haven't asked where we're going, if you're in need of coffee, it would be a good idea to get your own and not complain about the choices at Spoon's office, as they're not up to your standards."

"Another thing," Fab continued as though she hadn't heard me. "On occasion, these visitors of Marcus's go into the house. They never stay long, and when they come out, it's always with a large envelope in hand."

"We've talked about this before. If Marcus isn't doing something illegal, then what is he doing? We also agreed to find out what before pointing fingers, but we're no closer to knowing."

"If it's not illegal, I'll turn in my PI license." Fab spun through the coffee drive-thru.

I was right about her need for caffeine, as she took a couple of sips and then practically guzzled the dark brew. I passed, having had enough at home, and besides, I could get a rush just off the smell of the Turkish brew steaming up the cup holder.

"When do you plan on telling me what Spoon wants?" Fab rocketed back out to the highway and turned in the direction of the auto body shop.

"Didn't get the chance to ask; sounded busy in the background. I assumed it had something to do with the stolen Porsche. I'm hoping for a longshot and that Spoon was able to recover it."

"Longshot alright." A few turns later, Fab turned into the lot of JS Auto Body and parked. Seconds later, Spoon opened the door and beckoned us inside.

We took our usual seats.

Spoon settled behind his desk. "I've got not-so-great news. I asked you to come by, thinking you'd want to take a couple of pictures of what my guys recovered to share with your client."

"You got the car back?" I asked, excited.

"Not exactly."

Fab snorted. "Can you tell us what that means?"

Spoon leveled a stern stare at her. "I know you wanted a better outcome, but I can't give it to you. It took a couple of visits, but my guys caught up with Dent yesterday, and he was fairly forthcoming. They feel confident that they got the truth out of him."

"Staring down the muzzle of a gun will make most people chatty." Fab pulled the trigger on her finger gun.

"It's my understanding my men went armed with rifles—not condoned by me, but they didn't ask ahead of time." Spoon smirked. "Dent would have to be a stupe not to know that at close range, whatever was left would have to be scraped off the wall. Want to hear the rest, or do you have more questions?"

Fab answered with a squint. "I'm all ears."

"Dent claims not to know anything about the actual owner of the car, having only dealt with Cart, who wasn't a first-time customer and was hard up for money," Spoon said in disgust. "Turned out that Dent had a client who was restoring a Porsche—not the same year, but close enough—and wanted to pick off the parts he needed. Dent went for the quick money, not wanting to deal with the title issues and knowing that he was going to have to discount it anyway."

"If it was stripped, what would we be taking pictures of?" I asked.

"Gotta warn you—it's nothing more than a shell. Had it picked up on a flatbed yesterday and brought here. Been mulling the options." Spoon stood and motioned us to follow.

Once in the work area, he turned and walked outside, then down to the far end of the lot, where he had a freestanding six-car garage. He punched a code into the security panel, and the garage door went up.

When Spoon said shell, he wasn't kidding. The Porsche sat on jacks, both doors missing, the interior stripped. The hood was missing, and only one part had been left inside—not sure how it was missed.

"Apparently Dent forgot to remove the battery." Fab walked around, camera out, and inspected the once pristine sports car.

"What does one do with a shell? Junk value?" I asked in disgust.

"It can be sold as-is but won't bring much. There's restoration, but it will take money and patience to track down the parts. It can stay here as long as necessary," Spoon assured us. "Give Charlie my number, and we'll set up a time for him to come check it out and go over his options."

"Thank you for keeping us out of trouble on this one," I said as he closed the garage door.

Billy met us as we crossed the lot.

"I wish you'd go home," Spoon grouched.

I gave him a quick hug. "Good to see you up and around."

"Thought you'd want to know about my home visit with Kyle's caseworker yesterday," Billy said as we headed back to the office and took seats. "Brought my A-game and charmed the woman."

"That doesn't surprise me." I winked at him.

"Kyle is lucky to have you step up; most would let the system handle it," Fab said.

"I admit it was awkward at first when Coral stopped by," Billy said. "I'd already coached Kyle to answer any questions truthfully, which he did. Then Xander arrived and Coral talked to him, and he was equally candid."

"Happy to hear that they both did okay," I said with a smile.

"Lucky us — she mentioned having to drop off her computer at a repair place, and Xander told her he was happy to look at it. Coral jumped up and was out the door in a flash." Billy laughed. "She brought the laptop in from the car, and I assured her that Xander was the best and would get it running, which he did and at a much faster speed. He also gave her his card and told her not to hesitate to call if there were any glitches."

"She won't be having any problems," I said with assurance. "Xander keeps mine and Fab's up and running with no issues."

Fab nodded.

"Worked out to our benefit. I invited Coral to stay for dinner—barbecued hamburgers," Billy said. "We talked while eating and got all her questions answered and then some. When she left, she assured us that she didn't see any problems and would be expediting the process."

"How was Kyle when she left?" Fab asked.

"He liked the woman and was less afraid of what she might do. He had a genuine smile on his face."

"Did you update Emerson?" I asked.

"Got hot on the phone, and Emerson assured me that she'd follow up," Billy said. "She had more good news. That cop lied about the foster family filing a report against Kyle, so that's no longer hanging over his head."

"That's great," Fab said emphatically. I nodded.

One of the mechanics came in and needed both men out in the garage.

I stood and wrapped my arms around Spoon, giving him a hard hug. "You're the best."

"A bit disgusted that I couldn't get a better outcome for your client."

"At least Charlie's getting an answer. Tell your guys: dinner at Jake's. If Kelpie's bartending, have them flex their muscles and she'll give them special treatment." I shook my torso.

Spoon and Billy laughed.

Chapter Thirty-Eight

When we left Spoon's, Fab didn't need to be told the next stop was Jake's. She cut across town and parked around the back, and we entered through the kitchen. Cook was in his office. He looked up and beckoned us in, pointing to the chairs in front of his desk.

"Heard there was a big gunfight and it wasn't clear if the two of you made it out. Figured it was just someone's overactive imagination and happy to see I was right." Cook smirked.

My guess was that once that salacious story started to make the rounds, Cook investigated on his own and easily got the truth. The man had an ear for everything that went on in town. And if it had been true, he'd have been hot on the phone.

"It was one gunshot and not aimed at either of us." I struggled not to roll my eyes as he continued with an outrageous retelling of events that had Kelpie all over it. "The better the story, the more drinks we sell."

"Heard that one more than a time or two." Cook chuckled.

"I've got an update for you. It's not what we were hoping for," I said.

Fab grumbled something.

"Language, young lady," Cook directed his dad tone at Fab.

"You been hanging out with Mother again?" I asked to break the stare-down between the two. "She snuck in here for a whiskey and to get caught up on the latest goings-on, in and outside the bar?"

"She's a lovely woman."

"Tip: she'd rather hear she's a badass." I laughed, and this time, I was the one to earn a frown. "Where was I?"

"You were about to tell me that you weren't able to recover the car. In anticipation of that news, I've been working on another idea."

"Hold your shorts, Cooker."

His eyes shot to Fab and another stare-down ensued.

I looked down, my cheeks flaming, and bit my lip to avoid laughing.

"I'm not suggesting that I don't want the details," Cook said, eyeing Fab with a hint of humor.

Fab flourished her hand at me.

"This is what went down…" I told him about the confrontation with Cart and finding out who he sold the car to, then skipped to the two rifle-toters sent to confront Dent. "If you'd pass along Spoon's number to Charlie, they can discuss what to do next. I don't need to tell you this, but reassure Charlie that Spoon won't screw him."

"The part Madison left out of the confrontation with Cart is that she brandished her Glock to get the tight-lipped man to talk. I felt left out." Fab smirked.

"It was one of those days, and Cart's smarminess set me off," I defended myself.

"When I first heard the story from Charlie, I figured the Porsche was long gone, but a shell? Dent needs his butt kicked. Such a fine auto," Cook said on a sigh. "Charlie's been looking around for another deal and had to table the idea. He's a single dad, and his daughter got sick; the bills are going to clean out his savings."

"What's he driving now?" Fab asked.

"Third-hand pickup that's older than I am. It's made the rounds of a few people and barely runs. He's constantly got it jacked up for one repair or another," Cook said, his disgust evident.

"What if..." I swiveled and stared at Fab. She crossed her fingers in front of her face with a grin. "We, meaning—" I pointed at Fab, who'd had enough of me. "—get a car dealership to pony up a new ride? They heard about Charlie's plight and stepped up—think of the great publicity from helping a veteran. I can think of one man who's a pub-ho and a friend of yours."

"You expect me to call Brick and ask him to fork over an auto, and by the way, the only thing he's getting out of it is that warm feeling from doing something nice? Not even a certificate for him to boast about and hang on the wall with the rest of them?" Fab snorted. "We both know that you can't do it since you irritate his last nerve."

Cook sat back in his chair, enjoying the byplay. "Okay, you two. Your idea would work with mine. We have a big blowout here at Jake's—small cover charge and post a sign that donations can be made to a good cause. Then you get your friend—" He raised his brows at Fab. "—to offer up a rock-bottom deal."

"Brick's going to want me to go back to work for him." Fab sighed.

"Tough totes. Not happening," I said adamantly. "If he tries anything shifty, I'll just shoot him."

"Good. That means you're coming with me, and I'll hold you to it."

"Wouldn't miss it," I said with a maniacal grin. "Good time to renew old friendships. And it's been a long time since we exchanged glaredowns with the gun-toter who sits at the front desk."

"There've been a couple of women in that position, and none of them liked us," Fab said.

"So sad." I wiped away a nonexistent tear.

"Back to your blowout idea—what were you thinking?" Fab asked Cook.

"Fun, games, local entertainment. We put the word out, and you know everyone will come. It's proven that we do well with word-of-mouth."

I raised my hand. Fab pushed it down and

said, "I suggest you put Kelpie in charge—let her spread the word through her underground groupies and she'll have the place packed."

"In order to do that, she's going to have to offer up more than discounted beer." Cook snorted. "Gun fight? Brawl? How about target practice and use the ceiling?"

The poor ceiling. I squeezed my eyes closed. "Let's move this meeting out to the bar and bang on the office door, rout out Doodad so he doesn't yammer on about not knowing what's going on." I stood.

"There's only so much of the antics Doodad can stand, and then he holes up in his office, claiming he has a mountain of paperwork. Told him you used to work out on the deck and he ignored me, so to hell with him." Cook followed us out of the kitchen.

We made our way to the bar. On the way, Cook kicked the office door open and found it empty.

Kelpie unleashed a long, loud whistle. "Doo's out here."

Fab and I slid onto barstools. A couple of morning regulars at the other end sent a nod our way and went back to their beer.

Cook whistled for Doodad, who was hanging over the side of the deck. When he looked up, Cook waved him inside. Neither Fab nor I had to order; Kelpie set our usual choice of non-alkie drinks in front of us and did the same for Cook and Doodad.

"Meeting called to order. Anyone not here—if you think they need to know—pass it along and try not to exaggerate." I tipped my glass and pointed to Cook, letting him relay the latest on Charlie's case.

"I was hoping you were going to cough up a car." Kelpie made the distinctive sound.

The men at the end of the bar overheard and laughed. She jiggled her mammoth chest, ringing the bells she had looped around her neck.

"The other part of the idea is to put you in charge of the fun," I told Kelpie.

Doodad snorted. "You know that's inviting big trouble."

"Hey!" Kelpie shot him a glare followed by a grin.

"That's why there's going to be rules." I held up a finger. "Nobody dies." Another finger. "No arrests if you can manage that. And finally, no one tips off anyone in my family. They can find out on their own. I'll pay you more to keep quiet than Creole pays you to squeal." I stared her down.

"Deal," Kelpie said with no hint of embarrassment and more bell-ringing. "Give me two weeks, and I'll put together a night that no one will forget. That will give me time to get the word out for maximum results."

I raised my eyebrows at Fab, *Is that enough time?*

She nodded.

"Doesn't seem right that the so-called friend gets to walk," Doodad grumbled.

"Since Cart doesn't appear to have two nickels to squeeze out of him, the only other option is to send someone to beat the smoke out of him," I said.

"Although I highly approve," Cook said, "Charlie wouldn't. Besides, it's something that could come back to haunt him, and we don't want that."

"Anything else before we adjourn this little sit-down?" I asked.

The door flew open, and Termite barreled through, looking like he'd been worked over pretty good, his face bruised, eyes blackened. His eyes roamed the bar and stopped on me, and he shot me both middle fingers.

"You're not welcome here." I didn't have to yell since you could hear a pin drop.

"Call the cops," Termite sneered. "By the time they get here, I'll be long gone."

Fab drew her gun and pointed it at him. He flinched. "Spit out why you're here, make it quick, and then get the heck out before I'm tempted to shoot out what's left of your teeth."

Termite swayed on his feet. "You'll end up in jail." But he'd lost some of his swagger. "You may have managed to run off my lawyer and make the prick withdraw the lawsuit, but you haven't seen the last of me. I'll find one with testicles that'll get the job done."

I didn't know what he was talking about, but it sounded like good news to me. Wonder who I had to thank?

"If you're finished, get going." Fab shook the muzzle of her gun at him. He apparently wasn't moving fast enough for her because she pulled the trigger, sending a bullet buzzing past his shoulder into the wall behind him.

Termite leaped into the air with a screech. "You won't get away with this." He raced out the door.

The men at the bar clapped, and Kelpie danced around.

"Send the bill for repairing the wall to Fab," I told Doodad.

She smirked.

"Leave it," Kelpie practically shrieked.

"What was he talking about?" Fab demanded.

I shrugged. "If his rearranged face has anything to do with him trying to take my bar, I'd suggest he rethink that idea."

"You don't sound very broken up about his sad state."

I ran my fingers across my dry cheeks. "Happy now?"

Several customers walked into the bar at once and took up the rest of the stools, leaving one standing. Fab and I stood and moved off to the side.

"No problems until tomorrow or the next

day," I told Kelpie, who was filling orders. Then I grabbed a cherry from the condiment box and headed for the exit.

Chapter Thirty-Nine

"Lunch is on me," Fab said as she beelined out of the parking lot. "I've got the perfect place picked out."

"I bet you do. Sorry to disappoint…" I made a sad face. "Not in the mood for dress-up."

Her eyes scanned my t-shirt dress and flicked down to my shoes. "You're fine. At least you're not wearing flip-flops."

"If this were the Hummer, there'd be a pair in the back, and it would be an easy swap." I wanted to laugh as she scrunched up her nose.

"I can do casual. Just not all the time, like you know who? You," Fab answered herself as she headed south on the highway. "I've found a new restaurant. It's waterfront, and I've heard the food is good."

After a short drive, she cruised into the parking lot of the Beachfront Grill and easily found a space. The two-story A-frame building had lots of appeal, the bottom level a stilted area with several picnic tables. The restaurant and bar were upstairs, where an oblong covered patio extended out and overlooked the water.

"Hold up." I moved forward in my seat. "You

remember carjacker chick? Well, she's right over there. Appears she's upgraded to a slim jim and is circling that Porsche and peering in the windows. My guess is it's about to be her next victim."

Fab maneuvered around and backed into a space that gave us an unobstructed view of her every action. "She convinced some judge it was a girlish prank and she wouldn't be reoffending and got bail?"

"Not certain how it works with juveniles, but probably got released to her parents." I whipped my phone out, noticing Fab had done the same, and we both took pictures. "Should've had Xander flag any mentions of her case. Though since she's underage, there might not be any. The cops never called me with follow-up questions and neither did the district attorney's office."

"This girl's good," Fab said in admiration as she watched her easily get the door of the sports car open.

"Based on watching her in action previously, I thought she was a beginner. Her skills have improved. It would've been nice if she'd used a slim jim on my car instead of trying to smash my window," I grumbled. "Wonder who her mentor is?"

The girl slid behind the wheel, got the car started, and headed out of the parking lot.

"Be interesting to see what she does with the car." Fab waited until she turned onto the street and followed, hanging back.

I opened an app on my phone and made a note of the license number. "If they'd sent her to juvie jail and she had to stay more than a minute, you'd think she wouldn't be back to stealing cars so soon. Can't be that much fun to hang out with other teenage hoodlums."

"A few possibilities: first-time offender and a really good lawyer… or her side of the story made it look like a she said/she said, with no video to corroborate our side. Not sure why the cameras wouldn't have been working, but it's a possibility." Fab stayed a couple of cars back, following her through traffic.

"Just surprised that I didn't get a call that she's out and running around—she did try to attack me." I sighed. "Good thing we're not in the Hummer or she'd have picked us out in a second. Though I would've loved to see her reaction at coming face to face with us again."

"Unless she's carrying a gun this time."

Agreed on that one.

The girl turned off the highway in an area familiar to us—commercial, the entire street made up of warehouses, some with security fencing. Fab pulled to the side of the road and idled, and halfway down the street, the Porsche turned into the parking lot of two single warehouses that shared the same driveway. Fab inched forward as the sportscar disappeared between the buildings and around the back.

Based on the lack of signage or cars, both appeared to be empty.

"There's always an entrance in the back." Fab craned her neck. "The problem is we have no idea which building she went into, and based on past experience, once we pull around the building, there's generally no exit to the street one way or the other and we'll be stuck."

"I vote—" I raised my hand. "—to get the heck out of here. It's not our car, so why risk getting trapped and our butts kicked or worse?"

Fab pulled to the end of the block and u-turned, coming back and slowing to snap pictures. "If this was a business in full operation, the front door wouldn't be boarded over."

"I know that you hate not knowing the answer to something, but don't go jumping out and leaving me here."

"We could call the cops."

Now that surprised me. "Since we have no idea what's going on, it could easily put us in the middle of a crime. Based on what we already know—and the fact that we just watched her boost an auto—my guess is that she's just delivered a stolen car. Do we want to meet whoever she's involved with? I can answer that—no." I stared at the building again. "For someone so young, she's up to her neck in big trouble." She'd been dressed like she didn't need money—cute dress and a designer purse slung over her shoulder—but she could be living on her cut of the proceeds from the stolen cars.

"We've both dealt with criminals that think nothing of taking over an empty building until someone catches on. What I find interesting is there's no 'For rent' sign. So maybe the owner allows criminal activity, getting a cut on the side. Anything goes down, and the property doesn't get confiscated." Fab inched her way down the street, checking out the neighboring businesses.

"Drug dealers and growers use rental houses in much the same way." Boy did we know that to be true. "I'm thinking that tipping off an ex-cop friend—one that would keep our names out of it—would be a good solution. I know just the one to ask."

"We go with that plan, and it will make both our husbands happy," Fab said. "I could maybe stay out of trouble with mine for five minutes."

I nodded.

With one last look in the rearview mirror, Fab cruised slowly to the corner, checking out every business, then turned in the direction of the compound.

Chapter Forty

Inside the security gates, there wasn't a single person or animal in sight. "Since I can read your mind—sometimes anyway, because it gets pretty busy in there—" Fab stared at my head and smirked. "—I know what cop you're talking about, and since his SUV is in the driveway, we might as well get this over with so whatever's happening at the warehouse, they don't change location and move on." She turned into Casio's driveway and parked.

"If I get a vote, and I should, we go to my house, call him, and order his backside to come over and not dally."

"Casio doesn't like being ordered around; he likes to be the one telling people what to do." Fab laughed. "And we're here..." She got out, and I followed.

It surprised me when she knocked politely. Probably didn't want to scare the kids with one of her cop knocks.

Marcus opened the door and stared past us. "Where'd you get the ride?"

"Stole it," I said with a smile. "We'd like to speak to Casio."

He shut the door in our faces.

I huffed out a surprised laugh. "How about a small wager as to whether the door opens again?"

Fab ignored me and leaned on the doorbell. That set the dogs off, and they went into a barking frenzy.

The door flew open. "Ring once or twice, then knock it off," Casio growled at us.

Fab squeezed past him, making eye contact with Marcus and glaring. He grinned, picked up his phone, and left the room.

Casio closed the door and frowned at Fab's back, then turned on me. "The doorbell thing is damn annoying."

"I know." I smiled sweetly. He wasn't amused. "The kids around?"

"They're in their rooms, supposedly doing homework. They probably are, since they're not hellions like I was growing up."

I tugged on his arm and turned toward the kitchen. "How about we take a seat and you offer us something cold to drink? We'll both take bottled water." I waved a finger between Fab and me.

"I know who you meant," he grumbled as he stomped over to the refrigerator and took out three bottles, setting them on the island. "Whatever you two are up to better be good."

"Anyone ever tell you to calm your shorts?" That got me a brief smile.

Done checking out the living room and, my guess, wanting to know where Marcus disappeared to, Fab came over and joined us.

"I'm about to share something… but it would be better coming from Fab. But before all that, we need you to pinkie swear that you won't babble our names about." I held out my finger.

"When have I ever?" He linked his finger around mine and didn't squeeze the life out of it.

"That's the reason we're here. You have a proven track record of keeping your lips zipped." I made the motion. "What you do with the information is up to you." I nodded to Fab, telegraphing *your turn*.

"I thought you were going to tell him," she grumbled.

"If you were paying attention, a nod is all you need to get started sharing the deets. If you need reminding, here it is: you revel in it more than I do."

"Not sure if you heard about the Hummer…" Fab rehashed the events from the day of the attempted car theft, then what went down today.

"There's big money in stealing high-end autos. These operations move around a lot to avoid getting caught. The exception is when they're working out of a car lot, thinking they won't get caught. They do, although it often takes longer." Casio held up his phone. "Text me pictures and anything else you've got. I've got a couple of friends that work undercover; they'll be happy to check it out, shut it down, and haul everyone off to jail. The real score would be if they were able to bring down the ringleaders."

"Maybe your *friends* can squeeze the girl. It should be easy for one of your brethren to get her name from the police report on our incident so you know who we're talking about," Fab said.

"Kyle isn't the only teenager to be recruited to commit crimes; in fact, the numbers are climbing. I really don't like it going on in my backyard. Anything I can do to help shut it down, I'm in."

"Don't forget that you're taking a low-key approach to life these days," I reminded him. "I know you like running down criminals, but just be careful."

"Yeah, yeah, got it. It's a good reminder though, thanks."

"How's Melba doing?" The dogs were out of sight when he opened the door, and I didn't see one asleep on the furniture.

"New rule: When the dogs need to go out, the person that takes them out has to stay with them until they're ready to come back inside. Once the kids get home, the dogs glue themselves to their sides. They only go crazy when someone plays with the doorbell. As I just found out." Casio shot Fab a withering stare. She laughed.

"How's life with another teenager in the house?" I asked.

"It takes patience," Casio said with a strained smile.

"You're a great dad." I smiled.

Fab stood. "Even though we want to remain anonymous, we still want to know what happens," she told him.

"Happy you two didn't get involved, but you should know this is going to take a couple of days, so don't go burning up my phone. I'm tempted to jump in, but when I get those inclinations, I remind myself that I have kids. You can be assured that I'll be turning this info over to someone who will investigate and not drag their feet."

"Anything you need, give one of us a call," Fab said.

Casio walked us to the door. We waved and went back to the car.

Chapter Forty-One

Two days passed, and no call from Casio. I grabbed my laptop and a cold water and sat at the island. I really wanted to sit outside, but storm clouds appeared to be blowing in. Recent events had made me uneasy. Fab and I had gone out to lunch the day before, making up for the one we missed, and she'd found another restaurant that she wanted to try. When we got home, we parted ways in the driveway, and as soon as I stepped foot in the house, a weird sensation came over me. I knew someone had been in my house and wasn't sure if they were still there. Drawing my Glock, I walked from room to room and nothing. But someone had definitely been there. I didn't know when it started, but from the time I was young, I could walk into a room and know if something was out of place. I found a drawer hadn't been closed all the way, and the closet door in the guest bedroom was left cracked. I checked the windows and doors, and all except the patio doors were locked.

My laptop rang, interrupting my musings about the day before—Casio had set up a conference call with Fab and me.

"My detective friends took the information and, after some investigation, found it credible and were able to ascertain that they were onto a stolen car ring. A team was put together, and they converged on the warehouse to shut down the operation." Casio grunted. "Place was empty, but whoever had been there had made a quick exit, leaving behind trash, debris, and some personal items."

"They were tipped off? But how?" I asked in disgust.

"Good question," Casio grumped. "Before they went in, they found a guard at a neighboring business willing to talk. Guessing a few bucks changed hands. He told them that that particular warehouse had non-stop traffic at night, after all the rest of the businesses closed for the day. When asked why he never called the police, he said they were a rough crowd and he didn't want to take the chance that it would come back on him and he'd get his butt kicked or worse."

"We tell you about the warehouse—" Fab stared at Casio. "—and before the cops can get there, the thieves are gone."

"They investigated the first night; the plan was to go back the next night, but by then, they'd cleared out."

"Fab and I only told our husbands. Who did you tell?"

"Same question my detective friends had, and the answer is no one. The second night, when they surrounded the place and found it empty, they went back and talked to the guard. He told them that several cars pulled out in the early morning hours and there'd been no activity since."

"First the guys threatening Kyle are tipped off, and now this," Fab said in disgust.

"Hold on. One of the boys the officers picked up who'd been living in that house with Kyle was able to give them fairly detailed information on the group. Thanks to that kid, they've tracked the group to Miami, and they'll be arrested soon," Casio assured us.

"Let's hope that kid and the others don't get hung out to dry." I grimaced, knowing that the kids would never be seen again if that was the case.

"Not going to happen," Casio assured me.

"I'll be keeping an eye out for our car thief, since she seems to like this area. Be interesting to see where she leads us next," Fab said.

"Whatever you do, don't corner her yourself," Casio said gruffly.

"I promise for Fab," I said. "I'll remind her that it'll keep us out of trouble with our husbands."

"I'll keep you updated," Casio said and cut the feed.

"How about a 'gotta go' or something," I

grumbled to no one. I wanted to know who tipped off the car thieves; I didn't believe that they just got lucky.

Not sure what I expected to find, but I clicked away on my laptop and pulled up the security tapes for my house. I'd never looked at them before since there'd been no reason, but now I wanted to reassure myself that I was overreacting and it was just my imagination that someone had been in the house. I rewound the footage to the previous day and started it up. Shortly after Fab and I went to lunch, Marcus strolled through one of patio doors, looking around like he owned the place. He went room to room, opening drawers and cupboards; apparently nothing appealed to him, as he didn't take anything. Once he was done snooping, he slid onto a stool at the island and opened my laptop. A minute later, he slammed down the lid. From the disgust on his face, he didn't appreciate finding out it was password protected. He helped himself to a beer and left the same way he entered, closing the door behind him.

I got up and crossed the living room to double-check the pocket doors, then closed and locked them. What would his reaction have been if he were caught? I shuddered, thinking I'd better have been able to draw my weapon quick.

Did he try to get into Fab's house? Probably not, as it would've set off an alarm on her phone.

A comment Creole made replayed in my

thoughts: "Marcus must have a girlfriend. Saw a girl pulling out of the driveway in a pricey sports car as I passed," he'd remarked shortly after getting home last night.

Sitting down again, I texted Fab: *Forward me the outside security tapes.* I didn't expect her to come through the front door a few minutes later, lockpick and laptop in hand.

"You've never made that request before, and I had to come check it out." Fab grabbed a water before she sat opposite me. "What are you looking for?"

"I need the footage from last night around the time the guys got home. Creole commented that Marcus had some hotsy visitor in a sports car. Let's see what she looks like."

I knew Fab would access it faster than me, and a few clicks later, she had it pulled up. She flipped the screen around to show me where she had it on pause. My "what if" was answered—carjacker chick and Marcus were locking lips. A couple of frames later, Fab zeroed in on the license plate, and I copied down the number and texted it to Xander.

Then I called him, having forgotten to tell him to step on it. "You're on speaker," I said when he answered.

"Just sent you and Fab emails." His voice bubbled with excitement. "Made a new friend that's got police connections and is willing to do a favor now and again as long as I don't hound him. Chloe Bedford—the girl that tried to steal your car—her case was dismissed for lack of evidence."

"What the heck?" I said in exasperation. "You'd think they'd want to talk to the victim, and I never got a call."

"Ran a background check. No arrest record, and she's from big money. Daddy's got millions in his pocket."

"Yours was her first attempt at car theft?" Fab didn't look convinced. "Wonder who helped her improve her skills, as the second time we saw her in action, she'd gotten much better." She clicked away on her laptop. "Look at this." She flipped it around, and she'd matched the picture Xander had sent over of Chloe to the girl in Marcus's driveway.

"You just got a text from me. It's got the plate number of the car Chloe was last seen in. Want to know if it's registered to her family or stolen."

"It won't take me long," Xander assured me. "Also, I got easily a dozen license plate numbers from the security footage you sent over. Got names and addresses on all of them, three of whom visited more than once. Didn't see the girl, but I'll run through the list of names and see if I get a match."

"Can you tell us anything about the names you did run down?" Fab asked.

"All rich kids. The majority of the addresses are from Marcus's neighborhood up in Miami.

Two are out of Homestead."

"Wonder if whatever's going on is what Brick was trying to get Marcus away from," Fab mused.

"I haven't had a chance to tell Fab, so you're both hearing this next bit at the same time."

Fab's eyebrows went up.

I told them about reviewing my own security footage and watching as Marcus snooped around, leaving out the part about a weird feeling driving me to do it. I winced at what Creole's reaction would be when he heard—I wouldn't want to be Marcus.

"Did you do this before or after our conversation with Casio?" Fab asked.

"After."

"A meeting with Casio, and I know nothing," Xander said in amusement.

Fab gave him a quick update. "I've mulled over who could've tipped off the warehouse crew until my head hurts. Interesting that you should be checking your footage while I was wondering where Marcus was while we were telling Casio about the car theft ring. We know that he was home. We were in the kitchen, and there are several places he could've easily have eavesdropped from."

"We know Chloe's a car thief and that she was at the warehouse the day we followed her and at Casio's last night before the detectives raided the place. It only makes sense that Marcus tipped them off, which was the reason for their hasty exit." I rubbed my eyes and sighed. "What a mess."

"We need to know exactly what Marcus's involvement is, besides hanging out with a car thief and possibly tipping her off."

"Is it possible to hack into Casio's security system and find out where Marcus was while we were gathered in the kitchen?" I asked. Xander's chuckle had me quickly adding, "Not by you, but I know you have a connection or two who wouldn't blink at such a request and would cover their tracks."

"No problem. Even easier, since I'm guessing that Fab had it installed…"

"You'd be right. I have access. Up until now, nothing that's happened has been a good enough reason to invade Casio's privacy," Fab said.

"And now?" I asked.

"If Marcus was the one to tip them off…" Fab tapped the counter with her finger.

"You know…" I ignored her groan. "We've witnessed his guests going in the house, and they never stay long. So what are they doing? We've already stepped all over Casio's privacy, and a quick review of the interior footage would give us answers."

"Then what?" Xander asked. "You'll be in possession of information that could explode on you, and from more than one direction."

"It's possible Marcus doesn't know that Chloe

is a car thief, but the other stuff…" I said. There wasn't going to be an easy way to dump all this info on Casio.

"I can review the security footage quicker than you two. If Fab will give me permission to remotely access her laptop to get what I need…?" Xander said. Fab stared at me for a long moment, then said yes. "I'll call once I get something." He clicked off.

"There's no innocent explanation for what Marcus is doing, and we both know it." Fab groaned. "I'd like to know what he was looking for in your house. I'm surprised he didn't come to mine."

"Check the beachside tapes and see if he came lurking around," I suggested. "Once I tell Creole, Marcus will be headed back home."

"And when Brick finds out, we'll hear the explosion all the way down here in the Keys." Fab grimaced.

"Let's hope we're wrong."

I knew we were both thinking, *Fat chance.*

I got up and got us both cold drinks while we waited for Xander to call back. It didn't take long.

"Marcus stood in the hallway the whole time you were there. He didn't move until you all stood and headed to the door. Then he went in the living room and stretched out on the couch. Casio came back in the kitchen, made a couple of calls, then went to his room, and never noticed

Marcus, who then got up, went out to the deck, and made his own calls."

"At this point, who'd believe he wasn't the snitch?" I asked.

"I'm reviewing past footage now, and I can tell you that on at least one occasion, that big envelope you've seen someone leaving with had packages of white powder in it."

I gasped. But how surprised was I really?

Fab angrily shook her head.

"The reason I know is one of the guys upended it on the counter, took one of the packets, and slit it open for a taste test."

"Put together a video of anything else you find, along with footage of the cars coming and going and the passing off of envelopes and whatever else," Fab directed.

"Working on it now."

I disconnected the call.

Fab put her head in her arms.

"Want to come over for dinner?" I asked. No response. "We can't do anything without telling Creole and Didier first. We've accumulated all this information and can't sit on it; it's time to get their input."

"What goes good with vodka shots?"

"I'm thinking tequila."

Chapter Forty-Two

Before Fab left, I texted Creole and got an expected time for him to be home. Sharing it with Fab, I said, "Make sure you get your butt back over here. Since you haven't made a food choice, we're having pizza." I got up and opened the refrigerator. "I'll order their favorite beers—sets a relaxed mood."

Fab rolled her eyes like that was the stupidest thing she'd ever heard, and we both knew that wasn't true. "Make sure the vodka's cold and there's olives," she ordered on her way out the deck doors.

I got busy and ordered the food, then set the table outside on the deck. It was beautiful out, the blue-green water lapping the shore. I waved to the heron stalking the sand, who stared back with indifference. I then went back inside, for the first time double-checking to make sure the patio doors were locked, and went to take a shower.

Donning a turquoise t-shirt dress, one of my faves, I pulled my messy red hair into a ponytail high on my head and slipped into a pair of sparkly flip-flops.

Creole walked into the bedroom, and I gave

him a big kiss. "You need to step on it; our guests will be here soon."

"The neighbors? They're more like regulars." He kissed me again and disappeared into the bathroom.

I went out to the kitchen and grabbed an oval bucket, filled it with ice and bottles of beer, and took it out to the deck. Coming back inside, I got out a platter and arranged everything Fab needed to make her drinks. For me, I took out a pitcher and threw together a margarita concoction. Taking a sip, I licked my lips. I was tempted to drink straight from the pitcher but that would be a tip-off that the day hadn't gone as planned.

Creole came down the hallway in shorts and a t-shirt that stretched across his abs. I gave him a thorough-once over and winked. Grabbing a bottle of beer, I removed the top and handed it to him.

"Special occasion that's slipped my mind?" He eyed me warily.

I snuggled up against his chest, then stood on my tiptoes and brushed his lips with a kiss. "Every night's special with you, babes."

Creole laughed and gave me a scrutinizing look.

I stepped back. "We always have these get-togethers in the morning. Why not the evening, when it's heavenly to sit outside? The best part — pizza and antipasto salad."

We both turned, hearing Fab and Didier talking as they came across the deck. Didier grabbed a beer, and they came inside. Creole walked around the island, making a drink for Fab and handing it to her as they approached.

I held up the glass that Creole handed me. "To friends."

The four of us talked for a few minutes before the gate buzzer rang—pizza delivery was here. Creole let the driver in and brought the food outside, setting everything in the middle of the table.

We laughed and joked through dinner. A couple of times, Fab and I exchanged *Who's going to be the one to share?* glances. Once we were done, I jumped up and insisted the guys have another beer while I made short work of clearing the table.

"Food was great, company even better, but I've got the feeling something is up with you two and I'm waiting for… hopefully not an explosion." Didier grinned at Fab and me.

Fab and I engaged in a stare down, *You tell them. No, you.*

"Look what I just happen to have?" I pulled a quarter out of my pocket and held it up. "Heads or tails?"

"Let me see that." Fab held out her hand.

I flipped it in the air, caught it, and after a quick glance, said, "Oh look, you lose," and pocketed the coin.

The guys laughed. Fab, not so much.

"Since Fab is feeling a bit testy over losing another coin toss, I'll start."

"Totally rigged," she grumbled.

I ignored her glare, knowing she wasn't all that irked. "Casio called this morning with an update on the warehouse."

"He filled us in at the office," Didier told us. "He wasn't happy and wanted to know who leaked the information, as though one of us might have done it."

"You want me to rearrange his face?" Fab smiled up at Didier.

He leaned down and kissed her, and whatever he whispered in her ear, she smiled.

"Thought about that question on and off all day," Creole said. "Didn't want to believe that it was someone within the police department."

"Turns out that there's another option you couldn't have known about." I continued my story, telling them that Marcus had been snooping around our house. I got a raised eyebrow from Creole, silently asking, *What made you check the inside security feed?*

After slugging down another martini and finishing off the olives, Fab took over the retelling of the day's events and updated them on what Xander had uncovered so far. "We haven't decided what to do with the information."

"There's no doubt that Marcus isn't just a total

dick, but a criminal one," I said. "Because of Fab's association with Brick, he's gotten more than the benefit of the doubt, but now there's video evidence."

"When we first heard about Marcus's so-called friends coming and going, Creole and I chalked it up to friendly guy... more like we hoped that was the case," Didier said.

"Got to tell you, I figured he was up to something illegal but hoped, being Brick's son and living with Casio, he wasn't that stupid. Considering his age, he'll do prison time." Creole shook his head in disgust. "Not sure how we would've handled this situation any differently, given our friendship with Casio and knowing he's dealing with strained family relations."

"Now what?" I asked.

Creole took a long pull on his beer. "Put together a nice little presentation of everything you've found out."

"Great minds and all that." I pointed to Fab. "She asked Xander to piece together the activities in a video."

"My suggestion is to dump it in Brick's lap. He wanted to take a harder line with Marcus when he was in trouble in Miami. If he knew that his son was dealing drugs and whatever else, he should have known a distance of seventy-five miles wasn't going to put a stop to that enterprise." Creole sighed, shaking his head. "There's no doubt that he'll put the squeeze on his kid, and he's got the connections to bring down the illegal operation."

"If Marcus skates, isn't that letting him off easy?" Didier asked with a raised brow.

"Brick will come down on him like a ton of... well bricks. The last thing he's going to want is for his oldest son, or any of his kids, is to go to jail," Creole said with assurance. "Marcus might not become intimately involved with the legal system, but he won't walk away."

"Who tells Casio?" Fab asked. "His first thought will be his kids and how fast he can get Marcus out of the house."

"Let Brick break the news to Casio. Him coming clean with his brother might be the one thing that saves the relationship. Tell him if he doesn't do it within twenty-four hours, we'll do it for him. Get your presentation together." Creole nodded at Fab and me. "Then go see Brick ASAP."

"I'm not going by myself," Fab said adamantly.

"No, you're not," I assured her.

Chapter Forty-Three

The next morning, Fab and I met with Xander at the office to put together a concise report of the comings and goings of Marcus and his friends.

"There's more," Xander said and, after a couple of clicks, turned his laptop toward the two of us. The video he'd spliced together showed that on several occasions, the big envelopes contained cash and a lot of it. On those occasions, Marcus was handed the envelope, which he took inside, and there was no other exchange.

"What's going on there?" I asked.

"No clue." Fab sighed. "Once Marcus is gone, I'm changing the security codes. I don't want the kind of people that have been coming into the compound to come back."

"The video I put together shows everything going on inside and out." Xander scrolled past images of license plates and notations of their registered owners and addresses.

A separate report detailed what we knew about auto thief Chloe Bedford and the failed police raid. We believed her to be Marcus's girlfriend based on footage of the two of them kissing on several occasions. Between the three of us, we managed to put everything together in a concise fashion and back everything up with photographic proof.

Once finished, Fab called Brick and asked to meet him in his office the next morning, requesting that it be before the showroom officially opened.

The next morning, I left before Creole for once but not without a long encouraging kiss and an admonition to call as soon as we left the car lot.

"It's not too late—I can still come with you," he said with another kiss.

"If it were just me…" Creole's eyebrows went up. "I wouldn't go. Brick's going to be furious, but he won't hurt either of us. He knows we wouldn't hesitate to shoot him." That got a chuckle out of my husband.

One last kiss, and I went out to the SUV, not one bit surprised to see Fab already behind the wheel. On the ride north which we hadn't done in a while—and I can't say I missed it—we were quiet, listening to music.

On a hunch, I asked, "You're going to dump this in my lap, aren't you?"

After a long pause, she answered, "Kind of."

I sucked in a deep breath. "Figured as much. Based on your long relationship with the man, I was fairly certain that you wouldn't want to be the bearer of such sucky news."

"Brick's going to take the report and double-check everything. He isn't going to let it slide that his kid is a criminal," Fab said with assurance. "He wanted to come down harder on Marcus when he first got into trouble, but the wife stopped him. I have a feeling his son is going to find out all about tough love. As for the kid's friends, my guess is that Brick's going to inform the parents, and what they'll do, who knows."

Thanks to light traffic, we made record time up to Miami and exited the freeway. A couple of turns later, we pulled into Famosa Motors and parked in front of the roll-up doors, which were closed. Too early for salesmen to be lurking around, sipping their morning coffee.

We got out, and Fab grabbed her briefcase. The side door was unlocked, and we entered.

"Wonder where big-busted what's-her-name is?" I asked as we passed the empty receptionist's chair.

"Not sure which one you mean, since Brick has a type." Fab smirked.

We crossed the showroom and went up the stairs to Brick's second-floor office. For once, we didn't play games going up the steps, knowing it wouldn't get our meeting off to a good start.

Fab led the way, and I stayed behind her, taking a deep breath.

Brick heard us coming and beckoned Fab into his office with a huge smile. His eyes landed on me, and the smile was replaced with a *What are you doing here?* look.

The layout of the office hadn't changed, and I chose a chair in front of his desk. Long ago, he'd upgraded to something that didn't make one's backside ache. His philosophy for the previous chairs had been *people won't linger*.

Fab sat on the ledge of the picture window that overlooked the showroom, car lot, and busy boulevard below.

"Happy to see you," Brick said to her, his muscular bulk kicked back behind his desk. "You didn't say why you wanted the meeting, but I figured it must be important."

Fab stood and flipped around her briefcase, which she'd left in the chair next to me. She reached inside, pulled out a USB drive and an envelope, and handed both to Brick. "Just read this with an open mind and follow up with your own investigation." She backed up and leaned against the ledge.

"We want you to know that this information wasn't shared with anyone, and that includes Casio," I reassured him. "We'll leave it up to you who you want to tell. It would be nice if there were no secrets… at least, none that could come back to bite any of us."

Brick eyed the drive with suspicion, turning it over in his fingers as though he expected it to explode. When that didn't happen, he reluctantly plugged it into his computer.

I stood. "If you have any questions…" I tossed

a *help me* stare over my shoulder at Fab.

"Sit. Down," Brick ordered. "Neither of you is going anywhere until I know what this is all about."

Fab must've known what his response would be, as she hadn't moved an inch. I dropped back into my chair. Where was that coveted snack bowl he used to have on his desk? A girl could use a hit of sugar. And no, I wasn't about to ask.

Since neither of us could see the screen, it was hard to know which part he was looking at, but he sat up straighter, his features grew more intense, and anger filled his face. You could hear a pin drop.

Finally, he looked away, his eyes boring into Fab, and growled, "What the hell is this all about?"

"It's exactly what it looks like. If there's an innocent explanation, we couldn't come up with one," Fab said in a placating tone.

"I can't believe this." Brick's meaty fist pounded down on the desk, and several items wobbled around. "In light of recent history… that damn kid." He threw himself back in his chair and stared at the ceiling. "I had hoped… Guess I was the stupid one."

"If there's anything you need us to do…" Fab said.

I hoped not but kept my mouth shut—I was the last person he'd want to hear from.

Brick straightened and pointed at the empty

chair next to me. Fab took the hint and moved off her perch. He managed to hold us both in his wide-eyed stare-down. "I wish there were an innocent explanation but, like you, I don't hold out hope. Appreciate you bringing this to me, as most would've called the cops, and with your connections... If my brother had known about this before me, he'd have killed Marcus for bringing this kind of trouble into his house, and I can't say that wouldn't have been my reaction in his shoes."

"Like I said before—"

"Got it," Brick cut Fab off. "I'll need some time to, ahhh... Anyway, you'll be hearing from me."

Fab and I stood, and she motioned me out, then moved in front of Brick's desk and lowered her voice. I waited for her at the top of the stairs. She didn't leave me waiting long, and instead of sliding down the banister as she'd done almost every time in the past, we walked down, neither of us saying a word.

I slid into the passenger side and exhaled a deep breath. "That was intense."

"Brick's on the phone now, calling Marcus home to explain himself," Fab relayed. "Very happy I'm not that kid."

"I'm thinking that Brick's going to protect his kid and the criminals are going to end up walking," I said. "Do what they normally do—close up shop and relocate."

"Brick assured me that wasn't going to

happen. Not sure how he can keep his kid out of jail and bring down the rest of the crew, or if that's even the right thing to do. He didn't say, but I'm guessing that once he's done interrogating Marcus, he'll call in Casio."

"I'm hoping our relationship with Casio survives." I glanced at the dash clock. "It's too early for a drink, but maybe we could make an exception."

"We'll settle on something non-alcoholic and sit out on the deck for a much-needed dramaless day." Fab laughed. "I was waiting for you to bring up wanting a discounted truck for Charlie."

"Thankfully, I didn't think about that. But I still wouldn't have brought it up. There's a limit to my nerviness."

"I already dealt with it." There was a ta-da in Fab's tone. "Called after our meeting with Cook and pitched Brick the good deed idea and the positive press coverage we could get him, and it didn't take any arm-twisting. He didn't think much of the fundraising idea, assuming it would fall short, and will cover the difference."

Chapter Forty-Four

All in all, it was a quiet few weeks. I, for one, was happy and back to taking regular walks along the beach. During one, the Famosa kids were playing on the sand, and I stopped to talk to Alex, who told me confidentially, "Marcus went home. Good riddance."

"What happened?"

Alex shrugged. "His dad called, and he left. Never came back. After a couple of days, my dad packed up his stuff. Said he didn't know what happened and didn't ask."

"You never quite warmed up to having Marcus around, did you?" I asked.

"He was always sneaking around," Alex said with a shake of his head. "Hated the dogs, and he wasn't on their favorites list either. They tolerated him, though Larry growled at him a couple of times. If a dog doesn't like you..."

"I've heard that." I chuckled, thinking about one of my cats clawing a guy once. Turned out the cat had better instincts than me. I waved to Lark, who was walking over with the rest of the kids in tow, and Alex engaged them in a game of chase.

When the kids were out of earshot, Lark said, "Casio's working on some big case in Miami, even took the Chief along. The guys are tight-lipped about what's going on. It's hard to know who knows what, and they're not sharing, which is irritating."

"I haven't heard a word either."

"Something tells me you know something." Lark shot me a squint-eye.

I was saved from a response by the kids screaming for her to come play.

* * *

We had a blowout night at Jake's for the fundraiser. The feedback was great, and everyone had fun. The cover charges and donations didn't begin to cover the cost of the truck, but Brick kept his word. Although overwhelmed by the new ride, Charlie went along with the picture-taking that Fab had orchestrated at Famosa Motors. He'd been disappointed to only get back a shell of a Porsche and hadn't decided whether he'd ever restore. But he'd struck up a friendship with Spoon, and for now, the car was staying at the shop and there was no hurry to make a decision.

Fab and Didier had gone for the presentation, and the report I got back from her afterwards was: "Something big is about to go down. Brick didn't elaborate and I didn't ask, since he looked ready to explode."

Gunz called to tell Fab that he was on the mend but wouldn't say where. He told her he'd heard that Eva left the Cove. So that was why, despite the all-points bulletin, she hadn't been arrested. Eavesdropping on the call, I was happy when Fab wasn't insistent about finding the woman. Though she'd claimed that she didn't want any part of tracking Eva down, she was also known to change her mind. When they hung up, she said, "I was tempted to tell Gunz to ask his sisters if they knew her whereabouts."

I winced. Knowing what I knew of the Q sisters, there was no way they'd allow someone who'd shot their sainted brother to continue walking around.

* * *

The weekly get-together was at my house this morning, which I didn't mind. I imagined the hot topic would be the big arrest that had gone down in Miami and what had been shared and by whom.

I'd grabbed souffles and an array of breakfast pastries from the Bakery Café the day before and got a little carried away, but the rest would go to the office. I made one pot of coffee and a pot of brewed swill.

The skies had turned dark, rain threatening, so I arranged everything on the kitchen island. The doorbell rang, which surprised me. Creole, on his way down the hall, opened it, and Fab smirked at him as she walked by. Didier said something that had the two men laughing.

"Surprised you didn't pick the lock."

Fab rolled her eyes.

The four of us had barely gotten settled around the island when Casio walked through the deck doors. "I heard there was going to be an early meeting, so I thought I'd invite myself." He crossed the living room and claimed a seat. "Good to see it wasn't a lie about there being food."

"No food would never happen at one of our houses." I slid off the stool and grabbed a plate, poured him a cup of coffee, and set both down in front of him.

"This is a first." Fab eyed him suspiciously.

Didier nudged her with a smirk.

"I'm sure you've all heard about the multiple arrests that have gone down in the last couple of days," Casio grumped.

Fab leaned forward. "The news reports lacked basic information as to who was being arrested and why, except for 'criminal activity.'"

"A few reporters owed us favors and were asked to keep their flaps shut, since everyone isn't in custody yet, so they downplayed the story. That can't be said for them all, but the bigger names were helpful." Casio downed his coffee and held out the mug.

I grabbed it from him. "You want the 'guaranteed to grow hair on your head' concoction or the sissy one you just slurped down? Forgot to ask before."

"Sure, I'll go for the hair one—see what happens." Casio ran a hand over his bald head. I set the full mug in front of him, and he took a sniff and nodded. "When I heard of my nephew's criminal activities and figured out where the info came from, my first thought was so much for friendship. Then I gave brief thought to beating the hell out of your husbands, since I don't hit women."

"I'm assuming you're over your thoughts of violence, because if not, you should know it wouldn't end well for you." I opened the junk drawer, removed my Glock, and laid it on the island.

Casio held his hands up. "I'm unarmed."

"Not to brag, but your body would disappear," Fab said with a flinty stare as I went back to my chair. "The alligators around here need a filling meal once in a while."

"You're not the first person to think that would be a good way to get rid of my body... Good luck. Back to why I'm here." Casio smacked his hand down. "Speaking of disappearing, got a call that Marcus had gone back home. Then an urgent call from my doting brother, who wanted me to drop everything and come to his office, with a last-minute command to 'step on it.' First time I'd seen him overwhelmed, not knowing what action to take. Once Brick shared the information he'd received—good job, by the way—I knew it was better that I heard it all from him." He finished off his coffee, and Creole got up and refilled everyone's mug.

"Let me guess, you heaped on the brotherly love?" Fab asked.

Didier shot her a *be nice* look. She smirked in response.

"As I'm sure you're aware, I've always got a solution for everything, even if it's unsuitable. But by the time Brick was done, I was speechless. It was only late morning, but I still got up and poured us both a drink. It was easy to see that Brick was totally wrecked by the whole situation, and I really needed to stifle my inclination to kick the hell out of his kid."

"Good thing you can control yourself." I smiled at him.

"Where was Marcus?" Creole asked.

"After another refill of whiskey, Brick picked up the phone and ordered, 'My office, now.' I figured the kid was at home and it would be a while. But no, here he came, stomping up the stairs, looking like he'd rather be anywhere else. Tough."

I passed around the platter with the last of the pastries, and the guys finished them off.

"It took everything in me not to choke the a-hole look off his face, as the faces of my own kids flashed through my mind for the umpteenth time, along with thoughts of how much danger he'd put them in. Kind of surprised I was able to control my anger."

"Probably a good thing you didn't deck him," Didier said.

"I swallowed my anger, for the moment anyway, and told him that he'd better answer my questions or he was headed to jail and I'd take him myself. There wasn't a word out of Brick and I took that to mean I could do whatever I had to do to get answers."

"Did you give Marcus a detailed description of life in prison?" Creole asked.

"I went with all the worst-case scenarios and how he could spend a year behind bars before he even got to trial. Then gave him the highlights of how he'd spend his days." Casio shook his head. "Once he was sentenced, he could expect to spend years behind bars, as he was old enough to be tried as an adult. Spoiled rich kids don't fare well."

"Was he forthcoming with anything helpful?" Didier asked.

"Marcus told me to FO, and that's when I snapped and sent him flying face down on the floor. To my surprise, Brick tossed me a pair of cuffs, and I had Marcus back on his feet in a moment, saying, 'Say good-bye to your dad; you won't be seeing him for a while.'"

"Can't believe that at that point, he wasn't ready to say anything to get himself out of trouble," Creole said.

"It was only when he realized his dad wasn't going to do anything to stop me that he wanted to broker a deal. Told him that depended on what he had for me. The more he talked, the more I knew he was in deep trouble and walking away wasn't going to happen. Brick knew the same thing, and the color drained from his face."

"You need a drink now?" Creole slapped him on the back.

Casio's phone rang, and he looked at the screen. "Got to take this." He got up and moved into the living room.

Fab nudged Didier. "I may need your help if Casio thinks he's leaving here without telling us the rest of what went down."

I got up and cleaned off the island. "If any of you want more coffee, someone needs to make it."

"We know how to be good hosts." Creole laughed.

Casio pocketed his phone and detoured by the refrigerator to grab a water before sitting back down. "Marcus and a couple of his friends thought selling drugs would be a good way to make a few extra bucks. These are all kids of wealthy parents and never denied anything. They wanted the excitement of getting away with something and didn't think through the consequences, figuring there wouldn't be any."

"Watched those videos a couple of times, and based on what I saw, Marcus made some kind of good supplier connection," Creole said.

"That connection turned out to be his girlfriend's older brother. He's mid-level in the operation, and we got a couple more names out of Marcus. Once the first guy got arrested, the rest scattered. That guy requested a lawyer and didn't say another word; he knew it would be bad for his health if it got back to the ones that ran the operation."

"What about when they find out Marcus brought the organization down and is the reason they were arrested?" Didier asked.

"Called in the Chief. He got us in with the current police chief, district attorney, and a couple of detectives investigating the heads of the operation. Thanks to the new information, a series of arrests went down and that included Marcus. You know that saying, 'The first one to talks, gets the deal'? That's what ended up happening for Marcus. It was made to look like he was booked and held like everyone else, but if he continues to cooperate, he won't see jail time. If it wasn't done that way and it became known that he was the only one not arrested, he'd have a bounty on his head."

"Where's Marcus now?" Didier asked.

"He's at home, but on house arrest, mandated by Brick. Basically for his own safety. Once Brick gets the okay from the DA's office, he's going to send Marcus across the country to finish his senior year."

"What about the car thefts?" Fab demanded.

Casio chuckled with a shake of his head and a grim look. "That was an all-chick operation. A bunch of underage girls thought it would be fun to act like hoodlums. This group were not only privileged but straight-A students. When Chloe was arrested, the first thing out of her mouth was 'I want to call my lawyer,' and she had Cruz Campion on speed dial."

All of us laughed, as we knew the man, and well. Best criminal defense attorney in the world, just ask him.

"How did she get his number?" I asked. "Same social circle?"

Casio shrugged. "Would love to have eavesdropped on that call."

"Be interesting to see if he represents her, since he claims not to rep guilty people," Fab said.

"What happens now?" Creole asked.

"We've got a few more persons of interest in the wind that need to be rounded up. We're building a good case that will send the lot of them to jail for a long time," Casio said with assurance.

Chapter Forty-Five

Emerson and Brad were having a barbecue on the beach and had invited family and friends. I'd wanted to bring something but was told, "It's all handled." I suspected that Mother stepped up and didn't leave anything for anyone else to do.

I chose a coral sundress with spaghetti straps. Normally I'd choose cute sandals, but today, I reached for flip-flops to get me as far as the sand. I also grabbed a pair of sunglasses and a wide-brim hat.

Didier had stopped by earlier and grabbed Creole, and the two went down to Brad's to lend a hand moving chairs and an umbrella down to the sand.

I went out on the deck and looked over the railing, watching with some amusement as Fab pulled a blue collapsible wagon past my house. It had a cover on the top, so there was no telling from my vantage point what was underneath. I went down the stairs to the beach, leaving my flops on the bottom step and burying my feet in the white sand.

"What are you doing?" I stepped around her and lifted the cover. "Bar on wheels? Of sorts." I laughed, noting that she had everyone's liquor choices covered. "The Florida sun has finally gotten to you."

"There's a pitcher of margaritas on ice; if you're mean, I'll pour them out."

"We're not in a hurry; let's have a sip or two now." I licked my lips.

"No!" Fab shook her finger at me. "We stop to do some sipping, and we won't make it the rest of the way. What possible excuse could we give for not making it the last hundred or so feet?"

"I suppose." I sighed dramatically. "We can't miss Brad and Emerson's first party."

"Thank goodness we like her and she's not crazy."

I nodded. "I'm thinking..." I ignored her groan. "If barbecuing on the sand isn't a disaster, you should put one in at your house. We can all come over and use it, have more parties."

"That's what I thought was happening, but Didier said we're going back up to the patio when it's time for dinner.

"I like my idea better."

"Maybe I'll pitch it to Didier." Fab stared down the beach and groaned. "Isn't that Mama Lawyer over there?"

I glanced over and my groan matched hers. "The killer defense attorney wouldn't want to hear you calling her mama. You'd have to shoot her to stop her from feeding you to a reptile."

Emerson's mother, Ruthie Grace, now a

blonde, wore her hair swept back in a chignon, her tropical-themed dress inches above her ankles. She'd retired to run off with some dude—must have been the burly fellow with his arm around her shoulders.

"Glaring like you want to chew her leg off isn't friendly. Paste on a smile." I demonstrated.

"You need to go back to practicing your expressions in the mirror." Fab shook her head as I tried a couple out on her. "It's possible she's forgotten how annoying she thinks we are."

"Can I have that drink now?"

"The answer is still no."

We were the last to arrive. Everyone else had filled the seats—Mother and Spoon, Creole and Didier, the host and hostess. A long table down one side held cold beverages, and the kids played in the sand with a young guy I realized was Liam.

I ran over and wrapped my arms around him in a hard hug. "How did I not know you were back? Wish you could tell me your visit's going to be permanent."

"Here for a week and then going back to graduate." Liam's smile was huge.

He'd been adopted into our family long ago when Brad dated his mother. Their break-up had been amicable, as she was moving to Hollywood, where she was making it big. Liam had stayed in Florida to finish up his education.

Mila and Logan ran over, and I hugged them

both and kissed their cheeks.

"We're going to have to do something fun while you're here," I said to Liam over their heads.

"Sounds good."

I walked over to where everyone was sitting and took a seat next to Fab. Ruthie acknowledged us with a scowl but changed her tune when she found out that Fab had dragged over an assortment of beer in her cart. Didier at her side, Fab lifted the lid, and the two filled orders as they were called out.

Creole slung his arm around me, and we went over to Mother and Spoon. I kissed and hugged them both, then enveloped my brother in a hug. "You been behaving?"

"We both know I'm the boring one."

"Not always." I laughed.

Creole handed me a margarita and sat down next to me under the big umbrella facing the ocean.

Emerson and Brad stood in front of us all, both with drinks.

"To family," Emerson toasted.

"We have an announcement." Brad hooked his arm around Emerson and kissed her cheek. "I've asked Emerson to marry me, and she said yes." The two kissed.

The kids cheered the loudest.

"Congratulations to you both," Fab said, and Didier nodded.

"To my bro and SIL," I toasted. "When's the big day?"

"Right now," Emerson said with a huge smile. *Good luck with that.*

"What?" Ruthie glared at her daughter.

"So soon," Mother muttered.

"Maybe you'll like my idea better," Brad said with a smirk. "A Las Vegas wedding, and when we get back, we'll have a party."

"You're doing it here? How are you going to pull it off and have it be a valid marriage?" Ruthie asked, looking around.

"Happy we're in agreement." Brad kissed Emerson, then turned and motioned to a man who'd come down the stairs, while Emerson ducked into the house.

The Bible in his hands was a dead giveaway that he'd be the one performing the nuptials. The woman at his side, electronic keyboard in her hands, walked over to the table and set it up. The man walked down to the shoreline, and Brad joined him, Liam at his side.

The pianist played a soft melody.

Liam had led the kids off, and they were now back. Mila came down the sand in a frilly sea-green dress pulling a fish-shaped wagon with Logan inside waving a ring box. All of us waved at the kids. Mila exuded confidence, smiling like she was the one in charge. Liam lifted Logan out of the wagon, and he handed Liam the ring box. Then the kids sat down in the front.

The pianist switched to a wedding march, and everyone stood.

Her mother at her side, Emerson came behind the kids in a backless white A-line dress that showed off her curves, holding a bouquet of white peonies. Her face glowed with happiness, her lips parted in a wide smile. Her eyes sparkled, even from a distance. When she joined Brad before the pastor, the two beamed at one another.

Brad and I made eye contact, and he smiled. I made a heart symbol with my hands.

The ceremony was short. Brad and Emerson held each other's hands and recited their vows, after which the pastor announced, "I now pronounce you man and wife." We all clapped as Brad swept Emerson up into a kiss and the kids jumped up and ran to hug them.

~ * ~

About the Author

Deborah Brown is an Amazon bestselling author of the Paradise series. She lives on the Gulf of Mexico, with her ungrateful animals, where Mother Nature takes out her bad attitude in the form of hurricanes.

For a free short story, sign up for my newsletter. It will also keep you up-to-date with new releases and special promotions:
www.deborahbrownbooks.com

Follow on FaceBook:
facebook.com/DeborahBrownAuthor

You can contact her at Wildcurls@hotmail.com

Deborah's books are available on Amazon
amazon.com/Deborah-Brown/e/B0059MAIKQ

PARADISE SERIES

Crazy in Paradise
Deception in Paradise
Trouble in Paradise
Murder in Paradise
Greed in Paradise
Revenge in Paradise
Kidnapped in Paradise
Swindled in Paradise
Executed in Paradise
Hurricane in Paradise
Lottery in Paradise
Ambushed in Paradise
Christmas in Paradise
Blownup in Paradise
Psycho in Paradise
Overdose in Paradise
Initiation in Paradise
Jealous in Paradise
Wronged in Paradise
Vanished in Paradise
Fraud in Paradise
Naïve in Paradise
Bodies in Paradise
Accused in Paradise
Deceit in Paradise

BISCAYNE BAY SERIES

Hired Killer
Not guilty
Jilted

Deborah's books are available on Amazon
amazon.com/Deborah-Brown/e/B0059MAIKQ

Made in the USA
Middletown, DE
27 January 2022